Look at Us

Look at Us

T. L. TOMA

Bellevue Literary Press
NEW YORK

First published in the United States in 2021
by Bellevue Literary Press, New York

For information, contact:
Bellevue Literary Press
90 Broad Street
Suite 2100
New York, NY 10004
www.blpress.org

This is a work of fiction. Characters, organizations, events, and places (even those that are actual) are either products of the author's imagination or are used fictitiously.

Library of Congress Cataloging-in-Publication Data
Names: Toma, T. L., author.
Title: Look at us / T.L. Toma.
Description: First Edition. I New York : Bellevue Literary Press, 2022.
Identifiers: LCCN 2021001703 I ISBN 9781942658917 (paperback) I ISBN
  9781942658924 (epub)
Classification: LCC PS3570.O4295 L66 2022 I DDC 813/.54--dc23
LC record available at https://lccn.loc.gov/2021001703

This book's cover image, titled "African Grey Parrot, peeking out from under its wing," is by the photographer Avenue. No changes were made to the photograph. It is licensed under the Creative Commons Attribution-ShareAlike 3.0 Unported (CC-BY-SA 3.0) license. To view a copy of this license, visit https://creativecommons.org/licenses/by-sa/3.0/.

Bellevue Literary Press would like to thank all its generous donors—individuals and foundations—for their support.

 This publication is made possible by the New York State Council on the Arts with the support of Governor Andrew M. Cuomo and the New York State Legislature.

Book design and composition by Mulberry Tree Press, Inc.

Bellevue Literary Press is committed to ecological stewardship in our book production practices, working to reduce our impact on the natural environment.

❀ This book is printed on acid-free paper.

Manufactured in the United States of America.

First Edition

10 9 8 7 6 6 4 3 2 1

paperback ISBN: 978-1-942658-91-7
ebook ISBN: 978-1-942658-92-4

To Melanie

Niemand ist mehr Sklave, als der sich für frei hält,
ohne es zu sein.

None are more hopelessly enslaved than those
who falsely believe they are free.

—Goethe

Look at Us

PART I

CHAPTER ONE

PALOMA IS LEAVING. The news comes as a shock. She has been with the Fowlers for close to four years. In that time they have learned to rely upon her completely. Life before Paloma seems another life altogether.

She first started working for the Fowlers shortly after the birth of the twins. Martin and Lily had always agreed: Adults have children. Otherwise, you were just children pretending to be adults. Yet they did not have a family right away. They hoped to avoid that mistake. They had their careers to think about. They were saving to buy the apartment downtown. And they wanted to see more of the world first. They saw Paris, the Canadian Rockies, Saint Kitts. They sat behind the dugout in Yankee Stadium. Lily liked the fluke sashimi with miso at Motsunabe. They did all those things you do when it is just the two of you. Weekend mornings, they slept in.

But after eight years of marriage, Lily looked up one evening and announced, I'm ready.

She was thirty-six. Soon it would be too late. They tried that very night. They tried again that Saturday. They tried four times the following week. It was fun doing it, knowing you were really going to do it.

Nothing is ever as easy as it looks. As the months passed without success, it became less fun.

Lily insisted they both go for tests. A nurse gave Martin a plastic cup with a screw-on top and directed him to a toilet stocked with magazines. Naked women gazed out from the pages. Their expressions were sly and baleful. He could hear people, other patients and clinic staff, moving about in the hallway just outside the door.

Martin worried he might not be able to.

He came to an advertisement for a nonabrasive kitchen-counter cleaner. The woman in the ad wore a sundress and rope sandals. A bonnet wreathed in miniature tea roses and baby's breath adorned her head. She wandered through a citrus grove filled with rich hues of amber and emerald and saffron. She looked back not at him but instead smiled up at the trees hung heavy with fruit. The woman held her bonnet in place with one hand, and with the other she was reaching for a pair of plump lemons. Her eyes reflected the golden light.

Five days later, the Fowlers returned to the clinic for the news. They were both nervous. Martin had already decided: If they learned it was Lily's fault, he would shower her with understanding. He knew that love is not about finding fault. Love is just love. But if it did turn out to be Lily's fault, he was going to draw her close and remind her they could adopt a baby from Guatemala or China or Romania, or any of those countries over there. Or they could go the test-tube route. Their good friends George Davenport and Hannah Finkelmeyer had been down that road. Now little Tzipporah Davenport-Finkelmeyer at age three could already recite the alphabet to *qoph*.

Martin was concerned, however, about what might happen if they discovered it was his fault. Lily would probably act as if everything were okay, though he would forever wonder if this was only an act. And he did not want to discover there was something wrong moving around inside him. The thought made him anxious. Say whenever his wife met another man, she would think first thing that what swam deep inside this other man was fit and gunning to go.

In the end, the doctor assured the Fowlers they were both fine. The man counseled patience and prayer. He was of the old school. White hair grew from his ears like sprouts. Age spots mottled the backs of his hands like blight on a leaf.

These matters are ultimately mysterious, the doctor told them.

Lily doesn't believe in mysterious. Either everything makes sense or nothing makes sense. Driving home from the clinic, she called the doctor a moron. She said, If nothing's wrong, then what's wrong? She began researching the matter on her own. It's the kind of woman she is. She joined an online chat room where prospective mothers exchanged the latest tips. She downloaded an ovulation app on her phone and marked a calendar with large scarlet stars that she stuck to the door of the refrigerator. She made Martin swap his briefs for boxers and limited him to a single cup of coffee. She started to ingest megadoses of manganese, selenium, and essential fatty acids. She took up yoga to synchronize her biorhythms with those of the cosmos, stepping down into the subway clutching a polyvinyl chloride mat while wearing a leotard with an inscrutable Sanskrit inscription stenciled over her heart.

Evenings their lovemaking turned rote. They did it whether they felt like it or not. In bed they moved as if they were rowing a slow boat. Afterward, Lily reclined with a pillow beneath her rump and her knees tucked under her chin. Twice Martin dreamed of trussed turkeys.

Lily was reared in a household with three older brothers, so she hoped for a girl. Martin had grown up with four younger sisters. This made him want a girl, too. It seemed a happy coincidence, as if they were destined for each other. It took another year of trying before they learned they could expect twin sons. They were elated nonetheless. They went out to dinner to celebrate. They held hands across the tablecloth and looked into each other's eyes. The gender did not matter, they decided; children are children, gifts upon this Earth.

Lily got sick between the appetizer and the entrée. The tiramisu made her sick again. She was sick the following morning and the day after that. Lily was sick every morning for the next three months. In the meantime, her heartburn was searing. None of her shoes fit. She developed piles. She became a stranger to her own body. She endured fits of hormonal rage, unreasoning episodes. Panic followed by tears followed by dishes hurled smash against the wall.

Lily said, It's like I've been kidnapped by movie aliens who want to turn me into one of them.

It troubled Martin to see his wife this way. He worked at making her comfortable. He bought her upscale maternity outfits fashioned from dual-ply Egyptian cotton. He massaged cocoa butter into her belly to prevent stretch marks. He ran out at three in the morning to purchase pints of rhubarb ice cream dotted with crystallized ginger.

Nothing helped. The aliens were too powerful. The Fowlers felt helpless against them.

The delivery lasted a day and a night and half of another day. Lily threw up three times. She emptied her bowels twice. Toward the end she grew foulmouthed. Martin had once heard these very same words from a drunken fraternity brother in college, and on another occasion from a former coworker, an ex-marine who had just been let go—but he had never heard anything remotely like such oaths pass his wife's lips.

Martin was embarrassed in front of the nurses. They all stared at the floor while his wife yelled so-and-so. Nobody looked at anybody else. Later, a short woman in hospital greens took him aside. She had a mild, tawny complexion.

Martin would have called her Arabian or Eskimo or even Hawaiian; he could not tell. She said, They get like this.

She was only doing her job, Martin knew. But amid the mayhem of the obstetrics ward, beneath the shrill lighting, this nurse was a calming and benign presence. He wished she would spirit him away from here. He would have given anything to go home with her. He wanted to sit in her kitchen and have her feed him lamb kebabs or whale steaks or even poi, whatever it was he thought she ate. He imagined the years stretching ahead, years in which he saw this same smile again and again. At that instant, it seemed unfair and even cruel that this other woman giving birth in the next room, and calling him hateful and vulgar names, was the very person with whom he had vowed to spend the rest of what was left of his life.

And then the twins were born. Martin had not expected so much blood. It reminded him of a gruesome traffic accident he had witnessed as a child. The driver hung head-down out the open door. The passenger had gone through the windshield.

It was just like that.

The agony was not done. One baby had colic. The other refused to sleep. The Fowlers' quarters were soon strewn with an unfamiliar rubble: torn cellophane bags spilling diapers, jars of diaper-rash ointment minus their lids, the unused baby monitor still sealed in its box, a ubiquitous dusting of powdered talc, open tubs of desiccated baby wipes, the breast pump sitting naked and obscene on the back of the toilet. Whole weeks now passed in which neither Lily nor Martin managed more than two or three hours of sleep a night. They moved like stunned survivors through the postapocalyptic landscape of their rooms. Her nipples were cracked and sore.

Lily had arranged to take a six-month leave of absence from her law practice. But not eight weeks after the birth of the boys, Martin arrived home one afternoon to find her sitting at the dining room table with another woman. The woman had hennaed hair gone gray at the roots and tight eyes.

This was Paloma.

Lily said, I was just explaining how anxious I am to get back to work.

She had set out demitasses of espresso and a serving platter of macaroons. A small pitcher foamed with steamed milk. Brown cubes of raw cane sugar formed a miniature Mayan pyramid. From the living room came the ticking of the grandfather clock. It was March. Outside, dense clouds choked the sky. The towers of the city were gray in the windows. Down the hall, in the nursery, one of the babies bawled for a moment and then stopped. Lily glanced at Paloma. Paloma's own look was impenetrable, blank as a board.

The truth is, Lily went on, I am desperate to return to work.

That must seem horrible, I know, she quickly added, like she could have been kidding. Except it did not sound like kidding. I feel guilty just saying it, she confessed. A mother should be with her children. But I miss the office. I miss the job.

Lily said, I miss my life.

Martin looked at Paloma. He looked at his wife. Though it was the first he had heard of any of this, he said, That's perfectly understandable.

Lily ignored him. She said, My husband doesn't feel bad about going into work every day. Why should I?

When Paloma again didn't respond, Martin shifted in his seat and said, No reason. None at all.

Lily frowned. She reached for her coffee. She peered at the other woman over the top of her cup. Paloma came highly recommended. She had worked for a family up in Scarsdale and another in the Village. Yet sitting there, Martin could not escape the sense that it was they who were being interviewed, not the other way around. Lily picked up a cookie, gazed at it, and put it back.

She smiled at Paloma and said, I even feel guilty about feeling guilty.

Paloma, not smiling, replied, I'll need an extra twenty-five a week bus fare.

CHAPTER TWO

I T WAS PALOMA WHO PLAYED this little piggy. It was
Paloma who went peekaboo. She heard the boys utter
their very first words and watched them take their earliest steps. When one of the children falls or the other is
frightened, it is always Paloma they want. Waking from
bad dreams, they call out her name.

They have learned to count on awkward fingers: *uno,
dos, tres.*

Paloma isn't perfect. She spends too much time on the
phone. She has agreed to light cleaning, but she won't do
windows. She yells at Martin for leaving wet towels on the
floor. She demands all holidays off with pay. Before the
boys were toilet-trained, she kept tossing soiled diapers
straight down the trash chute.

She hates the super; the super hates her.

Paloma dutifully arrives at eight each weekday morning
to feed the twins their breakfast. She fills the kitchen with
her thick frame, bosoms the size of hams. Lily and Martin
both have good jobs, positions of responsibility, ample sala-
ries. But what do they know of life? Paloma knows life. She
kneels to scrub shit stains from the toilet and pull clogged
hair from the tub drain. She does two loads of laundry
before lunch.

On clear afternoons she strolls with the children to the park. The trio waddle down the sidewalk, a child on each side clutching one of her hands. They stop at the corner to purchase day-old baguettes. Paloma settles on a bench to watch as the twins hurl the bread from the banks of the pond. The ducks fascinate the toddlers. The ducks frighten them. Then the boys remember: When they are with Paloma, no danger is too great.

Later Paloma puts them down for their nap. She gathers up their toys, vacuums crumbs from the carpet. She hums to herself as she works. The sound permeates the room like an infusion of oils.

Paloma hung the spider plant in the bathroom. She made the mobile in the nursery from wooden dowels and cardboard cutouts. It was Paloma who knit the heavy throw draped over the arm of the love seat in the living room.

She is everywhere. Signs of her presence reach into every corner.

Midafternoon she settles on the sofa with the laundry. As she folds she watches her favorite telenovela on the Spanish-language channel. The TV matriarch is long-suffering but sage. The son is a reprobate; he arrives home dissolute and broke. The daughter may prefer women, but she is not sure. At a Mexicali strip club, the father stuffs fifty-peso notes into the G-string of a dancer named Mango.

At the end of the day, Paloma prepares the boys' dinner. These meals occasionally feature eye-watering sauces with too much cilantro. She places the food in covered dishes next to the microwave. At six in the evening, she boards the bus back to her three-story walk-up.

But now Paloma is leaving. She turned fifty-five the previous winter. She was widowed a decade ago, a span of empty, interminable evenings. In recent months, she has struck up a correspondence with a retiree in Jupiter, Florida. He spent forty years as a machinist in the merchant marine. In the photo he sends, he stands shirtless, a squat man squinting against the light. His torso is round like a boulder. His face is as creased as a dry riverbed. A green-and-indigo dragon breathing apricot flames spirals up and down each of his forearms.

Paloma uses the desktop in the Fowlers' study to read the man's messages. He writes about the throb of the surf and the shattering heat. She reads while outside a chill rain batters the window. He mentions the waving grasses of the savanna. He describes the dappled sunlight glinting off the waters. He writes, A great egret stands one-legged in the distance. My ashtray is the shell of a giant horseshoe crab. The tide sounds like the beating of the Earth's heart.

He writes, I sit every evening with a pitcher of mojitos made from the juice of limes I pick myself from a tree that grows wild not twenty yards from my doorstep.

After 47 emails, 296 texts, and one three-and-a-half-hour phone call, Paloma has decided to join the man in his mobile home amid the dunes.

But you don't even know him, Lily says.

Paloma shrugs. She is tired of knowing. She wants to feel once again. The gaze in her eyes is already far away. I will stay until you find someone else, she promises.

Though do not make me miss the start of the greyhound season.

Life will never be the same. It is hard to imagine these rooms without her. The Fowlers are not sure how to tell the boys. Paloma has been with them always. She is as much a part of their world as the skyline through the windows and the thump of the elevator behind the walls and the honk of traffic sounding far below.

I can't believe she would do this to us, Lily says that evening.

She's lonely, Martin reminds his wife. You can't really blame her.

But Lily can. Do you have any idea how hard it's going to be to find someone new?

The next morning she contacts an employment agency. She phones friends. She accesses a situations-wanted website. She scans the bulletin board at her yoga studio. Lily has always been a methodical woman. She knows how to get from A to B. At work she wears her blond hair up. She is tall and a little ungainly. A wide mouth and a strong nose. Her nostrils are deep. Her nose is like this monument to the rest of her face.

In no time Lily has compiled a list of names. She schedules interviews with five women and one man—she wants to be fair—over three evenings. During these meetings, Martin has trouble keeping people straight. One candidate blends into another. After a while, his gaze wanders to the view of the city as it stretches beyond the living room window, to the sudden upthrust of building after building. They rise like stalagmites beneath the dome of the sky.

The Fowlers live on Maiden Lane, at the bottom of the island, in a renovated estate house. The foundation dates from the earliest days of the city, back when Dutch still rang in the alleyways. The street name comes from the path young girls used to take down to the water. The building has grown higher with the passage of time, as if each generation were just one more floor. They both enjoy living in the very middle of history, though they can't get rid of the water stain in the corner of the bedroom ceiling. The plumbing clangs and bangs like pots and pans. The floorboards groan, the massive oak timbers settling with great age. A dropped penny always rolls east. While the original chandelier continues to hang in the lobby of the building, their bedroom door won't shut.

In the end Lily chooses a kindly and soft-spoken replacement, a smiling woman in her forties.

The one with the limp? Martin asks, remembering.

Lily looks at him for a while before saying, It's not that pronounced.

He doesn't want to argue. But he is not happy about bringing a total stranger into their home. The truth is, he has never been entirely comfortable with Paloma. Now he will have to be uncomfortable with someone new. He does not relish the prospect of her gimping about their rooms. Martin imagines a fire in which this woman will not be able to get out in time. He will have to risk his life to rush through the flames and save her. And he worries that if the boys spend all of every day with this woman, they might somehow start to limp themselves. These are absurd reasons, he knows, reasons that if you said them out loud, people would think there was something wrong with you. This does not keep him from having them as reasons.

The limp made me like her, Lily admits after a moment.

Martin regards his wife with interest. She occasionally says things that surprise him, that cause her to seem new in unexpected ways. It made you like her?

It made me sympathize with her. The whole time I was talking to her, I kept wondering about her childhood. I thought about all the names they must have called her on the playground. People, strangers, probably always stared.

Maybe she was lamed as an adult, it occurs to Martin.

His wife peers at him fixedly. She says, I keep thinking about all the men who must have rejected her.

On her last day of work, Paloma brings two pairs of mittens she has knit for the boys, a dozen sugar-coated rolls of her homemade *pan dulce*, and a bird that appears too big for its cage. It turns out that her merchant marine has a cat. Paloma's African gray parrot, her companion for the last decade, will have to stay behind. Martin learns too late that Lily has agreed to keep the bird in the failed hope that this and other last-minute gestures—she took Paloma to lunch in Union Square, she bought her a new luggage set—might make the woman reconsider. The bird is over a foot tall from beak to tail, with ruffled plumage the color of ash. The tips look dipped in a kind of sacramental whiteness, save for the tail feathers, which are a startling scarlet. The fowl hunkers on its perch in unimpeachable dignity. Its pate fits like a Greek helmet. Paloma named it Aristóteles because of its immense intelligence, with a rich and varied vocabulary.

This way you will remember me always, she says.

We will never, ever forget you, Lily vows.

That weekend, they accompany Paloma to Penn Station to help her board the Coconut Limited Standing on the train platform, Lily turns teary. She kisses the other woman on both cheeks and says, If you ever change your mind—

Paloma says, I won't.

The new nanny arrives promptly at eight on Monday to begin work. Martin makes sure not to stare at her limp. But two evenings later, the Fowlers discover cigarette butts in the trash bin and a scorch mark on the Tabriz rug in the living room. The next woman lasts almost a week, until Lily finds several porn sites bookmarked on the study desktop. The third hire fails to show as scheduled and is never heard from again.

When Lily learns of openings in a child-care center near Lincoln Square, she rushes to submit the twins' names. It will add almost an hour to her morning commute. The staff, however, are highly credentialed. On their fourth day, the boys emerge with notes pinned to their jackets. A classmate has nits. Included are detailed instructions for treatment and eradication. Lily spends the following afternoon washing linens while the twins move underfoot.

In the coming weeks the Fowlers try to juggle the child-care duties. They draft Lily's mother on occasion, though when the woman shows up tanked one morning, Lily has to stay home from work. They use Mrs. Nagorsky from downstairs a time or two. But it is not enough. Martin misses a meeting. Twice Lily is forced to reschedule appointments. She has to excuse herself midway through an important deposition, leaving an associate to finish.

Children know more than you think. The boys sense something is wrong. Gavin, the younger by fourteen minutes, tantrums repeatedly. Arnold starts going in his pants. It is as if the toilet training never happened.

It's like living with monkeys, Lily mutters one evening.

Martin once read that you can teach even a chimp to wipe itself, though now does not seem the time to say so.

CHAPTER THREE

HELP COMES IN THE FORM of the street vendor from whom Martin buys his almond bear claw each morning. The man stands in his tiny cart all day every day, big-bellied and grizzled, balding save for auburn tufts at his ears, three teeth missing in the middle of his smile. His wife's sister-in-law's niece has just arrived in the country.

Martin expects to meet a large woman, a female version of the vendor, though with incisors intact. She turns out to be short and slender, almost spritelike, with glossy hair the color of pitch, hacked bluntly at the nape. She has the delicate profile of a cameo, marred by a spray of acne at one corner of her mouth. She looks unformed, her face not yet all there. She looks more young than pretty. Her eyes are the same mild blue as the covers of Martin's exam booklets back in school.

She admits that she has never worked as a nanny before. Her experience consists of two seasons on the line of a fish cannery back home before it closed. But she has six younger brothers: Padraig, Éamon, Colm, Cillian, Liam, and Finbar.

I understand little boys, she assures them. I know what they want.

That makes one of us, Lily says.

The girl's laugh causes her features to swarm with

unexpected emotion. When she grows nervous or excited, however, her brogue turns incomprehensible. She tells them she has always loved children, or maybe she is saying children have always loved her. She says she wants to work for a few years in the United States to save money and then return home to attend university, or perhaps she means she would like to study American history. She says she has heard all her life about New York and read about it and seen it in the movies and she cannot believe she is really here, or else New York itself is so much like a movie it does not seem real. It is only toward the very end of their conversation—after discussing the hours and the pay—that the Fowlers realize she expects to live with them.

We could move the futon into the storage room, Lily suggests once the girl is gone.

Martin shakes his head. The futon won't fit.

Maybe it could.

It won't. Besides, I don't want a stranger always underfoot.

Lily waits before speaking. You'd rather have me underfoot.

He sits up. Just what is that supposed to mean?

It means you expect me to find a nanny. Until I do, you expect me to be a nanny.

Martin stares at his wife. Don't pull that one.

Which one is that?

You know which one. I work just as hard as you around here.

I didn't say you didn't.

I think you did.

She says, I didn't say you didn't, but do you think you do?

Lily adds, Do you really, really, really, really think you do?

She makes a show of leaving the room—arms swinging, heels knocking on the wood floor. Martin remains on the sofa. He knows already that his wife will not speak to him the rest of the evening.

They have been through this before.

Lily can be headstrong. Growing up in a house full of older brothers, she had to be. They twisted her arm, wrenched the heads off her dolls, locked her in the closet. She was smaller, weaker, outnumbered. She fought back in the only way she knew how: She became better at whatever she did. She studied harder and read more. She stayed up late to put the finishing touches on her English composition and rose early to check her answers in geometry. She was also a joiner. Anything to get away from the house. She joined the pep squad, wrote for the school newspaper, and was *el presidente* of the Spanish club. Every Saturday between the ages of ten and sixteen, she mounted her Friesian down at the stables. There are women, and then there are women who love horses. Anmer, standing at fifteen hands, with black fetlocks, was more trustworthy than any human she had ever known. Lily rode with her back straight, her chin up, the pommel of the English saddle just behind the animal's withers. A display case in the Fowlers' living room still exhibits ribbons from dressage competitions. They lie like feathers on a field of burgundy felt. But at home, the atmosphere remained savage. Her brothers teased her mercilessly: She would never get breasts. She had a horse face herself. The night before she left for college, she discovered the hole they had bored in the wall of her bedroom years before to spy on her.

Had Lily's mother been stronger, she might have shielded the girl. Yet Martin has seen the woman pie-eyed a dozen times over the years. She is one of those sloppy, falling-down drunks, waking incontinent on the floor of the bathroom. When Lily emptied a quart bottle of gin into the sink on a visit home early in their marriage, her mother—proud native of Dundee, Churchill's old constituency—slapped her daughter and screamed, At least I'll be sober in the morning, but you'll still be a cunt.

Her late father was rarely around. When she was young, he was old. Even she saw she was the result of a mistake. He didn't have time for equestrian events or parent-teacher conferences. He was always jetting here and there to deliver a lecture or chair a symposium. He would arrive home at seven in the evening from Reagan National and have to catch a 6:00 A.M. flight for LAX. He referred to himself as a gentleman scholar. In other words, the man never held an academic post. He didn't need an academic post. He used to say he spent more restocking his wine cellar than a professor earns—even though his monograph on Emerson has been cited hundreds of times. He made an annual pilgrimage to Walden, hiking the perimeter of the pond amid the brown and red leaves of October. He celebrated the inviolability of the individual and what he saw as the peculiarly American virtues. Let the French extol *fraternité* and the Germans *Ordnung*; here, the watchword is *self-reliance*. A few bend life to their will; the rest are broken by it. Exalted sentiments. Yet he thought about the dog more than he thought about me, Lily once told Martin. His dachshund, von Mises, won best of breed in 1998. And even when her father did notice her, his view was not always charitable. He used to give me chores—we all had chores—but only I among my siblings never seemed to get it right. He'd tell me to weed the garden or sweep out the garage, but when he came out later to check my work, he would take the spade or the broom from my hand and quote Napoléon: If you want something done right, better do it yourself. Six weeks before he died, she overheard him compare her to a ruined colt.

Such a childhood left its mark. As an adult, she is highstrung and often guarded. She suspects others don't like her. The man at the greengrocer's was rude. A woman on the treadmill down at the gym kept staring. During a deposition, opposing counsel ignored her. In response, Lily's demeanor turns rancorous. When angry or thwarted, she will round on you with caustic comments. No matter how wounding they may prove, however, when you step back and look at her remarks in the cold light of day, you discover they often contain a disconcerting measure of justice.

Martin feels wounded now. The fact is, he helps around the house. He helps out plenty. He sometimes bathes the twins. The other day he unloaded the dishwasher. Two evenings ago he went back out into the night to buy pacifiers. There must have been a dozen of the plastic nipples hidden in the sofa cushions and behind the refrigerator and at the foot of the closet, but neither he nor Lily could locate a single one. The boys were crying and refused to go to sleep, so Martin hurried through a cold, slanting rain to purchase three two-packs at the twenty-four-hour pharmacy six blocks over.

He starts a mental inventory of all the household chores he has done of late but instantly recognizes that this rush to list them indicts him already.

When he crawls into bed several hours later, he and his wife still have not spoken. She lies on her side of the mattress, a gentle hillock of shadow against the darkness. At such moments he is overwhelmed by an unexpected tenderness. She could go out tomorrow and be hit by a bus or stumble into the subway well while a train roared past, and he would live always with the knowledge that they spent their last evening together made mute by a squabble of absolutely no significance. He could be knifed in an elevator, or an aneurysm could go off in his brain, and his wife would survive for another forty years with a lasting memory of him as a moping lump in bed. These thoughts fester for a few minutes more before Martin says, I suppose we could give her a try.

What? Lily replies after a while, like maybe she is asleep. She is not asleep.

He says, If we start her on a trial basis.

Lily rises on one elbow to look at him. Through the

skylight, dark clouds churn in front of a quarter moon, hiding it one instant, then rolling on to reveal it the next.

He says, Though if the twins don't take to her—

They will, she says. I know they will. If they don't, we'll get rid of the boys and keep the girl.

She kisses his smile before jumping up to use the toilet. He watches her in her nightgown going away from him across the thinly lit room. He has seen her move this very same way hundreds of times, yet the sight always makes something deep within him stir. When Lily returns to bed, he waits for a modest interval so as not to seem too avid and then starts to stroke her back, but he stops when she says, I have an early morning.

His wife says, I want to clean before the new girl gets here.

Maeve is from Claddaghduff, a tiny hamlet on the Irish shore. Martin's phone shows an island like a squashed green bug, with Belfast where the eye should be. When they lead her down the hall to her new room, she pauses in the doorway.

It's not that big—

The girl shakes her head. It's brilliant, Ms. Fowler.

Call me Lily.

The new au pair stands holding a cloth suitcase in one hand and a jute gunnysack with sewn handles in the other. The Fowlers spent the better part of an hour wrestling the futon bed into place. It just fits, leaving a spare six inches on either side. You have to crawl over it to open the window. A battered bureau with a missing drawer handle sits opposite.

The bathroom at the end of the hall will be yours, Martin tells her.

The girl nods, then turns to the skyline gleaming through the window. The sun seizes the faces of buildings and bathes them in light. She finally settles on the bed with her hands folded in her lap. Her eyes range around the room, taking in the dresser and the small wicker chair next to it. She reaches out to smooth the quilted comforter. Sitting there, she seems subdued and a little frightened.

But she comes alive in the presence of the boys. The storm later that morning fails to dampen her enthusiasm. Arnold takes to her instantly, though Gavin won't look at her—until she suggests they bake a batch of shortbread biscuits. After lunch they draw "Jack and the Beanstalk" using wax crayons and six paper bags, one for each panel of the story. The magic beans are the color of rubies. As the light outside the windows begins to wane, she drapes the wool throw over two chairs in the dining room and makes a tunnel, a bear's lair, a fort.

She tells the twins timeless tales of pillaging Vikings laying siege to the coast.

It turns out the girl likes to cook. Though Lily has a multitude of talents, food preparation has never been one of them. She can easily parse the nuances of a seven-thousand-word appellate brief, but ask her to go from milliliters to teaspoons and she loses her way. For his part, Martin enjoys culinary shows on TV. The chefs always seem so earnest and richly suited to their places in life. After watching such programs, he occasionally goes out to purchase a slew of exotic ingredients at an upscale market in Chelsea. He brings home lemongrass and Kobe beef, or Caribbean spice rub and conch, or a whole duck with the makings of a cherry and port wine glaze, and then trashes the kitchen on the way to producing an unnervingly greasy meal that costs seven dollars a bite.

The au pair, on the other hand, knows food. While Paloma could quickly throw together a serviceable if fiery meal, Maeve will, if given the time, spend several hours crafting dishes of surprising depth. Her bangs stick to her forehead with a sheen of sweat, but beneath it there is that smile. The aromas that fill the house belong to another time and place. In short order, Martin comes to look forward to her lamb stew, her sherry-soaked trifles, to savory servings of poached salmon and new potatoes dotted with butter and fresh dill. Hearty dishes—you push yourself back from the table with a groan. He develops a craving weakness for her shepherd's pie.

When you compliment her on the food, she blushes richly and says, 'Tanks.

This is only the first of many changes. In the weeks immediately following Paloma's departure, dirty laundry overflowed the hamper. Mildew accumulated on the bathroom tiles. Grime crusted the burners. Here, too, the girl's energy proves unflagging. Freshly pressed shirts magically appear in Martin's closet. The kitchen counters shine. She separates the aluminum from the plastic. She leans halfway out the windows to clean the other side of the glass. From fourteen stories up, Maeve strains for a smudge in the corner.

She has even assumed care for Aristotle, the African gray. Lily complains that the animal smells. Martin is irritated by its squawk. But the girl dotes on the creature. She has made its home in the study. The broad windows allow the sun to flood inside. She changes its bedding every day. She installs a new swing perch with a bell and a mounted mirror. She sits before the cage door, talking to the parrot. The bird stares back, its pupils expanding and contracting with modulations in her voice.

The Fowlers, meanwhile, do their part to make the Irish au pair feel welcome. One Sunday Martin takes her and the twins to a Broadway matinee, the stage alive with mythical creatures, marionettes the size of pickup trucks. On another afternoon, Lily invites her to the Vermeer exhibition at the Metropolitan Museum. When her phone rings, Lily excuses herself to step into the rotunda, only to return a few moments later to discover Maeve standing before Canova's *Perseus with the Head of Medusa*. It's one of my favorites, Lily says, peering up at the god armed with his sword and the hat that renders him invisible, and, most important of all, the mirrored shield to protect against the Gorgon's gaze that will turn you to stone. The girl focuses intently on the marble nude rising before her, the detail exacting, until she catches herself and reddens.

It's okay to look, Lily assures her.

At the same time, the new nanny's presence sometimes bewilders Martin. More than once he has caught her studying him. He will be eating dinner and glance up to discover her eyeballing him across the table. She likes to sit with him and watch TV—baseball, police procedurals, politicians railing against diseased rapists intent on storming the border—her look moving from the screen back to Martin, as though the true meaning of the images might appear on his face. He and the twins always tune into an old favorite, a Western serialized from the 1960s. Whenever bank robbers or cattle rustlers get the drop on an unsuspecting innocent, they level their six-shooters and say, Reach for the skies, hombre! and she stares as father and sons all immediately throw their hands in the air. Or Martin will be reading a book in the big leather recliner in the den, and she will appear with a book or magazine of her own to ask if she might join him. He will say, Of course, though he cannot help but notice how her gaze keeps drifting above her text, seeking him out. Her look is neither friendly nor unfriendly, fond nor indifferent, but instead clinical, almost anthropological. It feels as if he—as if his whole life—is on display. Something about her expression stays with him, haunting him through the afternoon and into the evening, reverberating in his memory like an ocular echo.

It occurs to him that her eyes may be a little off-kilter, one sitting slightly oblique of the other. While most would never notice it, Martin fixes on the notion that this feature somehow permits her to triangulate her glances in such a way that she can pinpoint his position in the world with uncanny precision. But then he will look again and conclude her eyes are in fact evenly spaced in her head, which makes him wonder at the possible derangement of his own vision that first led him to think otherwise. Though he has yet to decide whether a genuine asymmetry marks her features, he cannot escape the driving impression that something about the naked force of her scrutiny strikes at his very core.

Equally perturbing is the unexpected percussion of her toilet at dawn. These explosions startle him out of his dreams. They serve as constant reminders their home is no longer entirely their own.

Previously, Martin had always been the first out of bed. He was used to moving down through the darkness of their rooms, pausing to turn up the thermostat. In the kitchen, he would grind the coffee while watching the first bands of sunlight stream from the east. He watched the news van moving slowly down Broadway, bound bundles of the *Post* banging against the storefronts. He heard the rumble of the subway trains as they emerged from beneath the ground to climb the elevated tracks.

The world made a kind of sense at that hour that it would not make again for the rest of the day. But now Maeve is always already up, padding around in a worn housecoat and tattered slippers. She has gotten a head start. He feels strangely robbed, as if she has stolen these first moments out from under him.

If the nanny rises early, she also retires late. The floor-boards in the old building complain with each step. Because the Fowlers had previously used the girl's new quarters to stow those things they had no use for but could not bring themselves to throw out—a nineteenth-century camelback sofa; boxes of pewter candlesticks, brass steins, and cast-iron trivets; a steamer trunk that accompanied Lily's uncle Rupert all around the world, plastered with stickers from Tampico, Amalfi, and Macao—the room never experienced much foot traffic, and so Martin rarely noticed the creaking timbers. But now with her constant passage, he can track the girl's progress up and down the hall. From within the master bedroom, he hears the groan of the planks crescendo as she approaches and then fade as she continues on, dopplering weirdly. One evening the footsteps pause, and he lies in bed in the gathering silence. When they do not immediately resume, he sits up and stares hard into the darkness, stares until a shadow finally edges past the door that always stands slightly ajar.

Let's ask the super to rehang it, he tells Lily in the morning.

In the meantime, he has taken to propping the door closed with one of her old texts from law school. She keeps them stored in the maple bookcase along the far wall. The embossed lettering glitters on the spines of the leather bindings.

Use *Property*, his wife suggests. It's the biggest.

CHAPTER FOUR

MAEVE WANTS TO KNOW how the Fowlers first met. The question makes Lily sit up. She likes remembering. She dips into the details of the anecdote as if she were easing down into a piping hot tub, beginning as she always does with a morning in a diner long ago.

Martin has heard this story before, of course, countless times. Lily tells it to friends, usually to other couples, on those occasions when talk turns to love and its beginnings. Yet it is not the story he would tell if he were doing the telling. He would tell a different story.

Martin would tell the story behind the story.

He had been in Manhattan almost two years when he first encountered his future wife. He had come east to take a job in investment banking. This had not been his original plan. He had long hoped to complete his doctorate at Indiana A&M in mathematical physics and then teach. In his dissertation, "A Stochastic Demonstration of the Principle of Sufficient Reason Using the Saperstein-Hideaki Conjecture," he meant to use probability theory to demonstrate irrefutably why there is something rather than nothing.

Martin's early progress had been steady. After ten months of writing, he finished chapter three out of a proposed five chapters. The first two chapters had already been accepted for publication in respected peer-reviewed journals. Dr. Häggström, his dissertation adviser, had proclaimed him a scholar of quote-immense-unquote promise. Martin began to fantasize that in the years ahead the Saperstein-Hideaki Conjecture might come to be known as the Saperstein-Hideaki-Fowler Conjecture or even the Fowler-Saperstein-Hideaki Conjecture. He had already lined up a teaching position at Eugene V. Debs College, a small school near the Kentucky border. It was a ramshackle campus with dilapidated dorms and outdated labs, and was by no means the most esteemed institution, but it lay within commuting distance of his hometown, where he planned to return with his degree in hand and settle down.

Though it has been two centuries since it was last pronounced like your sibling's daughter, Nice, Indiana, was first settled by fur trappers from the Maritime Alps. Even today you can put up at the Chamonix Inn and dine at the Grenoble Café. The courthouse is on Avignon Street.

Several years ago, Lily went online and traced Martin's family name all the way back to the ninth century. The Fowler lineage includes Henry I, the duke of Saxony and king of the Germans, and Richard Fowler, a skilled bowman who fought with Richard the Lionheart at the Siege of Acre during the Third Crusade. (Bartholomew Fowler, broken on the wheel for piracy in the 1400s, doesn't come up.) For their anniversary, Lily hung a commemorative plaque in a stressed cottonwood frame in the study. From his seat at the computer, Martin can look up at the Fowler coat of arms, a helmet on an azure field along with three lions—standing *passant guardant*—above a silver chevron. A scroll at the top bears the family motto, *Sapiens qui vigilat*: He is wise who watches.

Despite such airs, Martin's parents are both soft-spoken and pastoral sorts who have bumped cheerily through life. They never heard of the duke of Saxony. His father is a tow truck operator who has spent the better part of forty years going out at three in the morning in streaking blizzards or tumultuous rains to rescue some lost bastard from Michigan who drove into a ditch. In his spare time, he collects buffalo nickels in slotted folders of royal blue. As far back as Martin's memory goes, the man dutifully paused every evening to search his pocket change in the dream of one day laying hold of the impossibly rare 1937 edition with the three-legged bison.

While Martin's father is lean, with features sharp as a flint, his mother is round. She was round as a child and she is destined to die round. Yet the couple has always struck Martin as singularly suited to each other. Standing side by side, his parents remind him of the number ten. If his father busies himself in the relentless pursuit of the numismatic shaggy-haired ox, his mother goes door-to-door soliciting money for the leper colony on Moloka'i. She sets out birdseed in winter and butterfly nectar in summer. His mother is one of the only people he has ever met who takes unalloyed joy from the thought of the well-being of others. She favors knit sweaters and fleece pullovers during the holidays that feature turkeys and pumpkins and ears of Indian corn, or reindeer and snowmen and elves—entire little sagas going on right there on her front.

Martin is older than his four sisters. They all ran free in the hills just north of the Ohio River. He must have at times experienced heartache and disappointment, though these are not the emotions he associates with childhood. He recalls the dinner smells of roasts and simmering greens, the spilled sugar of stars in the night sky overhead, and yellow elm leaves on wet pavement.

For the whole of his time in graduate school, Martin had a girl back home named Wendy Chalmers. Wendy had been raised on a small farm west of the limestone quarry. Her father grew alfalfa and soy on two hundred acres. The man was a deacon down at the Methodist church. Wendy taught music appreciation for the local board of education. She drove from one school to the next, giving music lessons. She knew the basic fingerings for everything from the trumpet and the clarinet to the cello, along with how to beat the tympani drum. Evenings she liked to play the old spinet piano in her father's living room. Her mother had died a few years earlier from a lingering illness. The experience imparted to Wendy's features a discernible melancholy. Martin looked at her and his heart was like a berg in this age of global warming, enormous slabs of it shearing off. Wendy still lived in the farmhouse, taking care of her father and her two younger brothers. Summer evenings she would set the metronome going in the living room and play "Für Elise" or the overture from *Carmen*, or one of those pieces everybody knows without always knowing they know it.

Wendy and Martin talked about getting married. People said what a great couple they made. They would marry and save their money, and one day build a house of their own. They whiled away whole afternoons making sketches in which they designed the entire layout of their future home. There would be a kitchen floored in the latest laminate out of Indianapolis and a massive stone fireplace with a mantel of spruce, and a screened veranda that circled three sides of the house. Upstairs the master bedroom would open onto a widow's walk, and a gabled window would face east to reveal the sunrise. They would raise tomatoes, sweet lettuce, and heirloom potatoes in a rolling yard. Martin would build a place for grilling meat out back. Wendy would give private piano lessons during the day, and he would arrive home in the evening from teaching at Eugene V. Debs College. They would be together always.

They even had the site of the house picked out, an acre and a half sandwiched between the river to the south and a broad run of goldenrod and wildflowers to the north. Sometimes they would drive down to the lot and sit in the car and gaze out over the meadow. In the waning twilight, they watched the fireflies appear. Once in the fall a twelve-point stag came along the ridge and stood big-antlered looking over at them, and on another evening they could just make out the bats swooping and diving in silhouette against the cobalt sky. They sat in each other's arms and stared off into the darkness and saw in their minds the future as it would one day come to them. Time somehow slowed at such moments, and everything important in their lives lay right there before them. Everything looked simple and fitting and perfect.

While Martin made rich progress through the first three chapters of "A Stochastic Demonstration of the Principle of Sufficient Reason Using the Saperstein-Hideaki Conjecture," something happened when he hit chapter four. He remained mired in chapter four. He could not get past page 119. While the details remain abstruse, it's enough to say he intended to use Heisenberg's uncertainty principle, along with kindred advances in quantum mechanics that suggest experiencing something necessarily changes it. He hoped to show that the universe could only exist in a definite state if observed, so that we must assume probabilistically that God originally existed to do the observing; otherwise, we were left to conclude that vast regions of space-time did not come into existence until we trained our telescopes in their direction—an obvious absurdity. But in the pivotal chapter four he ran into a problem, in that we must assume God Himself is observed in turn. If we put all the scientific arcana to one side, the problem is this: If everything must be seen before it can exist, who sees the Seer? Which means we need something else to observe God, and then something still further to observe this something else, and on and on and on, until we are left with Schrödinger's proverbial cat chasing its own tail.

Martin had stumbled down an infinite regress and could not climb back out. He had sped through the first 118 pages, but at page 119 he was stopped dead. Though Martin was the most promising candidate in mathematical physics Indiana A&M had ever produced, Dr. Häggström gently advised him to lower his sights and rethink his dissertation. Humankind had been trying without success to answer the big questions of existence for over five thousand years; one could not expect to do so in eighteen months. Yet Martin was confident he could offer a compelling, if not conclusive, argument. He approached the project with such determination it never occurred to him that he might fall short. He redoubled his efforts, intent on proving not only Dr. Häggström but all naysayers everywhere wrong. Martin spent the whole of the following semester trying to bridge the gulf separating page 119 from 120, but it was a threshold he could not cross. Whenever he got close, he lost his conceptual footing and slid all the way back down to page 34 or 79 or 111, only to dicker with arguments he thought he had already dispatched long ago. His faculty appointment depended upon the completion of the degree. Without the degree, there was no job. As the deadline approached, Martin grew more and more agitated, until his agitation tipped over into outright despair. He had initially decided his inability to progress further signaled a fundamental failure on his part. Failure is a part of life, of course, and if that was to be his lot, then he was prepared to accept it, however bitter a prospect. Yet he eventually arrived at a far more unsettling conclusion: He began to suspect that it was not he who had failed, but the universe that had failed him.

When the dean at Eugene V. Debs College wrote to withdraw the offer of a position, Martin was devastated but not surprised. Dr. Häggström was naturally disappointed, but being the man he was, he kindly arranged through his many connections for the job at the currency desk of an investment house in New York. Dr. Häggström said the financial industry was always on the lookout for bright minds in statistical analysis, and as far as he was concerned, Martin was one of the brightest. When Martin admitted that he hoped to teach and do research and one day publish work of such merit that the Saperstein-Hideaki Conjecture would become known as the Saperstein-Hideaki-Fowler Conjecture or even the Fowler-Saperstein-Hideaki Conjecture, Dr. Häggström said, Let me tell you a little secret: Teaching is for saps. Teachers are underpaid and overworked, and with more illiterates than ever matriculating at today's schools, the academy will soon be dead. Martin said, But I hoped to prove something of significance and lasting merit about the nature of the universe and the ways of the Almighty.

Dr. Häggström said, Don't be such a hayseed. You will make more money in the financial sector in one year than you will see in five on a college campus. This is a blue-ribbon outfit. You will develop a bevy of extraordinary contacts and undreamed-of opportunities that will leave you in good stead for the rest of your life no matter where you go in your career. And you will get to live in New York. New York is the capital of the world. New York is better than the capital of the world. New York is another planet.

You will, Dr. Häggström insisted, experience freedom of a kind that you have hitherto never imagined. And when you are free, who needs God?

But when Martin told Wendy Chalmers about Dr. Häggström's generous offer, the couple fought. She did not want to leave Indiana. She did not want to abandon her family for somewhere new. Martin said, Because I cannot get past page one nineteen, Eugene V. Debs College has withdrawn the offer of a position. I have no choice. Wendy said, You can teach for the local school board. She said, I will put in a good word. They are desperate for math teachers. Martin said, I was this close to having a famed conjecture named after me, and I will not stoop to teaching fractions to sixth graders. She said, So teaching the oboe to sixth graders is good enough for me, but it is not good enough for you. Martin said, That is not what I meant. He said, The oboe is not mathematics. He said, The investment firm that has offered me a position is one of the oldest and most successful in New York, a blue-ribbon outfit. He said, It means a bevy of extraordinary contacts and undreamed-of opportunities. It means a kind of freedom that we have hitherto never imagined.

Wendy Chalmers said, But I want to sit out on a porch and hear the wind as it moves through the meadow and carries with it the scent of goldenrod. She said, I bet you cannot do that in New York. Martin said, Of course you can. He said, Aside from the latest plays and the best restaurants and the world's greatest museums and galleries, they also have this little thing they call Central Park if you want to look at fields and meadows. Maybe you have heard of it.

Wendy Chalmers said, You don't have to take such a tone.

I'm sorry, Martin said. But think about what this means. You would not have to work.

She said, I like teaching. I like to work.

You could have anything you desire.

I desire to live here with you in Nice and make a family.

Martin lost his patience. He said, I cannot believe you would ask me to forgo such an opportunity. I cannot believe you would ask me to give up New York and financial success and professional security all because of the smell of some weeds.

Wendy Chalmers said, I am not asking you to do anything. You do what you want.

They went around and around about it, but something had gone sour. They could not get the good feelings back no matter how much they tried. Martin was convinced it was only a matter of making her see reason, yet the more he pressed her the more reluctant she became. He arrived one overcast Saturday afternoon in September at her family's farmhouse to deliver an ultimatum. He had worked himself into a state. She escorted him into the living room, where she played a Chopin nocturne on the old spinet to calm him. She was not halfway through before he interrupted her to explain that he had thought the matter over at great length and it was clear to him that if she loved him, if she truly truly loved him, she would accompany him to New York. If she refused to accompany him, this could only mean she did not truly love him. If she did not love him, it would be best for all concerned if he were to depart for Manhattan on his own. QED. Martin thought that once he posed the matter so starkly she would relent, if only to confirm the depths of her affection for him. He made the mistake of actually saying QED.

Instead of relenting, she swiveled on the piano bench to peer at him with a frozen glint in her eye and a look of such controlled fury it made him shrink in his chair. It was a look he had never seen on her before. Speaking in a tone so subdued that he had to strain to hear, she said that if he truly loved her, he would never demand she leave her home and family and all that she had ever known to move eight hundred miles away to a place where she knew no one. But it seemed, she added, her words now flashing like blades, that he had already decided there was no love to be had anywhere. Before he could object or seek to explain or try to backtrack, she rose suddenly, slamming closed the fallboard on the old spinet—it sounded to him like the sound of his heart shutting down—and marched out of the room. He sat there for some minutes, waiting for her to return, but she did not return. It took him some minutes more before he realized she was never going to return. He drove home through a heavy downpour and that very evening brought his luggage down from the attic. He left Nice two days later and settled in a one-room apartment on Avenue B on the Lower East Side, where he took the train to midtown every morning. Even though the vast majority of city residents are themselves imports from elsewhere, he felt conspicuously out of

place. It was as if you could see Hoosier in the shape of his
nose or the way he scratched his ear.

For the whole of that first year, Martin was miserable. He
missed Indiana. He missed the feel of the rain on his face filtered through the branches of a dogwood tree, the call of the
wild turkey, and the sight of red admirals drifting above the
falls of the Ohio. He ached with longing for Wendy Chalmers. It was a hard, a palpable ache. The idea that he had made
a terrible mistake preyed on him. Every so often he pulled
out all 119 pages of his uncompleted dissertation, "A Stochastic Demonstration of the Principle of Sufficient Reason
Using the Saperstein-Hideaki Conjecture," and looked it
over, imagining that one day he would manage to finish it,
though after ten minutes of reflection he always came back
to the fact that he had bypassed for good the kind of happiness for which he had always longed.

Martin reminded himself he was free. He was free to eat
at the most famous dining spots in the world. He was free
to attend live performances of the latest plays. He had access
to the New York Public Library and the Museum of Modern Art. He was free to ice-skate at Rockefeller Center and
to book a seat at Carnegie Hall and to go sailing in New
York Harbor. He went out and did many of these things. He
brunched on dim sum in Chinatown. One clement Saturday
afternoon, he napped in Sheep's Meadow. Another weekend
he stood before Goya's *Naked Maja*. He took the train to
Coney Island, where he spun around on the roller coaster and
ate famous hot dogs. But whenever Martin did anything, he
wished Wendy Chalmers were with him. When he dined on
steamed pork buns, he imagined Wendy Chalmers was there

watching him savor the taste. He imagined Wendy Chalmers snapping a photo of him posed next to the triceratops at the Museum of Natural History. He wanted it to be Wendy Chalmers who heard him scream when he rode the Cyclone. He was not living his life. He was living his life as he imagined it would be seen by Wendy Chalmers. Everything he did, he did with the idea that Wendy Chalmers should have been right beside him, looking over his shoulder.

If God needed something to see Him, maybe Martin needed Wendy Chalmers to see him.

For some months he wrote Wendy twice a week, thinking that she might come around and make the move out here to be with him. She never answered his letters. In time, he heard from a mutual friend back home who had seen her at the Nice autumn harvest festival with Stanley Cavalcante. Stanley Cavalcante was a woodshop teacher at one of the middle schools where she taught the basic fingerings for everything from the trumpet and the clarinet to the cello, along with how to beat the tympani drum.

CHAPTER FIVE

B UT MAEVE WAS ASKING how Martin and Lily first met. Every winter the investment firm threw a New Year's Eve party. Now Martin generally kept to himself at work. While he had started the job with the understanding he might one day be named head of the currency desk, it soon became clear that he was regarded as an outsider. His colleagues had graduated from the best business programs in the world. They had gone to the Booth School in Chicago, to Wharton, to Judge at Cambridge. Most were clueless about pure mathematics. This made him the object of office fun. He frequently found his email in-box flooded with ads for erectile aids. He returned from Labor Day weekend to discover his desk and computer console in the Ladies. But new associates could not not go to the end-of-the-year party. So Martin went and stood to one side and nursed a near beer, not talking to anybody. He was waiting for a decent-enough interval so he could convey his thanks and go home.

Lily was the tall limber woman in the corner. He noticed her right away. She was friends with someone in international arbitrage, or maybe it was derivatives; Martin can no longer recall which. She had a high forehead and a swept-back mane of raging blond hair. Above her beaded vest, a shallow burst of freckles misted the bony ridges of her sternum. She gestured emphatically as she spoke, a goblet of wine cupped in her palm. Martin could not have said at the time what first struck him about her, and if pressed, he could not say now after all these years. Though her voice wasn't loud, it carried across the room. If you listened closely, however, you heard a tremulousness to her tone. Beneath it all, her vowels quivered like plucked strings. Her beaded vest and harem pants said she was trying too hard.

She was by no means unattractive, though her beauty was unconventional. She was one of those women who in a certain light looks exotic, but later you notice her eyes are too close together above the powerful nose, and while her rear is heavy she is small up top, as if she has been pieced together out of two different women. Still, Martin thought the disproportion oddly beguiling. It seemed to him that she writhed where she stood.

He could not help but wonder how pleasure might contort her features. He was young. Like most men that age, he was in the habit of immediately transporting any woman he first met to a mental room outfitted with a bed. Martin's particular mental room was hung with magenta tapestries and festooned with trumpet vines. The bed was large and the pillows bulged with eiderdown. The windows were long. The sunlight was shattering. He would slowly undress women in its glare and subject them to masterful if imaginary lovemaking in which he turned them this way and that. But his idea of this woman the first time he met her refused to enter the mental room. She remained a cipher. His mind got no further than her long-limbed body curled into the shape of a question mark.

Martin meant to introduce himself, but a member of the catering staff, a girl with a head of kinked red ringlets and a garnet stud piercing her left nostril, invited him to sample one of the vulcanized prawns on decorative skewers from her tray. Her bearing was decidedly flirtatious. He did not want to be rude. He had not been in Manhattan long enough to learn that rude could be a way of life. So Martin exchanged pleasantries with the girl for several minutes, but when he looked again, the other woman was gone. He searched for her throughout the remainder of the party, but he did not find her. He was sure she was gone out of his life for good.

The evening focused the whole of his discontent, which had been building for months now. Martin switched from near beer to real beer. Also real wine and finally real whiskey. He left with the girl from the catering staff with the burning Afro. She was working her way through Fordham. They went back to her dormitory, where the two of them reclined on a beanbag chair while she recited poetry in his ear. This was poetry she had written herself. In one poem a coal company executive was ravaged by a convocation of eagles. In another, a research chemist for a major pharmaceutical combine succumbed to a deadly antigen. In a third, a slumlord was torn apart in the middle of an urban street by a pack of feral dogs. In each poem Gaia revenged herself on the forces of benighted self-interest and shortsighted technocracy. Her verse, like her hair, was apocalyptic. After another seven poems, she stood and without ceremony shucked off her clothes. Her pubic hair was the same color as the hair on her head, though only half grown back. Her sex looked stark and raw. What little hair there was prickled. Making love to her was like plunging again and again into a thicket of flaming nettles.

Toward morning he staggered across campus to catch the subway back to his apartment. The train screamed through the Bronx dawn, past abandoned warehouses and tenements. At one stop, a lone pair of trousers turned inside out hung from a clothesline strung across an alleyway. The pockets of the trousers were preternaturally white, trembling in the breeze like flags of surrender. Here Martin decided to forswear women altogether. Their presence in his life seemed the source of an ongoing litany of grief and regrets. He would give up women and devote his energies to rock climbing or ukulele playing or learning Swedish—some pastime that would enrich his existence in unexpected ways and make him a better person. But he happened upon her one Saturday six weeks later, sitting in the window of a luncheonette uptown. Not the girl with kinked red hair, but the other one—the tall limber one from the party.

Martin recognized her straightaway. She would not recognize him, he knew. She had never registered his presence in the first place. He again tried to picture how the transports of love might reconfigure her features, but he could not. She was like this black hole in the night skies of his experience, from which no meaning could escape. He stood outside the luncheonette, summoning the courage to go in. He aimed to make a profound first impression. But as he hesitated, she pushed herself back from the counter and edged out the door, moving past him without a glance. She walked bent forward slightly at the waist, as if her hips had trouble keeping up with her head.

He returned to the luncheonette the next Saturday and the Saturday after that. She adhered to a strict schedule. She always ordered the grilled cheese sandwich on sourdough and a cup of minestrone. It was winter. Dirty snow lined the gutters. She frequently wore blue jeans and a heavy cable sweater, though once Martin saw her in black leggings, and another time in the same harem pants she had donned for the party. The harem pants were all wrong. They emphasized her rear in an unflattering way. He found this vulnerability curiously touching. He liked her in a way he would not have liked her had she had the ass of a fashion model. She ate with her books spread out on the counter before her. She studied amid the tink of dishes and the splat of simmering grease.

This became his hobby on weekends. Martin took one of the booths so he could stare at her with impunity. A mirror ran along the wall behind the counter. He watched her reflection straight on as she ate. Her presence was dense and vivid. She pursed her lips to blow into the hot soup. Her teeth tore at her food. Her throat moved as she swallowed. Her face dipped once more, striking at the sandwich. A time or two, her head came up and her eyes drove right at him through the mirror, but then her gaze tripped on past. She did not see him, he could tell. He did not exist for her. Sitting in the crowded coffee shop, it seemed he had become invisible. This made Martin feel strangely empty inside, as if he had ceased to exist altogether.

One crowded morning Martin waited until the stool next to her became vacant. Her proximity made him dizzy. She was almost as tall as he was. She exuded a certain nervous energy, a kind of heat. Sitting next to her was like sitting next to a large animal coiled to spring. He tried once again to imagine the words and gestures she would bring to the bedroom, but he could not.

Martin had, over the course of his youth and the early years of manhood, worked at envisioning all manner of women at the very pitch of the moment. He imagined the school-crossing guard, the woman at the dry cleaner's where his mother took his father's mechanic overalls to be laundered, and the parson's wife. He imagined Professor Tatyana Botvinnik, the instructor in his two-semester college sequence on the Russian novel. When she lectured on Nabokov, Martin got excited under his desk. He imagined a network news anchor, a world-class decathlete, and Margaret Thatcher all thrashing elatedly. He had pictured in exacting detail each of these women seized by passion, but no matter how hard he tried, he could not conceive of the look and the noises his future wife would exhibit at the pinnacle of rapture.

Sitting at the counter, Lily turned the pages of her antitrust text with a whipping action of her hand. In the mirror her reflection turned pages, too. She seemed impatient, possibly angry at the world. Martin sat next to her, an untouched almond bear claw in front of him, and practiced asking her out. These would be the first words he spoke to her. He wanted to get them just right. He would speak to her, and she would lift her head to look back. Her gaze would flood the emptiness inside. Martin imagined asking her in a clever and memorable way to dinner or a movie and then later, over a drink, admitting to her that he had gone to the diner every Saturday for a month to look at her. In time, he would tell her his deepest secrets and fears and hopes. She would tell him hers. He imagined a conversation that once begun would never stop. They would have so much to say to each other. For instance, he would tell her she should rethink the harem pants.

He imagined marrying her and years later the two of them laughing over how he had spied on her while she remained unaware. In the mirror behind the counter, his face now smiled, getting ready to laugh in the future.

But Martin did not ask her out. He did not speak to her. He kept putting it off. He returned again and again in the coming weeks, sitting a stool or two over, waiting for when he would turn to her and say whatever memorable words he eventually hit upon. He cherished these moments. To his mind, they were really all the same moment. He came back to it whenever he entered the diner. Here time stalled altogether. It was the moment before he would say the words that would change his life forever.

Riding the subway into work every day, he thought about when he would next visit the diner.

Sitting down to a staff meeting, he heard once more the sound of her turning the pages of her book.

Eating dinner by himself in his room at night, he remembered the way she looked blowing into her soup.

It occurred to him that he could do this for weeks more on end. He could return again and again for months and even years to come. He could live such a life.

Martin was happy inhabiting every second as if it were the penultimate one.

And then one morning almost two months after he started coming to the café, she asked him to pass the salt. He saw the way her reflection turned to face his own. It took him a second to connect the words he heard with the mouth moving in the mirror above the counter.

He wheeled on his stool to stare at her. She peered back, waiting. Her face looked different from the way it looked in the mirror. He could see the tiny pores in her cheeks, and the faint white down along her jawline, and the tight whorl of her ear.

Martin reached for the salt, anxious to comply, but the shaker magically leaped off the counter and smashed to the floor. The sound was sudden in the diner. It left a hush in its wake. She looked down. Broken glass shards sat amid the gyre and scatter of the white grains. A single arm of salt soared out along the dark pattern of the linoleum, spiraling like the photograph of a remote galaxy. The metal cap shot through with holes rested on its side. Martin saw everything; he took in the smallest detail. She shifted on her stool to look up at him once more. Her eyes settled on his face only at the final second, as if she had sought him out from an unfathomable distance. This became the story of how they met, the story she would repeat later. As far as Lily is concerned, it all started right there at that instant.

I won't ask for the pepper, she had said to him then.

By the time Lily finishes telling Maeve her version of their first meeting, the fire has burned down. Red embers smolder in the grate. Glancing at his wife now—the story has made her face shimmer in the dying light—Martin stands and stretches and says, I'm going to turn in.

Lily follows a short while later. He lies in bed as she puts on her nightgown. She undresses with her back to him. After she breast-fed the twins, she complained that she dropped from a B cup to an A, though a year or so back on a shopping trip to the mall, Martin learned she in fact wears a double A. Her need to lie both touches him and acts as a powerful erotic spur. He has assured her repeatedly he likes them even better than before. While she refuses to believe him, it is true. Slight as they are, they turn up sharply in the way of Nordic ski jumps. Looking at them, he experiences a sense of weightlessness like one vaulted high into the air.

When she disappears into the bathroom, Martin gets out of bed to prop the door closed with *Property*. He adds *Civil Procedure* just to make sure, and then crawls back under the covers. The bed shifts with his wife's weight as she eases in next to him. When she turns off the bedside lamp, he pauses for what seems a decent-enough interval so as not to seem too eager, and then begins to run an experimental finger up and down her arm, but he stops when they hear the unmistakable creak of the floorboards from out in the hall.

Lily whispers, I have a breakfast meeting anyway.

CHAPTER SIX

MARTIN LIES AWAKE UNTIL far into the night, unable to sleep. Time enough to contemplate the ironies. For if what initially drew him to Lily all those years ago was his fervid anticipation of her countenance in the throes of love, when the opportunity finally arrived, it was shrouded in shadows. She asked him to dim the lights. Though he assumed that in due course her reticence would soften, it never really has. To this day, she still occasionally retires to the bathroom to change clothes. She refuses to piddle in his presence. After a dozen years of marriage, she continues to prefer at most a weak bulb or single candle at bedside. For this reason, their lovemaking has almost always happened in ill-lit rooms with the shades drawn and often amid the aroma of smoldering paraffin. Anything above twenty watts and she can't climax.

Martin has entertained dozens of theories to explain Lily's sexual diffidence. He is familiar with the idea that successful people often manage to sublimate lustful drives by concentrating on social or professional advancement, though such talk seems to rest on a dubious hydraulics of libidinal flow that reduces personality to plumbing. Some might cite an overreaching religious training, yet the truth is, Lily's family are lapsed Calvinists who strayed from the flock almost a century back. When Lily was growing up, the Van Slykes made it to church only twice over the course of twelve months, on Christmas Eve and Easter morning—except not always on Easter and not always on Christmas, either. For a period of several years early on, Martin was sure Lily's inhibitions in this area issued from the high regard she had for him and his talents; he became convinced that were he a common day laborer or ditchdigger, she would gleefully inaugurate him into a slew of bedroom antics rarely seen outside a Tijuana bordello. For several years after that, he went the other way, wondering if her unresponsiveness resulted because her esteem for him had, in fact, dipped so low; if he were a shipping magnate or a Nobel contender, she would gleefully, et cetera. He eventually came to view both prospects as the product of an unhealthy preoccupation with his own role in the scheme of things. And so while he continues to be drawn to the notion that there may be trapped inside his wife another woman, a wilder woman capable, given the right circumstances, of unleashing colossal forces of concupiscence, his current perspective remains agnostic. He tells himself that maybe Lily's difficulty in this quarter is not necessarily a drawback or a hindrance, but strong evidence of her discriminating temperament.

Early on he came to realize it was best to sneak up on the moment. He had to spring an erotic ambush. If he was too clumsy or quick, then all was lost. If he was too subtle or lingering, all was also lost. The trick was to lurk nearer and nearer—you had to come up like a thief—and then at just the right instant fly at her. Fly at her with everything he had. After all these years, Martin never knows exactly when or how much is enough but not too much. Even for a man accustomed to calculating the most recondite probabilities, the variables are too many. It is not a science. It is even before art.

It is cavemen trying to capture lightning on the way to discovering fire.

Martin's memory of their first time together still makes him cringe. He was done before she had begun. Not that Lily complained. She lay back and smiled up at him with sweet forbearance without uttering a sound. He felt both humiliated and curiously cheated. To his mind, the acoustics of the act always figured prominently. He anticipated a little whoop and holler. But she remained as mute as the pillow on which she laid her head. When it was over—when Martin was through—she hopped up and padded to the bathroom. Listening to her trying not to pee too loudly left him weirdly forlorn.

It was the same the next time and the time after that. He tried all he could think of to gratify her, but her responses were so listless, he feared there might be some feature of his character or physique that rendered him repulsive in her eyes. He had never considered himself particularly handsome, though a woman or two had on occasion remarked on his looks. He had been a tall and rangy boy, narrow as a staff, and he liked to think that despite the accumulation of years and pounds, his body continued to carry some distant echo of those days. He trawled his own recollections in an attempt to draw up a detailed roster of what techniques had succeeded with other women and which had not. His experience was, admittedly, limited. He was far from a bedroom adventurer himself. But if there was a telltale thread to his conquests, it eluded him. He checked sex books out of the library, with their line drawings of cock and mons, yet the postures reminded him of circus contortionists. It occurred to him that perhaps his lovemaking might be too quick, and so he strove to delay his own pleasure by rehearsing in his head famed arithmetic chains—Recamán's sequence, Mersenne primes, Fibonacci numbers—though Lily continued to lie beneath him placid as a log.

Martin began to despair about their future. But then one evening—they had been together for almost four months—she suddenly started to tremble. She had never before trembled in just this way. Martin had no idea why this was so. He did not know what he had done. Maybe he had not done anything, and something about her day or her state of mind or pheromones in the air had joined to launch her near to finishing. Maybe the stars had hit upon a propitious alignment. Whatever the reason, it was apparent that she was coming close. He thought, Finally I will get to see her in the full attitude of love. She had as usual insisted on killing the lights, and so the room existed through a thin membrane of illumination from a neon marquee outside her window. In its bare glow, they loomed nearer and nearer.

At the very pitch of the moment, however, Lily whispered, Don't look, and she reached up to cover his eyes.

She shuddered mildly, once, and went limp. Only then did she let him look, but it was too late. He did not see her on that evening nor has he on most evenings since. She trembles only rarely, with not much more regularity than a lunar eclipse. She has trembled in a mountain cabin, a rural bed-and-breakfast, and once just off the promenade deck on board *The Flying Duchess* within hailing distance of Quintana Roo, but he has sighted her pleasure sporadically and always too briefly. In all their time together, he has never really gotten an honest and straightforward and unimpeded appraisal of his wife in the full heat of carnal transport, because whenever this instant approaches—whenever she begins to shake—she asks him not to look. He must filch such glimpses as he can. His mind is left to fill in the gaps. He makes love not to his wife, but to some mirage of his wife steeped in the simmerings of his brain.

What Martin fails to see is that the frequency and intensity of the Fowlers' couplings fall well within the usual statistical parameters. He clings to the idea that their love life is hobbled by Lily's self-consciousness. He does not see how his own expectations in this area were, in fact, wildly skewed by one of his very first lovers, a middle-aged divorcée who moved into town the summer between his junior and senior years in college. She was in his mother's sewing circle. The woman had fled Fort Wayne to escape a bad marriage. As she told it, her ex-husband was a domineering, physically repulsive man who went too long between baths. She was so taken with Martin's sexual pliancy and the scent of carbolic soap on his skin that in bed she went off repeatedly like a Roman candle. He does not see that this woman was the exception and not the rule. He does not see that the legions of reports in the popular press regarding female sexual underperformance are due almost entirely to the ham-handedness of husbands whose understanding of basic anatomy comes from the etchings on the wall of the Boys at PS 84. He does not see how the relentless barrage of online images, print ads, and TV commercials replete with half-clothed, sinuous women that he has endured through his more than two score years on this Earth has left him with the barely acknowledged but nagging suspicion that somewhere there exists a toweringly stunning nymphomaniac who secretly pines only for him. He does not see that this prospect is no more credible than talk of Bigfoot or Nessie. Martin does not see how women feel keenly the need to make themselves attractive to men and yet remain just as keenly aware of how humiliating and craven this need can make them. He does not see that by the time she is twenty-eight the average woman will have slept with 2.9 men who promised to phone the next day but are never heard from again. He does not see that at this same age the average woman will have been called a cold and heartless cockteaser by the 6.3 men she refused to sleep with. He does not see that at this age the average woman will have dated for over five months at least one man who frequently spoke of marriage yet not only refused to introduce her to his parents but also turned out to have a wife and three kids and a miniature schnauzer named Banjo residing in a split-level in Weehawken, New Jersey. Martin does not see that living in a world where you are paid eighty cents on the dollar and must devote six hours more than your spouse each week to housecleaning and four and three-quarter hours more to child rearing and three hours more to grocery shopping and an extra two hours and ten minutes to making up your face—and we won't even mention your hair—leaves you so weary and bleary-eyed that when you do manage the time to lie down with your husband, odds are you are going to come away feeling not only inadequate and confused but also used and resentful and just a little sick to your stomach. He does not see that the tales Paul Bogdasarian—a commodities broker (Ethiopian coffee, Chinese tea, Puerto Rican rum) and the closest thing Martin has to a friend down at the office— relays regarding Sheila Bogdasarian's sexual appetites are likely utter fabrications. Martin has met Sheila Bogdasarian. She is a dangerously thin woman with a faint mustache. She has a high nasal voice and teaches kindergarten. She looks and sounds like no one's idea of a bedroom dynamo. But according to Paul Bogdasarian, his wife is unquenchable. According to Paul Bogdasarian, most women don't exhibit similar passion because they have lost sight of themselves in the deepest part of their being. According to Paul Bogdasarian, these women merely need a kind and sensitive and accommodating man to introduce them to who they really are. According to Paul Bogdasarian, Paul Bogdasarian is an emotional genius. He introduces his wife to who she is on a regular basis in the bedroom. He introduces his wife to who she is bent over the living room ottoman. He introduces his wife to who she is on the area rug in the foyer. According to Paul Bogdasarian, Sheila Bogdasarian just the other evening twisted his shirtfront into a fist and said, Do me in the basement, so they went downstairs and he introduced her to herself next to the circular table saw. After one such conversation with Paul Bogdasarian, Martin went home and stole up behind Lily while she was preparing dinner. He planned on nuzzling her neck and then introducing her to who she is on the kitchen linoleum. But Martin does not see that Lily inadvertently stabbed him in the thigh with a tenderizing fork not because of sexual reluctance on her part but because in her surprise and fright she mistook him for an intruder when she was intent on rendering an inexpensive cut of chuck roast edible. Martin does not see that somewhere deep in a woman's brain there survive select snippets from Simone de Beauvoir and Andrea Dworkin and Mary Wollstonecraft and Aristophanes that have fermented for decades, such that every six months or so you come bolt upright out of a sound sleep with the momentary but crystalline urge to murder every man within a fifty-mile radius, starting with the load of flesh and gore snoring next to you. Martin does not see— he hasn't the slightest glimmer of—the smug satisfaction he derives from thinking how understanding he is toward what he takes to be his wife's difficulties in the sack.

Several years ago Martin tried broaching the subject with Lily directly. He would have done so sooner though he feared the conversation would prove both awkward and turbulent.

With the birth of the twins, however, the frequency of their couplings ebbed even further. It seemed they were fast approaching the point of no return. He told himself no man should have to spend the last half of his existence loveless. Moreover, he felt he owed the woman in his life honesty in all things. He hoped that she would so value his candor they would have a mature and thoughtful and soul-searching discussion, at which point she would fall into his arms and Roman candle again and again.

His plan backfired spectacularly. He talked at length, citing varying physical expectations, their respective sexual histories, society's repressive taboos, the difficulties and inequities of being a woman in this day and age. It was a wide-ranging speech he had spent some time preparing. He cited Kinsey, Theodore Reich, and Engels on the family. He talked for maybe twenty minutes, after which she looked at him and said, Are you finished? He hesitated before saying, Yes, I guess I am. She said, I did not realize you were so unhappy. I'm not, he countered. I don't want to make you unhappy, she whispered. You don't, he insisted, but before he could say more she left the room.

He saw he had embarrassed and offended her. They circled each other like wary gamecocks for the next three days, but on the fourth evening after they had retired she reached for him unexpectedly and pulled him on top of her. A moment later she began to mew. Her reaction was so uncharacteristic he knew it was far from genuine. But he was heartened by her willingness to feign enthusiasm. To show his appreciation, he grunted in reply. She sensed this grunt was part of an act meant to show just how desirous he found her—though she had to wonder why, if he found her truly desirous, he needed to act—and so sought to reward him in kind. Lying beneath him, she began to cry out. This was far, far more noise than she had ever made. He responded by groaning and thumping above her. Soon each gesture, every little sound was reciprocated, and now reciprocated again, in a rising dialectic of chirps and bleats and oinks, a veritable barnyard of spasms and gropings and facial rictuses. These tics and noises came in such a rush that whatever intentions first spawned them vanished under their mounting accumulation. Every convulsion and bark was no longer just itself, but instead a prop in an elaborate bit of stagecraft meant to affirm just how earnest and unstaged their affection was. In this way, the distinction between the real and the apparent was garroted right there in their bed. In no time they were each gibbering. If sounds are the bricks by which we build the house of meaning, here was its aftermath, a smoking rubble of noises.

They both stopped at once, having simultaneously realized they could go on like this forever and never arrive anywhere. They stopped, though neither had gotten off. They lay for a long time afterward. She found his hand and squeezed it and said, That was lovely. Wasn't that lovely, Martin? He looked over—in the darkness the moon came through the skylight and painted the planes of her face the color of silver ingots—and said, It was wonderful.

Yet when all is said and done, Martin counts himself lucky. If asked, he would insist theirs is a solid partnership. He often experiences a ballooning gratitude at his good fortune. He tells himself Lily's physical reluctance is a small price to pay for the familiar rituals and constancy of marriage. It feels petty to fixate on such troubles when there is her quick mind. There is the way she will rest her head on his shoulder on the cab ride home. He always comes back in the end to the pair of dimples that frame her natal cleft like his own personal punctuation marks, written in a private language incomprehensible to the outside world. He knows deep down that should she suddenly be torn from his life, his sense of himself would be so upended he would never manage to right it again. He once heard marriage compared to a large building, or perhaps it was an immense ship. It was a ship. Marriage is a ship, and if you do not undertake the thousand and one repairs necessary, the craft will founder. You must secure the matrimonial forestay and recaulk the gunwales or you, too, could go under.

This is why Martin wakes her with Asian-pear biscotti and spiced coffee on her birthday. This is why they always take a Caribbean holiday in winter. She receives a pound of Belgian truffles on the fourteenth of February and a single orchid shipped overnight from the Peruvian rain forest on the second Sunday in May. It is why through the years he has obligingly played backhand to her forehand in doubles and north to her south in contract bridge, though her serve is wretched and she can never keep track of the auction.

He joined her in a six-week wine class at the New School, nine two-hour dance lessons (ballroom, boogie-woogie, and bossa nova), and a book club in which nobody read. He misspent a bug-ridden summer coaxing dysmorphic squash and spindly broccolini from the soil of a community garden up on Sixteenth Street. It is why he never objects when one or the other of Lily's brothers persists in calling him "Marty." And this is why he makes it a point to stay always and forever unswervingly faithful.

CHAPTER SEVEN

ALWAYS AND FOREVER, though he's had his chances. Some six years into their marriage—a time when conjugal preoccupations fixed on her penchant for hogging the remote and his failure to recap the hemorrhoid salve— there appeared at Martin's investment firm a staffer who began looking up from her desk three rows over whenever he passed through the data-entry concourse on the way to his office. She was slightly gap-toothed. Otherwise, her eyes ruled her face. They seemed to hide an unspeakable hurt. Her skin was the color of a betel nut. Something about her demeanor suggested the casbah, though the fact is, she was from Yonkers. The first few times she caught his eye, Martin quickly turned away in bewilderment and embarrassment, but then one day when she smiled at him, he found himself smiling in reply. The gap between her teeth was no bigger than the width of a caraway seed, yet its mass was sufficient to open a trapdoor beneath his heart. He came home that evening to find Lily in a rage over some slight one of her superiors had ostensibly directed her way. She was up for promotion that year and saw herself as the target of a host of lawyerly intrigues and professional indignities, real or imagined. The pressure on her was enormous. If she made partner her future was assured, but if she was denied she would have to switch to a smaller firm, a firm with somewhat lower billings and therefore far less prestige, and hence start all over again. Martin listened as his wife recounted the episode, though his mind kept straying to the look the staffer had leveled at him. It was as if her smile pulsed even now in the way the blood flowed through his veins. In the coming days and weeks, these smiles grew richer and more constant and lingering. Evenings he sat patiently while Lily talked about another junior associate she had long regarded as a friend but who had had the temerity to stab her in the back, she talked about the ways in which the support team of secretaries and paralegals refused to treat her with the respect she felt was her due, she talked about how even the janitorial staff were obviously out to get her, having failed to empty the wastebasket beside her desk—but the whole while he kept imagining a perhaps not-too-distant day in the future when he and the woman from the data-entry concourse went from smiles to talk and then to whispers and on to who knew what else. But before they got to who knew what else, the woman was transferred to the D.C. branch.

And then there was the woman some three years on who started boarding the subway at Spring Street. She was a champagne blonde with ongoing legs and the sculpted features he associated with Finnish nobility. She wore furred boots and a sable hat. Her skirts had slits up to here. She always sat in the third car. Martin started to ride it so he could steal glances at her skirts. He stood just so in the aisle. One day she caught him staring, and he quickly averted his gaze. When he chanced to look a few minutes later, the slit had widened. It widened still farther as the train trundled north. Meanwhile, her own look narrowed with a knowing pleasure. By the time Martin got off at his stop, he believed he could see her underwear. Every weekday for the next two months, Martin boarded the third car. Her panties were often white, sometimes sky blue or a mild yellow, twice polka-dotted, and once an eye-jarring carmine. These hues named the color of his thinking for the rest of the day. He promised himself that the morning would come when he would not get off the train, but instead ride as far as the slit in the skirt would take him. But a conductors' strike shut the line down for a week. When service resumed, his queen had disappeared. For the next month, he boarded the first car and worked his way to the last, but he never saw the woman or her skirts again.

Not a word was exchanged in either of these intrigues, yet the looks that passed between Martin and these women were of such force that even today they continue to rise in his memory like lit obelisks at night.

There was one final incident from a year and a half back that Martin refuses to dwell on. He has never mentioned it to anyone, and he never will. In the time since, he has done everything in his power to forget—which is why we must talk about it here.

He had promised to attend a Saturday fund-raising luncheon. He and Lily usually went to these fêtes together. They felt at times a social responsibility. They were lucky, they knew. They had long ago outgrown the absurd belief that those who have more work harder. The data was clear. Despite anecdotes to the contrary, the notion of social mobility is largely a myth.

That said, the future looked dire. Humanity was running out of fuel, water, rain forest, fish, topsoil, coastline, birds, and bees. Lily sympathized with those tech tycoons who hatch plans for designer villages on mountaintops or behind floodgates, who dream of terraforming Mars or colonizing the moons of the outer planets, schemes for secreting the very best humanity has to offer away from all the rest, safe and secure once the planet begins to cook. A few master life, while the rest are mastered by it. When faced with Armageddon, could you really be blamed for opting to save yourself and your own? In the end, she was her father's daughter.

Yet she was not unfeeling. So Lily and Martin duly partook of this or that charity function. Plus, she liked to see the Wainrights, Naomi Woodbine, and the Honorable Douglas Blankenbaker. Four months earlier, the Fowlers had attended an evening wine and cheese party for a desalinization plant on the banks of the Dead Sea, and the previous spring, he and Lily had donned trademarked T-shirts and walked three miles for cleft palates in the Andes. On the morning of the luncheon, however, Lily woke complaining of a migraine. Martin did not want to go alone, but he could not think of a reason fast enough that did not sound like a sorry echo of her own. So he dutifully took a cab to a hotel in the West Sixties, where he made his way to Banquet Room B. He ate cold curried chicken salad (raisins, red onion) and watched a video on river blindness among the Phů'doc of the Mekong Delta. It featured blank-eyed toddlers staring numbly into thundering torrents of water. The keynote speaker was a squat woman in an unlikely lamé pantsuit who had worked for twenty years at a Catholic mission in Indochina. Her thighs looked imposing beneath the fabric. Her hair was long and dark. Streaks of gray filtered through it like filament. While he guessed her to be at least five years his senior, he thought her striking and robust. Because his own wife was willowy in aspect, Martin had over the years developed a growing but unspoken fascination with stout women. It didn't hurt that she used to be a nun.

Standing at the podium, she explained that the cure for river blindness was already at hand. No laboratory break-throughs were required, no massive research programs. All that was needed was the economic will. For a miserly sum, the children of the Phů'doc would see once more. The woman spoke at length. Her voice was unmusical but edged with probity. Martin seemed to be one of those faces in the audience her eyes returned to again and again. He found himself nodding in reply, urging her on. At the close of her address, many rose to their feet and clapped. Martin rose to his feet and clapped. He wrote out a check and dropped it in the basket that made its way around the room.

Martin was filing out of Banquet Room B with the rest of the crowd when the chicken salad seized his entrails between turmeric talons. He about-faced to reach the restroom just in time. He did not emerge until twenty minutes later, febrile and wan. Banquet Room B was dark. The chairs sat stacked on the tables, and all the tables had been pushed to one side of the hall. He passed Banquet Room A, where the Ximinez quinceañera was in full swing, and boarded the elevator. Here came the keynote speaker, making her way up the hall, a white cane prodding the carpet before her. Her eyes looked the same as yours or mine, but it turned out that she was blind as a vole. Martin did not want to ride in an elevator or anywhere else with a blind person. He stabbed the CLOSE DOOR button repeatedly, but he was too late. She and her white cane stepped into the Otis. Martin quietly pressed his back to the wall and went still. The elevator began to descend. He held his breath and took the opportunity to study her. She had a large front. A Saint Lucy medal hung by a gold chain from her neck. She suddenly turned and asked, Is someone there?

I am, Martin volunteered after a pause. The pause felt sinister. He thought he should say something more to assure her he was not a purse thief or a masher. He said, I enjoyed your speech.

Addressing his shoulder, she said, Thank you.

I saw you up there and I couldn't even tell. Not for a million bucks could I have said.

She again turned in his direction and said, I've had lots of practice.

Her tone was wry, but her words were so full of lament— the close quarters, along with the slight but unmistakable atmospherics that told them they were going down down

down, encouraged a surprising intimacy—that Martin could not help but add, It must be hard.

She tilted her head and looked at him with what he would have described in any other context as interest, but of course it was not a look. It's lonely, she admitted. But you get used to it.

Martin heard himself say, Can I buy you a drink?

In the hotel bar when she ordered a vodka, he said, Two. The other patrons looked at her cane. They looked at him. He sat straight up on his bar stool. She asked his name. Bob, Martin told her. She brought the glass to her mouth. He watched her throat move.

He asked, How long?

Three, almost four years.

This was in Asia?

That's the funny thing. I was diagnosed with glaucoma in Tulsa, Oklahoma. The one doesn't have anything to do with the other. Sometimes things just happen.

Nothing ever just happens, Martin said, because he did not like to believe it did. He smiled so she would know he didn't mean to be disagreeable, but he remembered she could not see that, either.

She shook her head and insisted, Everything just happens.

He considered what it must be like to be blind. He did not think about never getting to see a sunset or the stars at night or the faces of your loved ones. He thought instead about how hard it would be to cut a steak, match your pants with your shirt, or trim your toenails. When the woman said she needed to return to her room to pack—she had an evening flight out of La Guardia—Martin offered to help her find her way.

She regarded his ear for a long time before saying, Are you sure?

They rode up in the elevator. No one said a word. In the hall she handed him her key, but he couldn't get it to work. She took it back and opened the door herself. He hesitated before following her inside. He watched her tap the cane along the carpet. The curtains were drawn. The television played with the sound muted. On the screen, a pack of hyenas was trying to separate a wildebeest calf from the herd. A Gideon's Bible lay on the nightstand, opened to Exodus. She eased down onto the bedspread. It was a colorful diamond-back print, possibly Navajo.

Martin settled in the chair opposite. She sat with her hands in her lap. He looked at her eyes. They looked like anybody else's. He gingerly waved his fingers before her, but she did not react. He noticed his reflection in the mirror above the dresser. Martin wished there were someone sighted sitting next to him so he could look into a gaze that would tell him what to think.

He asked, Would you like to touch my face? He had once seen this on TV.

She smiled. No, but thank you.

Martin looked around the room. He looked at the lamp and the nightstand and the possibly Navajo bedspread and the Bible. The fact that she could not see them made these objects feel not all there.

I lied, she suddenly announced. You never get used to it.

Martin nodded but then remembered nods were pointless. On the screen, one hyena had hold of the gnu's foreleg; another had sunk its teeth into the animal's haunch. When the woman leaned toward him, they kissed. She kissed with her eyes open. He could see his own image mirrored in them. Then he closed his eyes.

He pretended he was blind, too.

She stood and began to unbutton her blouse. It felt wrong to look when she could not see him looking. He looked anyway. Martin thought of the twins. He thought of his wife. He thought of Lily's disappointment—of her pain and anger—should she ever find out. He wondered if she might leave him. No. She would kick him out and keep the boys. He thought of the shame, the public scandal. He wondered how it would look if word got around that Martin Fowler had fucked a blind woman.

Here he experienced a curious epiphany. He was not a man given to revelation—his thinking these days tended to plod, not leap—but he was seized by the unexpected insight that neither marital outrage nor social censure would prove his undoing. He could weather both if he had to. Far more troubling than the likelihood that Lily could one day uncover such an indiscretion was the deeper and almost incalculable eventuality that she might never discover it. This struck him as grim. He saw himself sneaking about for months or even years, duping his wife. He imagined the innumerable falsehoods he would have to engineer, the countless misdirections he would need to sustain, the mounting burden of an unending masquerade. He was not sure how he could live knowing that she remained clueless about the depths to which he could sink. Martin had long believed that a spouse is the prism through which the colors of the self are refracted. If he became a stranger to Lily, then he would almost certainly end as a stranger to himself.

When the woman unhooked her bra, the Saint Lucy metal flashed between her breasts. They were large and ungainly. They kept moving even after she had stopped. She shifted position and two seconds later they were still going. It seemed a tutorial in how life won't hold steady. He understood suddenly that the woman's blindness would serve to mitigate his guilt, as if her inability to see him somehow meant he wasn't all there. And if he wasn't all there, then the fucking was not fucking, not entirely. Admittedly, his logic was fractured, but he felt far from the shores of common sense.

He understood then what he had never grasped before: If only one person sees something, then nobody sees anything.

Another man might have welcomed such a realization. It

appeared to confer a copious liberty. He could stand an ex-nun on her head in the mirror if he wanted. Martin, however, was not another man. He experienced not relief, but a rising panic. He felt bizarrely spectral, airy as a meringue. He held his hand in front of his face and looked at that. He looked at the possibly Navajo spread. He looked at the Bible. The woman's inability to see bled the room of its substance. Maybe this is what things look like when no one is there to see them. It seemed once she stepped out of her undies, he might vanish altogether from the face of the Earth.

Martin began to shake. He shook where he sat. He shook uncontrollably, as if his lymphatic system understood things he did not and never would.

He stood suddenly, making his chair complain. The woman hesitated at the sound. On the screen, a trio of hyenas gnashed at the supine wildebeest, disemboweling it altogether.

Bob? she said to his elbow.

Here Martin ran. He was not his elbow. He ran out of the room. He ran along the hall. Just this side of the elevator, the Honorable Douglas Blankenbaker stopped to stare, and Martin ran past him, too. He pushed through the fire door and took the stairs, two at a time, down four flights. In the lobby, he bumped into a mariachi player, knocking the man over and making the strings of his round-backed guitar twang, but Martin kept going. He tore through the doors of the hotel and out into the sunlight. It was as if he had been delivered from a moral cave.

At home he found Lily still in bed, felled by her migraine. He joined her beneath the covers, gathered her in his arms, and hugged her. He had never been so happy to see her.

He had never been so happy to be seen by her.

Martin, she finally said, you're suffocating me.

Though this exploit is less than eighteen months old, the memory now seems centuries distant. The idea that he once came this close to capsizing his marriage feels as if it belongs to someone else. Martin grudgingly attributes this in part to the au pair; her presence in their lives has added happy heft to the here and now. Time and again, she manages to insert herself between them and disaster. It is Maeve who finds the car keys on the morning Lily is running late for a hearing. It is Maeve who comes upon Gavin trying to turn on one of the stove burners. It is Maeve who manages to unstop the toilet when Arnold flushes his stuffed dinosaur. And when she asks, Martin happily relinquishes the chore of winding the grandfather clock, showing her how to insert the crank into each of the three winding points behind the crystal face. The chimes make her smile.

Both Martin and Lily suddenly find they have far more energy to devote to themselves and their interests than at any time since the birth of the twins. And even Martin will concede that the girl has readily adapted the rhythms of her days to fit their own. When she isn't working, she is careful to keep out of the way. Some afternoons when the twins are napping, she sits at the kitchen table and flips through one of Lily's many catalogs. She looks at ads of women in jeweled gowns, of women carrying Burberry handbags, at photo spreads where girls her age sun topless on the decks of yachts. Or she rides up and down in the service elevator. She occasionally thumbs through the paperwork Lily brings home, the contracts or the pleadings or the prospectuses, marveling at the legal phraseology and the Latinate. Or she visits with the doorman, an older gent in a hat and an overcoat like a Soviet commissar's. He offers her wrapped Almond Roca candies, which she happily accepts.

More than once Martin has rounded a corner to come upon her sitting quietly with her hands in her lap, as if she is trying on the room and the things in the room—the things in their life—for size. Other times she climbs the stairwell to the small rooftop garden (the hinoki cypress, the corkscrew willow; she likes the purple honeysuckle best of all) next to the water tank and the disconcertingly low railing, where she stands amid the soaring high-rises as they pierce the sky. She stares out at them as if the buildings are not mere structures, repositories of people and businesses, but instead mysterious artifacts of untold age, titanic runes the meaning of which you might read if only you knew how.

For all her diligence and the sweetness of her disposition, there continue to be moments when the girl makes Martin uncomfortable. He turns about every so often to discover her peering at him keenly. It's as if she is looking not at him but through him, as though the center of his being were behind him somewhere, haunting him like a shadow he can never really lay hold of. He has the sense she can see things about him he never does. But then he will look at her once more and conclude such suspicions are venal and unwarranted, the outpourings of a damaged personality. He will notice that she has swept his study or sewn a missing button back onto one of his favorite shirts, or he will hear her absentmindedly mouthing the lyrics to some heartfelt if despondent ditty—he will see her, in other words, as dutiful and guileless, daughter of timeless ways—and so censure himself for having such an ill-tempered cast of mind.

She has a high and direct and dulcet voice. She sings to the boys, she sings to herself when she is alone, she sings while working. She sings to Aristotle, the African gray, roosting in its cage. She can't not sing. She sings rock anthems, show tunes from the fifties, Catholic dirges, eternal Gaelic ballads. Meanwhile, her needs remain modest. She takes tepid three-minute showers, even as Lily keeps assuring her there is plenty of hot water. The girl has two pairs of blue jeans, a pair of linen slacks, three blouses, a skirt, and a dress. She owns two pairs of shoes: canvas sneakers and a pair of low black pumps that she wears always and only to the 10:30 Mass at Our Lady of Victory. A thin Celtic cross of hammered brass hangs from a chain at the base of her throat. Two small green stones—the famous Connemara marble, mined from prehistoric outcroppings—occasionally appear at her ears. Otherwise, her face, her fingers are always bare. She doesn't take coffee but instead brews tea, straining the leaves through a small sieve blackened with tarnish.

They give her two days a week off and one weekend a month free. She sometimes spends these afternoons in her room, listening to the radio Lily placed on the bureau. Maeve has a friend, a plump Dubliner, a girl several years older who works as a domestic on the Upper West Side. The two of them frequent a pub on the Bowery where a band from Kilkenny often headlines.

One evening Maeve serves a meal of lamb chops and mint jelly that is among the most toothsome food Martin has ever had—and he has eaten in a number of Michelin-starred establishments in both New York and foreign capitals. After dinner he and his wife sit quietly at the table, sipping their coffees, stunned by the amount and the quality of the food. But when the boys clamor for ice cream—Arnold has seized Martin's wrist; Gavin tugs at his trouser leg and begins to cry—the parents rise with a groan. The five of them stroll down to the shop four blocks over. It is a temperate evening. Outside, the sun has just set, striations of clouds in the peach twilight. Here, Lily takes Martin's hand, and the feel of her palm in his makes his heart swell. Maeve and the twins trip ahead of them along the sidewalk. It is one of those nights that shrinks his woes, and gives to the universe a benign shape, and makes life feel like a munificent gift.

Maeve is bewildered by the variety of flavors. She has never heard of macadamia cheesecake, peach wasabi, or maple and bacon. When Lily invites her to sample Martin's cone—a Persian faloodeh the color of snow, infused with rose water—Maeve steadies his arm before leaning forward to shear a big bite off the top. Still clinging to his elbow, her eyes widen with unexpected pleasure.

How many scoops? the counterman asks her.

She holds up her fingers: Tree.

CHAPTER EIGHT

SEPTEMBER BRINGS TROUBLE. The Irish au pair receives a notice from Immigration to appear for a hearing. Failure to do so may result in the revocation of her visa and the initiation of deportation proceedings.

I'll go with you.

You have better things to do, Ms. Fowler.

It's true. She has a scheduled partners' meeting—though they will spend most of the time arguing about what color to paint the conference room and likely decide in the end to put it off for another year. And because she bills at twelve hundred dollars an hour, it would make more sense to ask a junior associate from the firm to accompany the girl and report back if any problems arise.

But I learned long ago that if you want something done, do it yourself. And call me Lily.

On a drizzling Tuesday afternoon, they arrive at the appointed time but are made to wait over an hour in a crowded anteroom. They wait between a man wearing a dashiki and two women in saris. In time, the women are replaced by a fellow in a yarmulke, who is replaced, in turn, by a woman in a burka.

I should have worn me da's caubeen, Maeve mutters.

She sits clutching her passport with the harp on its face.

Can I see? Lily asks. She turns the booklet in her fingers. In her photo the girl looks squarely into the camera, unsmiling, her fragile features framed starkly by the small ears at the sides of her head.

You're very pretty, she says.

Maeve reddens. Oh, no.

I have some concealer that would do wonders for that acne.

When their turn arrives, a uniformed guard directs them to a tiny cubicle in the rear where a short man in an ill-fitting suit introduces himself as Mr. Xanthopoulos. He sits propped in a swivel chair. Every once in a while he goes for a brief ride in it, pivoting about on its coasters, knocking back and forth, seized by a fierce restlessness. On his desk sits a framed triptych of photos. In the first, a much younger Mr. Xanthopoulos stands with his arm around a petite grinning woman. A second photo shows this same woman, much broader, seated behind three heavy children. Though the third photo is facing away from her, Lily cannot escape the notion that it displays Mr. Xanthopoulos and his family as they will appear years from now.

He announces that unless she is a relative, Lily will have to wait outside.

I'm her attorney.

Mr. Xanthopoulos asks Maeve a number of questions about the date of her entry into the country, the port of entry, the point of origin, the names of her father and mother, her place of birth, their places of birth. He then asks the same questions in a different order. It takes Lily some while to understand the problem has come about because the girl failed to sign and return a form she should have received in the mail. She explains that Maeve changed address when she came into their employ. Likely the form has gone astray. If you can supply her with another—

It is not that simple, Mr. Xanthopoulos says. The form must be signed within twenty-one days of receipt, and now the twenty-one days have lapsed.

Bloody 'ell, Maeve whispers.

The man turns to stare at her. Lily leans forward into his field of vision and says, The twenty-one days have lapsed because my client never received the form.

Mr. Xanthopoulos scoots back and forth in his swivel chair and says, Her failure to submit the form in a timely fashion has triggered an automatic review of her visa. She will need to produce a number of documents, including not only her passport and visa stamp but certified copies of her birth certificate, as well as proof of all places of residence since her entry into the country. Such proof may be in the form of utility bills or bank statements.

If we could just— Lily begins.

She will also need to document all employment since her entry. This documentation may consist of pay stubs or letters from her employers detailing the duration and nature of her employment. She will need to submit a new visa application along with the required fee. She will also be expected to supply medical records that attest to the state of her health and childhood vaccinations, along with letters of recommendation from three persons legally resident in the United States.

But you must have those on file, Lily says.

Mr. Xanthopoulos's eyes narrow. You're not listening, he says.

Lily sits back. She regards him coolly. It is her courtroom look. I am listening, she says, but you're not saying anything new.

A tremor seizes Mr. Xanthopoulos's chin and then releases it. I should add that as recent directives have tightened immigration requirements, the outcome of your client's application—in light of her failure to submit the appropriate paperwork in a timely manner—may prove . . . problematic.

The word drops like a crossruff in cards.

What a right tosser, Maeve says.

This time she does not bother to whisper. Lily places her hand on the girl's arm before turning once more to Mr. Xanthopoulos. When those all around are losing their heads, Lily will settle into an extraordinary calm. Long experience has rewritten the synaptic map of the parietal lobe of her brain. She says, You must have considerable discretion in such matters.

The man shifts about in his seat, swivels all the way around once, and says, My hands are tied.

Then we would like to speak to someone whose hands are free.

Mr. Xanthopoulos hunches forward. He rests his elbows on the desk. He makes a small temple with his palms and peers closely at Lily. You are an attorney, yes?

I am.

You are by chance an immigration attorney?

No.

Ah. He sinks a bit lower, his tone growing intimate, yet insinuating. And exactly what kind of attorney are you?

Lily looks at a point in the middle of his forehead. It is a practiced look, a look of immeasurable patience. The air in the room turns corrosive.

I am the kind of attorney who knows how to file the appropriate grievance and, if necessary, to pursue an injunction.

Outside, it has stopped raining. The sun ranges overhead. They blink against the light.

I'm so very grateful, the girl murmurs. She sounds breathless, as if she has just run a long way.

It's nothing.

Maeve shakes her head. She knows better. This is everything. I wouldn't have known what to say, and even if I had, he wouldn't have listened.

Let's celebrate, Lily says.

The boys—

I told Mrs. Nagorsky we wouldn't be back for hours.

Arm in arm the two head down the street. They draw admiring looks. They could be mother and daughter, or teacher and student. They could be lovers in the war against men. They veer together into a tiny café that lies behind an unmarked door. You would never find it unless you knew it was there. The waitstaff wear crisp white shirts with lapis studs. Lily orders pastries and wine. A fountain in the center of the dining area consists of a single monolith of siltstone. The water runs down it in an unbroken sheet, so evenly it seems unmoving.

You made him angry, the Irish au pair says now. She seems to be seeing the other woman for the first time.

Except he wasn't angry at you, Lily explains. He was afraid.

Afraid. The word leaves the girl's mouth as if she has misheard.

Lily imagines he came here years ago, or maybe it was his father who first came, or his father's father. It doesn't really matter. In the end, everybody is always from somewhere else. You drop everything and pick up your life and move to the other side of the planet, praying that when you arrive, they will let you in. I suppose I'm not telling you anything new. Did you know that when émigrés used to be turned away at Ellis Island, some became so distraught they jumped from the ship that was taking them back home? Their families had pooled all their money and their hopes so a cousin or a brother or a nephew could have a chance. Having failed, they could not face their disappointed kin and so they leaped into New York Harbor, desperate to stay. A few even drowned. You've got to help me eat these. Just sitting this close, I can feel my hips growing. When I think of Mr. Xanthopoulos's childhood, I picture him making long walks from a well, balancing a heavy urn of water on his shoulder, or turning the crank to squeeze the last of the oil from an olive press. These are clichés, I know, but the thing about clichés is they are often true. I imagine him sitting down to dinner in a tiny kitchen crowded with three, four generations. I see the goat dung on his shoes. These days, he probably flosses daily and drinks filtered water and exfoliates every night and pauses each morning in Grand Central to get his shoes shined. But somewhere deep inside, he still lives in fear that others might smell the dung. You scrub and scrub and scrub, but what if it is still there? This is the one terror in his life. Whenever anyone doesn't treat him with what he considers the proper respect, Mr. Xanthopoulos panics. They say America is the land of immigrants. But it really is the land of people afraid to be found out.

But you're not afraid, Maeve says straightaway, as if she has realized something about her employer she never understood before.

Lily is oddly touched by the other woman's admiration—odd because Lily is no stranger to respect. It is Lily who has won the firm's Golden Gavel Award three out of the last five years. It is Lily who is included in the "most notable" list of the state bar's annual review. Lily has a host of friends, women and men, highly regarded in their own right—one heads up the mayor's reelection campaign; another has an upcoming exhibition at the Natsional'nyy institut keramikiin in Saint Petersburg; Hannah Finkel-meyer, associate professor at Barnard, recently published an article on the Kabbalah and Walter Benjamin—each of whom eagerly seeks out her company and counsel.

Yet this is different somehow. The esteem in which these others hold her is always marked by a slight, a competitive undercurrent. Here, however, the girl's regard seems untouched by envy. She is not busy calculating how the rising fortunes of others might offset her own prospects. Her admiration is so naked and unadorned it strikes Lily as richer by far. It means more, suddenly, than professional accolades or the approval of a local pol or the prayers of a whole minyan of Jewish mystics.

And what frightens you?

Maeve does not answer right away. She pauses for so long that Lily thinks she has not heard, or maybe she has heard but she chooses to ignore the question and pretend as if she hasn't, in which case, Lily decides, she will pretend she did not ask it, but finally the girl looks over with a look Lily does not recall ever seeing on her before, and says, I am afraid of not knowing what I should be afraid of.

It sounds at first like a silly thing to say, all but meaningless, an attempt to be clever that isn't really so clever, but the girl's tone is so quiet and reflective that Lily understands she is not being clever, she is being disarmingly honest, which is as far away from clever as you can get. And the older woman sees now that the girl has found herself suddenly moving through the world of the city, the world of adults, a world dense with hidden dangers, and is left on her own to decide what matters and what does not, a distinction she must learn right away, before it is too late, if it is not too late already.

Lily refills their glasses. You know who is afraid? Men. All men are immigrants in a way, if only because they are birthed by women. Think about it. They emerge from this hole in the body that they lack. Girls come from there too, but it's different. It's familiar. Women come from a place they can call their own. Living in the womb, adrift within the amniotic membrane, girls feel safe. Maybe it will be for the first and only time in her life, but in there at least a girl is home. Men on the other hand find themselves surrounded by foreign tissue, awash in unlikely hormones. Men are never at home. They never had a home. They are countryless from the very beginning. They don't know anything else. Maybe all of life is a foreign nation to them. Say it's a wound you never entirely recover from. At any moment you could be kicked out. Men, whether they realize it or not, are always looking over their shoulders. I know what I am talking about. My whole life I have been surrounded by men. I grew up in a house full of men. You and I, we're alike in that way. When I went to law school, most of my classmates were men. I was one of two women hired by my firm as a first-year associate, along with fourteen males. The other woman left in year three to have a baby and never came back. When I depose a witness, I am almost always the only woman in the room except for the court stenographer and the woman who makes the coffee. When I go home, I have three men waiting for me, or a man and two boys. Or three boys. Men have always been everywhere in my life. And what I have noticed throughout is that silence scares men. In silence you can hear the footsteps coming. Even when they relax, they can't really relax. Have you ever seen men try to take it easy, to play, to take a break? It's the rare man who can sit back and read a book. They have trouble enjoying something so simple as a sunset. They have to watch TV or go golfing or turn on the computer. Why look at the sun when you can go skydiving or strap on some scuba gear or check your emails. Men are never truly at home, and so they spend their whole lives trying to prove to themselves and anyone else that they deserve to be home.

Lily says, Women know better. You can't bear a child and not understand that he or she is pure innocence and whatever happens from there on out is not their fault. Life is not fair. It has never been fair. Men don't believe in fair, not deep down, but they think everyone else does, so they'd better pretend they do, too. This is the advantage women have. Women know nobody believes in fairness, not really. Fair is a story we tell men so they won't treat us too harshly. And why are they so harsh? Because they worry they don't belong and have never belonged and will never belong, and this terrifies them.

Even Mr. Fowler? Maeve asks.

The question catches Lily off guard. But after a pause she says, Especially Mr. Fowler.

I like your husband, the Irish au pair admits. She sips from her glass. He's very handsome.

Lily looks over. Thank you, she says after a time.

And he makes me laugh.

Lily smiles. I like him, too.

Do you? Maeve asks.

Of course I do.

The two of you don't touch. You don't kiss.

Lily stares. We kiss.

The girl shakes her head. Never, she says. She is positive.

Lily puts her napkin on the plate. She sips her wine. She could take offense, but the nanny's expression is so naked and genuine she won't. Maybe a marriage is like a good book, Lily explains. The best parts aren't the first things you see.

Gesturing toward the food she says, Now help me finish.

In the street they hail a cab. The driver wears a turban. The ceremonial dagger sits hidden beneath his belt. But he knows. His God knows. This is what matters.

The vehicle lurches from the curb and merges with the traffic thronging down Seventh Avenue. The buildings flash past. The final minutes of the autumn sun rush in.

You don't know how much I appreciate your help, the nanny says once more.

Thank me again and I'll start charging you by the hour, Lily says. Maeve laughs, then leans across the seat to kiss the other woman, a brief but moist brush of the lips. The girl smells of sweat and cheap perfume. Pimples dot her forehead. Her left knee bears a small scab. And then there are those teeth. Yet when she grins, you end up grinning back. Lily finds herself holding Maeve in her arms for that one extra beat of time, the girl's face against hers, her hands on the girl's narrow back.

Then the older woman is sitting forward to rap on the partition separating them from the driver. Why are you taking Bleecker Street? she demands. That's the long way around. It's not like we're tourists.

Chapter Nine

LILY DOES NOT DO IMMIGRATION LAW, but intellectual property. It is the chess of the legal system, more metaphysics than law. Life in the twenty-first century boils down to one question: Who gets what? Natural objects have defined the boundaries of the world for the past forty thousand years. This goes here, that goes there. But nature isn't what it used to be. It turns out nature has never been what it used to be. Nature is back there somewhere, buried for good.

Despite his own years of study, Martin has long sensed that Lily grasps connections that escape him altogether. Where he sees merely simple, self-contained units—an upholstered settee or a toaster oven or a ten-speed bicycle— she sees an innovation hatched at 4:00 A.M. by a twenty-three-year-old commercial designer two months behind in his rent. She sees an iron foundry in China's Fujian Province. She sees the rubber tapper who goes home at the end of the day to a dinner of noodles and fish balls. She sees the dockworkers of Liverpool. She sees in pixels, schematics, blueprints, brands. The real never just is. It is to be mined, harvested, caught, molded, cut, polished, stamped, packaged, shipped, bought, and sold.

The real for her is always already on its way to something else.

Some men are intimidated by brainy women. Not Martin. It gets him going.

Lily has devoted most of the past three years to a single case. Her client, a small tech firm out of Poughkeepsie with fewer than a dozen employees, is suing Schlüsser-Bonhoeffer, the German software behemoth, for patent infringement. The issues are highly technical, non-Euclidean, virtual. Throughout it all, she seeks to chart the provenance of an insight, a pathbreaking technique. She follows an inspiration as it winds its way down through the decades. All the greatest assets have long since turned intangible.

While she has detailed the issues to Martin repeatedly, the case continues to mystify him. The specifics are straightforward enough: The suit involves her client's solid imaging materials (SIM) patent. The SIM is the prototype of a program that will one day transmit three-dimensional shapes and solids, much as a fax machine currently transmits type and images. Though such machines now exist, they are nothing more than crude novelty items. Projections are that this new design will in fewer than ten years revolutionize materials transport.

Imagine the implications, she says.

Martin sits at the kitchen table and aims an eye at the ceiling, trying to imagine.

How close will what this thing transmits be to the real thing?

Very close, she says. Identical.

Not identical.

Identical. In time, we won't be able to tell the difference.

He shakes his head. Impossible.

Possible, she says. Inevitable.

Will it transmit even people? he asks, and he smiles.

Okay, maybe not people.

It sounds like something out of science fiction.

Ten years, she repeats. Maybe less.

He says, But what about the world?

He says, Just where does the world go?

Consider all the good that will come, Lily insists. Think of the savings in shipping alone.

At what cost?

At a cost far less than we spend now.

Martin rubs his eyes with the heels of his hands. This isn't what he means. He says, Isn't something, somewhere, lost?

You're being sentimental.

Maybe.

Don't worry, Lily assures him. By the time it happens, it will seem not only unextraordinary but natural.

Martin does worry. He cannot help himself. If a machine will in a single afternoon be able to furnish a room with items it once took weeks or even months to build and to ship and to install, he worries that in no time duration itself will become just one more manufactured good among others.

He worries that we stand at an unwholesome frontier, at

the very cusp of unexpected and relentless changes. Maybe we have shot beyond it already. Say there are events that sneak up on people, surprise and ambush them, overtake them in ways that remake their lives behind their backs— transformations that remake our lives even as we sleep, so we wake to find everything has irrevocably changed, changed in ways we can't ever go back on.

Or maybe he is being sentimental.

More and more such thoughts keep him awake at night. He will lie there for hours, trying to will himself to sleep, but when he is unable to, when such concerns threaten to overwhelm him altogether, he quietly climbs from bed and makes his way down the hall. Sometimes he will sit up and read, or check the markets. But one evening when he arrives at the study, he discovers Maeve kneeling on the chair with her face mere inches from the door of the bird-cage, in a scene of unexpected intimacy.

She stands when she sees him. The white band of her underwear is just visible beneath the fabric of her night-gown. If I woke you— she begins.

No. I couldn't drop off.

Me, neither.

They briefly gaze at each other before turning back to the parrot for somewhere else to look. In the cone of light from the lamp, the creature hunkers in implacable grandeur, as still as a trophy. But when the Irish au pair reaches between the bars to gently stroke its flank, the bird comes alive, bending into her finger. Martin watches its head bob.

I've never heard it talk, he says.

Aristotle turns at the sound of his voice and sidles a single step along the bar.

Maybe he is keeping a secret, she says, and she smiles. She continues to work her finger. The animal curves and dips against it.

I don't think birds have secrets, Martin tells her, and though he knows absolutely nothing about avian psychology, this strikes him as true.

She regards him thoughtfully. She speaks with the certainty of a farm girl: All animals keep secrets. Even if it's only from themselves.

Aristotle spreads his wings once, briefly—the span is astonishing; the bird swells to fill the cage—then sinks his head into his breast as Maeve smooths the long feathers down his back.

It's beautiful, Martin admits.

You can pet him, too, if you want.

When he hesitates she adds, Aristotle won't bite, and she smiles again.

He looks at the parrot and then at Maeve. She nods. He steps forward and tentatively slides a single finger between the bars. But just as he is on the point of touching the creature, the girl grabs his arm with terrific force and hisses, Watch out!

Martin lurches back violently. She snorts at his reaction, her laughter tripping, an undisciplined hee-haw all out of proportion to her slight features. It is a sound so raw and unexpected vast continents of her personality seem to shift into view, and he feels at that instant as if he can glimpse the whole of her history as a young girl on a distant isle. He envisions a blackened hearth, he smells the dank mold, he even imagines the sound of a storm dinning on a stone roof that has been corbeled to a steep pitch, the rain roaring over the eaves, and her in the corner of the room, laughing at something someone has said.

I scared you, Maeve goes on. Her eyes are pinched with a huge pleasure, of the sort he had not guessed she might be capable. She remembers too late to cover her mouth.

No, you didn't.

You were feckin' terrified, she says.

Maybe a little, he says, and he laughs now, too. Only now does it occur to her to loosen her hold on his wrist. Standing there, he feels strangely, unaccountably happy.

Martin feels less so several nights later, however, when—having barricaded the door with *Property*, *Foundational Texts in Criminal Law*, and *Constitutional Law: Principles & Policies*—he and his wife are once more interrupted by the thunder and roar of the toilet down the hall, followed by the diligent scrub of a toothbrush. When the girl pauses to spit, they edge away from each other. After several moments he whispers, So I guess we're just never supposed to fuck again.

Lily's head turns. In the shadows it turns like the head of a hawk.

Don't say *fuck*, Martin. Not in the bedroom.

The super has lived with his wife and three of their children—there is another daughter, the eldest, who moved to California several years earlier for reasons no one ever goes into—and their spouses and grandchildren in nine rooms in the basement of the building for the last eleven years. Before that the man worked as a carpenter's assistant on Staten Island, and before that he washed dishes at a pizzeria in Queens. As a youth he apprenticed to a glassblower outside Tallinn.

Paavo Kuusik's office lies just off the boiler room. His walls are lined with shelves filled with broken electrical appliances, old plumbing fixtures, and boxes of cracked tiles. The shelves extend all the way to the ceiling, looming overhead as if they are about to collapse down about his shoulders. A roll of mustard-colored carpet stands like a pylon. Above it, tools hang from pegboard. Paavo Kuusik sits in the middle of it all, repairing a lamp. When Martin appears, the super continues to work the needle nose pliers. He is a short man, in his late fifties, maybe sixty, and swarthy, with coarse black hair along his arms and a tussock of the same hair, kinked with gray, poking above the open collar of his work shirt. He inhabits immense silences, taciturn, brooding, as if words were a curious implement he came to late. He has a head like a block of wood and a nose the shape of a scimitar.

Martin explains about the bedroom door: It won't shut, not all the way.

This old building, Paavo Kuusik says after a while.

The two look at each other. The super bends back over his lamp. Martin cannot recall how much money he slipped into the man's envelope the previous Christmas, though he wishes it had been more. Meanwhile, the old Estonian wields the pliers. They are small in his large hands. Still, his movements are nimble. He cradles the shaft of the lamp as if it were a girl's leg.

The truth is, Martin feels uncomfortable with men such as Paavo Kuusik. Martin is incapable of rewiring electrical appliances. He cannot hang drywall. He could not begin to tune a car, bleed the brake line, or replace a water pump. He does not know how to change the washer in a tap.

Paavo Kuusik knows. He can also yoke an ox, gut a deer, and geld a goat. He knows how to pleasure a woman. Martin frequently happens upon the super's wife polishing a newel post in the stairwell, or mopping the foyer in front of the mailboxes. There is something bad-tempered about the way she eyes him, almost pugnacious, as if in the past Martin delivered to her some deep, untraceable offense. Beetroot occasionally stains her fingers. Her shoulders are round and full. She wears sleeveless blouses that gape wide to display memorably peppered underarms. She is a loud and sloe-eyed woman with rows of silver bracelets clanking at her wrists. He supposes Paavo Kuusik must imbibe huge quantities of kvass on Friday nights in order to mount his great waxen wife, hurling himself at her again and again, like a man trying to break down a door. Whenever Martin pictures the woman in the throes of sexual euphoria—and he has done so one or two or fourteen times—he imagines her lying beneath her Paavo with a telling leer on her face while her broad haunches widen to receive the man into the rich woody boscage of her sex.

Martin feels awkward among such people. They commune at a level of existence rooted in the humus of centuries past, while he is consigned to trip and stumble across a broken landscape that he has neither authored nor fully understands. He worries they sense his discomfort as they say a dog senses fear.

Martin tries once more. The door. If you could take a look, he says.

Paavo Kuusik digs the prongs of his pliers deeper into the switch housing and says, When I was a child? Me and my four brothers and my parents and my grandparents all lived in three rooms on the island of Hiiumaa in the Baltic. A cold land in a cold, cold sea. You had to heave the bucket down the well with all your might to break the crust of ice on the top. We huddled together to stay alive. Everybody saw everything. We heard everything. It didn't matter. We were family.

Paavo Kuusik's face turns fierce, proud, tribal.

We have a new nanny for the boys, Martin explains. She moved in not too long ago.

The other man cocks his head. I think I seen her. She Ukrainian?

Irish, Martin says.

But the super is adamant. Trust me. All Ukrainians are thieves. I know this firsthand.

CHAPTER TEN

ARTIN'S BIRTHDAY COMES on Columbus Day. He is one of those men who feigns surprise if you mention the date, though should you forget, he will be hurt. Yet forty-four sounds old to him in a way that forty-two or forty-three never did. He tries to console himself by dwelling on the oddly propitious character of the number: the four noble truths of Buddhism, the four rivers flowing out of Eden, the four Gospels. But then there are the Four Horsemen of the Apocalypse. Twain uses the number 44 to refer to Satan's nephew.

In Chinese, the word for four sounds just like the word for death.

Martin has always appeared young for his age. Everyone says so. When he hit thirty, people thought he was twenty. At forty, people thought he was thirty. It has begun to sink in that this cannot go on forever. Faint but undeniable signs have started to appear. Small half-moons of shadow shore up his eyes. Lines have entered his neck and forehead. His nose always looks larger in the mirror than he remembers, the pores in his flesh more pronounced. He suspects he may turn out to be one of those who looks eerily youthful for most of his life, until he rises one morning in his sixtieth year to find he has somehow transmogrified overnight to look a doddering eighty.

So while the date always brings with it a tincture of despair, he is nonetheless buoyed when he arrives home early from work to hear barely constrained snickering coming from the living room. He pauses in the foyer to set down his briefcase, does a pistol thing with his hand, and yells, Reach for the sky, hombre! and the twins squeal with laughter, emerging from their hiding place behind the sofa to charge toward him, hands high overhead. In the kitchen, he discovers Lily and Maeve decked out in matching aprons. His wife shoos him into the den where she deposits him in the big leather recliner, a glass of Bordeaux in his hand. On the menu: medallions of venison and steamed artichokes. Martin has always found the meat gamy and he does not like the bother associated with artichokes, though he feels heartened by their efforts. He would eat an old boot if they served it.

Once the twins are down for their nap the house grows quiet, save for the muted voices of the women and the ticking of a knife against the cutting board. He listens as they talk about the boys. Lily mentions how much Gavin still loves to play peekaboo, whereas Arnold grew bored with it long ago. Maeve says, Speaking of Gavin, he seems listless lately; I wonder if he is coming down with a cold. Lily says he is listless because he is probably worn-out trying to keep up with Arnold. The sound of their laughter reminds Martin of the running of a gentle brook. Here their voices fade further, and Martin jerks awake just as he is on the point of dropping off. He is not so old that he wants to sleep through his birthday. He turns on the TV and is rewarded with golf. He plays every once in a great while, though he is not very good. Many of his coworkers are enthusiasts. Martin has never understood the appeal. You whack the ball and chase after it. Then you whack the ball again and chase after it. Whenever he plays, he has the strange impression the ball has all the fun.

Oddly enough, he likes watching matches on TV. He enjoys it just as he enjoys cooking shows, real-life narratives of arctic crabbers, and curling in the Olympics—though he has an iodine sensitivity and he can't spend ten seconds on the ice without falling. But Martin has a grudging admiration for golf pros. He believes athletes are members of one of the last genuine aristocracies. Even when golfers win upward of a million dollars or more for four days' work, they seem strangely unsullied by money. The lesson of their days is not merely that life resembles a game—what is a bunker, after all, but a grown-up's sandbox—but that perhaps the laws of nature, however divinely conceived, receive no finer expression than when a man hurls a lance, hurdles an obstacle, or makes a ball vanish into a hole. He has long suspected that the reaches of human emotion extend further in sport than in almost any other human endeavor, be it commerce, statecraft, or the arts. If you have ever been on a court or a field with a mob of fans rooting you on in the final moments of a close contest, and looked around to see your teammates peering back at you with a fear that is a sort of joy, then you have known an intensity of feeling that, to Martin's mind, differs in kind from the cherished wishes of a parent, or the love of a woman, or even the tender concern of a God for His people. And so on this afternoon when a South African linksman shanks the ball into a hazard, and looks not just surprised but deeply aggrieved, Martin grieves for him. And when the man stands and with a mighty swing and a great display of flying grit hopes to turn things around, it makes Martin cheer. He cheers for the man; he cheers for the sport; he cheers for the species.

It is warm in the room. The wine makes straight for his brain. Despite his best efforts, Martin nods off. He comes to in a dream. He dreams he is out on the golf course. Hundreds look on. He wears a neon pink shirt and bozo lemon yellow pants, but no matter: The crowd applauds his every shot. They applaud when he blasts the ball three hundred yards from the tee. They roar when he sinks a rolling thirty-foot putt. In his dream Martin stalks the fairway, the gallery pressing against the ropes. He strolls the front nine very quickly—a dream is its own time machine—but on the eleventh fairway, just as he is about to take his second stroke, aiming for the green and a possible eagle on the hole, a crow soars in from the run of live oaks to the south (he had not seen the crow; he had not noticed the oaks) and neatly snatches up the ball in its beak, its caw piercing. The cry grows louder, until Martin wakes to discover he still hears it. He hurries to the kitchen, where Lily clutches one hand in the other above a half-diced onion, her knife at the side of the cutting board. A narrow tributary of blood streams down her arm to dot the countertop. She holds the injured hand out before her as you might hold a leaky bottle.

The sight scares him. His mind runs for the corners. What he has always liked about numbers is that there is only one route they can go: up or down. Life, on the other hand, is liable to explode, scattering shards everywhere. The sight of his wife's blood sends his thoughts somersaulting ahead to the prospect of hours spent in the ER, feeding the boys cheese and crackers from a machine while fighting with the triage nurse, who keeps deferring his wife's treatment in favor of the gunshot wounds and head-on collisions that clog the entryway. Then he wonders if venison might contain some fungal spore that can infiltrate the merest paper cut and turn one's inner organs to goop. Next it occurs to him that a part of her finger may be lying on the counter or on the floor or even nestled among the deer steaks. He briefly casts about to see if he might come upon it, though he stops when he realizes he might come upon it.

If the moment paralyzes Martin, it galvanizes Maeve. Unassuming as she may at times appear, she moves with a lithe coordination, setting her mixing bowl on the counter and reaching for Lily. Her demeanor is curiously authoritative. She lifts the older woman's hand to inspect it and, in the next instant, closes her lips around the finger. Tending to a clutch of younger brothers, perhaps this is the treatment of choice in County Galway. The Fowlers stare as the girl's cheeks narrow, her features contracting. His wife's eyes next lock onto his. His thinking hums with her meanings. Everything now slows down. Time feels as if it is walking on its knees. Lily tugs free and looks at her hand as if it is someone else's hanging at the end of her arm.

The Irish nanny says, It hasn't stopped, but before she can stick the finger back in her mouth, Lily places it under the tap. She lets the girl apply a bandage. You know, it's nothing, Lily insists. Indeed, the injury proves minor. In no time, the drama is over. They return to preparing the meal, though a strained silence takes hold of the kitchen. Back in the living room, Martin turns off the TV. He finishes his glass of wine. Forty-four sounds worse than ever. But the food, when it comes, is served with unexpected fanfare. The twins, fresh from their naps, don party hats. They toot paper horns. Maeve rubber-bands a hat onto Martin's head. He toots a horn of his own. The dinner grows festive. Lily uncorks a second bottle of wine. The women surprise him with a chocolate cake they have decorated themselves. The candles are lit. "Happy Birthday" is sung. The flickering flames enchant the boys. A primitive wonder, one of the very earliest. They stand in their chairs and help Martin blow the fire out. Presents appear. The gift wrap tears, crinkling loudly in his hands. His wife gives him a wireless phone charger for the car. Maeve gives him a scarf knit from Aran wool the color of oats. His two sons have worked diligently all morning to compose a portrait of their father on construction paper.

Martin has four toes on one foot, seven on the other, and a face like Picasso's bull.

Later, Lily bathes the boys and Martin puts them to bed. He
tries reading from Robert Louis Stevenson, but they clamor
to look at videos on the computer pad. They watch one featuring a poodle that can croon the national anthem and
another about a talking banana and another in which a construction worker falls two stories into a form of freshly laid
cement. He climbs out and walks away unscathed, but the
twins insist on watching again and again, laughing harder
each time. It takes Martin half an hour before he can extricate himself. Back in the living room, he volunteers to find
a movie if Maeve will make a bowl of popcorn. In the meantime, Lily opens a third bottle and sets it on the sideboard
to breathe. The wine, with its deep hints of pepperwood
and molasses, whets the mood. The Fowlers settle on the
sofa, edging to one side to make room for the girl. She opts
for the large leather recliner instead. She rocks back in the
seat, poking her bare feet out before her. They are small but
sturdy, the joints knobbed, the arch severe. Martin wants
to watch an old black-and-white oater in which an Apache
war party has encircled a western outpost. Maeve wants to
watch a musical featuring a barmaid, a steeplejack, and a lost
locket. Lily wants to watch a horror film set in the aftermath
of some unnamed cataclysm.

They watch the horror film, the bowl of popcorn passing
among them. The last survivors are few in number, holed
up in a library where they are besieged by an army of zombies. This final human remnant feeds volume after ancient
volume—good-bye, Augustine; so long, Thucydides; adieu,

Descartes—into the flames to keep the threat at bay. Presumably once the fire of knowledge is extinguished, civilization will succumb completely to the unthinking forces of savagery. Martin cannot remember if he saw this same film decades ago or if it has become such a cultural fixture in the years since that it just seems he saw it.

Maeve stares, her eyes alert. During a particularly gruesome part—one of the undead gnaws a human femur—Martin says, We can change channels if this bothers you.

The girl shakes her head. I want to see.

Just when you think all hope has been extinguished, a gnomish librarian whom time has forgotten—he has continued to work dutifully in the book bindery, oblivious to the impending apocalypse—steps forward to lead what is left of the race of the living through a subterranean passage. They surface in an urban park, where they take shelter not behind pages pulped from wood, but among actual trees. Nature, nature to the rescue. The music swells. But the zombies are not done. They trail the fading hopes of humankind through a deserted rail station, a ransacked candy shop—viscera amid the cashew brittle and Turkish delight—and across the nave of an ancient cathedral. They pursue them into a shopping mall, hats and leather goods having been wrenched from the shelves while mannequins stand frozen in the windows. The librarian is killed in a computer store, crushed by a falling display case filled with the latest gaming consoles. The few ragtag survivors flee down a manhole, a horde of the soulless loping after them.

Maeve says, I'd want to die right at the very start, and be done with it.

Lily and Martin both turn to the girl, who adds, I want to be one of the first to go.

Lily shakes her head. Not me. I want a fighting chance. Give me the hope of getting away.

They both look at Martin. He picks a popcorn kernel from between his teeth before saying, Make me one of the zombies, already.

Really? Maeve says.

Really? Lily says.

At least I'd be alive.

But would it even be you? the girl asks.

The movie ends with an immense fireball that incinerates the army of the mindless—we see a blackened foot, a severed head aglow with embers—while the final three humans on Earth stroll into a shimmering sunset, the giant orb banded in shades of yellow and orange and red. Two of the survivors hold hands. The third walks with a rifle slung over her shoulder.

Maeve and Lily rise now to clear the dishes, his wife pouring the dregs of wine into a single glass and drinking that. Martin goes to stand at the living room window. At this hour the lights of the adjacent buildings rise all about like constellations that have wandered down from the sky.

He hears the soft clink of crystal in the kitchen, the low murmurs of the women. When the girl reappears she says, I think I'll go to bed. She pauses to shyly peck him on first one check and then the other. She offers him a long hug, pressing her face into his neck.

Happy birthday again, Mr. Fowler.

You helped make it a wonderful birthday. And call me Martin.

Lily has paused in the doorway to watch. My turn, she says brightly. She pushes off the door frame and picks her way around the furniture to buss him briefly on the mouth. She draws back to peer at him, her eyes mere inches from his own. Here something new moves into his wife's face. He can tell the very instant. It falls across her features like a veil. She kisses him again, wetly this time. He closes his eyes and listens as a soft sound comes from deep in her throat, a noise straight out of nature: the sibilance of prairie grasses, leaves scattered before a breeze. When he looks again, Martin sees his wife's eyes are large, and set hard on Maeve.

I'm going to bed, the au pair says again, though she does not move. This is when Lily begins to unbutton his shirt. Martin feels her bandaged finger against his skin.

Unless you don't want to, his wife murmurs.

She continues to undo his buttons. When Lily reaches the last one, she hesitates, her glance going to Maeve once more. The girl responds with an opaque expression, as indecipherable as the knot on a tree. She slowly crosses her arms and leans back against the wall, waiting. The three of them stay perfectly still, as if surprised to find themselves suddenly inhabiting these lives. Time swells the moment until it seems it is about to shatter. They stand listening to the silence, which is not silence at all, but a sound beyond all meaning. It is the sound of nerves failing.

And then the moment is gone. Maeve turns finally to head out of the room, her footsteps tracking slowly down the length of the hallway. Lily moves to the far wall, just to the right of the mantel. She and her husband look at each other like boxers retiring to their respective corners. Neither speaks for a long second, until Lily takes her place on the sofa. Martin sits, too, his hands in his lap. The grandfather clock ticks in the air above their heads like a bomb waiting to go off.

Where's the remote? his wife asks.

Two evenings later, however, Martin wakes to an elbow in his ribs. His wife nudges him again. Sometime during the night, it has started to rain. The rain batters the window. The streetlights each give off a haloed nimbus, as if dozens of campfires burn.

Martin sits up. A ghost stands in the doorway. The ghost wears a bathrobe and frayed slippers. The quiet mounts slowly. Time feels as if it is still incubating, not quite ready to hatch the future.

The girl comes full into the room. She pauses to remove the Celtic cross from the chain at her neck, places it on the dresser, and then drags the vanity chair to the foot of the bed to sit down and watch.

PART II

CHAPTER ELEVEN

THE FIRST SATURDAY in November, they wake to the sun filtering through the curtains. The temperature climbs throughout the morning. It quickly turns into one of those outrageously beautiful days that seem to arrive out of nowhere, entirely without warrant. Over breakfast, Martin tells the twins that it is called Indian summer because the early settlers used to leave their storehouses unguarded once cold weather moved in, but if an unseasonal warmth arrived, Native Americans would stage a final raid.

Maeve puts down her fork. Is that true?

Light pours through the windows, glinting off the cutlery. Though he had planned on working that morning, and Lily was supposed to meet Naomi Woodbine for brunch, at the last minute Martin suggests they throw their plans over and all go on an outing to the park. The twins cheer. The five of them emerge from the subway in front of the Plaza Hotel and begin with a carriage ride, Lily and Martin sitting on one side and Gavin and Maeve opposite, while Arnold insists on riding up front with the coachman. At the playground the boys rush toward the monkey bars, the nanny right behind them. The Fowlers settle on a bench and watch their sons scramble to the top, each desperate to get there first. The girl, meanwhile, is surprisingly agile. She beats them both. At the summit, warmed by the sun, she pauses to strip off her sweater and toss it to the ground. She hooks her legs through a rung and hangs upside down, her arms hanging limp, no thicker than the arms of the boys, her blouse riding up to expose her midriff, a narrow expanse of flesh made even paler in the sunlight.

When she pushes the twins on the swings, side by side, each with his head surging forward, straining to go higher and higher, Arnold yells, I'm flying.

No, I'm flying, Gavin yells back.

That evening Martin and Lily lie in bed and wait to see if the girl will appear. She shows every third or fourth or fifth night. They never know when to expect her. Once she does arrive, a curious drama unfolds. If the Fowlers have never been particularly adventuresome in bed, their movements now grow more unadorned than ever, almost chaste. Lily looks at the ceiling. Martin looks at the sheets. They start and stop and start again. Even the Pilgrims were wilder. Yet each act no matter how small feels highly stylized, almost Kabuki. Meanwhile, the girl sits across the way, her hands gripping the armrests of the chair.

But there erupt unexpected episodes of fierce, bristling ardor. They flare like the head of a match. At these instances, Lily gambols about the bed in a way that incites him profoundly. As he hovers above her, she throws out her arms. She clenches the sheets in her fists, her body twisting. He bends toward her breast as if he were an infant, his mouth moving blindly.

During the day they are careful not to talk about it. Instead, they go about their routines, determined to act as if nothing has changed. But Martin is tempted at times to ask what passes through Maeve's head as she observes them. He cannot decide if she is excited, repulsed, or frightened, or, by turns, all three. And he would like to understand how it came to pass that the same boy who was baptized at age eleven by the Reverend Wilford "Bud" Vogel of the Second Congregational Church of Nice can grow into a man who snorts like a steed while the girl looks on, his heart slamming away in his chest. He would like most of all to know what peculiar cocktail of causes, what bizarre jackpot of factors has rendered his normally demure wife a good deal more brazen.

But to answer this question he would have to first get clear on what it was that lay behind her sexual timorousness all these years. You understand the one by understanding the other. Yet here, too, he remains utterly in the dark. Maybe her initial reluctance issued from the sense of helplessness, the gaping vulnerability to which one subjects oneself in the midst of orgasmic display. Predators in the wild sometimes wait to catch their prey in mid-rut before springing. Or maybe because her romantic expectations are so high—ginned up by the narrative onslaught featured in reality TV and rom-coms, in tabloids filled with photos of Hollywood weddings, in fairy tales heralding yet another damsel rescued from the clutches of an ogre / troll / wicked in-laws / a cad / highwaymen / the Dark Duke—the reality is bound to be a disappointment. Or because she had an unfortunate experience early on that soured her forever on a whole corridor of human experience. Or because one of her first trysts proved so shatteringly electric that everything since seems a pale imitation. Or because some anatomical idiosyncrasy on her part puts ecstasy beyond reach. Or because something about Martin's own genital architecture dooms their coupling. Or because her father brutalized her mother, leaving Lily to listen to an unending series of reproofs and imprecations through the matrimonial walls. Or because her mother mocked and taunted her father, engineering a virtual castration of what was otherwise a proud and imperious man. Or because the clamor and stink of the boudoir strike his wife as too strident and barbaric and animalistic. Or because these very sounds and fragrances are too weak and unfocused to trigger the sexual brio that lies dormant deep in her psyche. Or because she once coupled with a woman and the memory of that escapade so overshadows all subsequent episodes that she squanders her energies in a futile quest either to recapture it or deny it altogether. Or because she once coupled with two men who came at her with so much energy and from so many directions, a many-appendaged creature bent on pleasuring her manifold erogenous zones in a virtuoso performance every bit as polymorphous as it was riveting, such that the ministrations of a single man with only two arms and two legs and a lone cock necessarily feels stinting and miserly. Or because she became so adept in her formative years at playing the keyboard of her own vulva, of dealing a hand of carnal solitaire—he imagines her teen self lying back, legs akimbo, eyes scrunched closed in a momentary effort to keep the world and its failings at bay—that the presence of another is not only not an incitement to pleasure but its opposite, a guarantor of frigidity in its most arctic dimensions. Or because the proscriptions against self-experimentation were implanted so early and at such length, she in fact never hazarded to uncover the ins and outs of her own psychosexual cartography, so that she is left to wander alone and lost like a blind castaway, marking the passing of days and months and years by scratching pidgin braille on a cave wall, unaware that the inflatable that would return her to civilization lies conveniently just the other side of the lagoon.

The possibilities are many, uncataloged, often contradictory, and always inconclusive. He cannot begin to grasp how the familiar patterns of marriage, the well-blazed trails and the worn pathways they have padded down so uneventfully for all these years, have suddenly veered off deep into the wilds, leaving them to bushwhack their way through uncharted sexual hinterlands. It is almost as if she—as if they all—have become other people on these evenings, as if he himself has turned into someone else altogether. Indeed, looking at his reflection above the sink first thing in the morning, Martin increasingly has the sense he no longer sees what the mirror sees. He would like to ask whether what they are doing is in any way wise or prudent. He would like to ask whether it might be wrong, and if they should consider ending it.

But Martin doesn't ask, because then they might end it.

If Martin and Lily never talk about such matters, here is what they do talk about: One evening after dinner, when Maeve rises as usual to clear the dishes, Lily puts her hand on the girl's arm.

You've done enough, Lily says. I'll get them.

I don't mind—

Sit, Lily says, please, and she stands now to carry the plates into the kitchen. Maeve eases back down in her chair. She hears the scrape of a knife across bone china, followed by the growl of the disposal. When Lily reappears in the doorway, wiping her hands on a dish towel, she says, Martin and I were just saying to each other how much you do.

He says, You work hard.

The Irish au pair gazes from one to the other in bewilderment and says, I like making this a nice home.

You make it a wonderful home, Martin tells her.

We were saying how it isn't too soon to talk about a raise, Lily says. She names a sum.

The girl eases deeper into her seat. A month?

A week, Lily says.

Maeve looks at them both. Her eyes go back and forth in her face.

You don't have to do this, she tells them. She shakes her head. You shouldn't. She speaks as if they are acting unwisely, as if she has their best interests at heart.

Neither responds. They don't need to. The matter has

been decided. Instead, Lily makes a paddle with one hand to brush crumbs from the tabletop into the palm of her other.

Watching them, meanwhile, the nanny is struck by the sheer physical exertion. The Fowlers appear to be swept up in a grueling task, an effort that pushes them to the very limit. She is strangely touched by how hard they work. As a child, she saw men sweating and groaning in much the same way while digging up the last of the peat bogs of Roscommon.

Their movements are fluid at first. There is a supple quality to the way Lily stretches an arm, lifts a leg. Gradually, she and her husband begin to pick up speed. It is like watching a finely calibrated mechanism. They move faster still. But somewhere along the way—one can never tell the exact moment, the awareness always comes after the fact—the rhythm begins to disintegrate. The bed starts to thump beneath them, make a real racket. In a span of three or four seconds, they lose the tempo altogether. The machine has slipped its housing. They turn into a tangle of warring limbs, heads bouncing at the ends of their necks. There is a dismaying, appallingly raw power to their bodies. Lily begins to cry out. It is like the cry of an animal caught in a trap. Martin grunts through gritted teeth. His thrusting is undisciplined, wild, his buttocks clenching. The au pair knows she should not be seeing this.

Nobody should see this.

⤛

She never speaks during these evenings, or almost never—
the power of words is diminished in such a setting—but one
night Lily says to her, You know, if there is ever anything
you want . . .

The Fowlers sit side by side across the room, leaning back
against the headboard of the bed. Maeve glances from one to
the other. Anything I want, she repeats.

Something we could do, Martin suggests. Though he and
Lily have not talked of this, he understands instantly.

Something we could do for you, Lily adds.

The girl turns now to gaze out the window. She sits that
way for a long while as the Fowlers trade looks. She doesn't
know what she wants. She has no idea of what to say. But
four evenings later—it is almost as though she intends to
parcel these visits out, as if there can be only so many—
Maeve says, Kiss her.

She speaks softly, her words barely audible, yet so entirely
unexpected they seem to pulse the air like wings.

The couple looks at the girl, and then at each other.
Martin obliges by leaning over and kissing his wife gently
on the lips.

Not there, the au pair says.

Except it comes out Not dare.

They sit unmoving for several seconds—they could be
posing for a photo—until Martin says, All right.

He positions himself between his wife's thighs. Lily hesitates before parting her legs. She does it slowly, like a woman
stretching after a nap. Her face turns very red. Her husband

bends before her like a supplicant. His are the sounds of a small animal drinking quietly. His wife rests a foot on each of his shoulders. She lies with her head back, her neck long. After a time, she reaches down with both hands to tug gently at his ears. His pate moves slowly in a sideways figure eight, as if he means to inscribe infinity on the inside of her thighs. Her face, her neck, the space between her breasts are all red. At the end, Lily closes her eyes. She closes her eyes, but her mouth opens in a broad silent O of pleasure.

They are quiet for a long while afterward, until Maeve speaks up once more, saying, Now you, to Lily. The girl's voice has a breathless, strangled quality to it. Small beads of perspiration appear on her upper lip in the light from the lamp.

Martin is quick to say, Lily doesn't like to.

When the girl doesn't respond, he says, This isn't something she feels comfortable doing.

The girl looks from him to Lily. Her eyes settle on Lily.

I don't think you understand, he begins again.

Shut up, Martin, his wife tells him.

True, she has always found the posture and the sounds demeaning. Only now does it occur to her that perhaps this is the very point.

She puts her hand on his chest and eases him back down on the bed. She sits at his side, her legs tucked under her. She curls over it, her features narrowing in concentration, as if she is performing some complex calculation, doing long rows of sums. Her hair moves up and down.

Martin lies with his head back. He closes his eyes and opens them. He watches how the girl looks at him from her chair at the foot of the bed. She looks at him as if she sees who he is when he is no longer trying to be who he is, at that secret place where we all really live.

Lily, he says after a time, maybe you should stop.

The seconds beat past slowly, like birds crossing the open sky.

He says, Lily.

Lil.

He says once more, in a voice not entirely his own, Lilith, you had better stop.

But she does not stop.

CHAPTER TWELVE

W ORD COMES DOWN without warning: Schlüsser-Bonhoeffer has been docketed for the winter. After years of preparation, the motions and depositions sifting across the seasons, it appears as if the case may soon go to trial. Lily begins arriving home at nine, ten, sometimes eleven o'clock at night. She rides in the rear of the black Lincoln car hire that takes her down the empty avenues, the streets wet with rain.

During these evenings her chair at the dinner table stands vacant. It feels odd to eat with his wife away, all wrong somehow to sit across from the girl with the boys on either side of her.

It's awkward, he complains. I can barely look at her.

For God's sake, Martin, she isn't going to bite.

Yet however uneasy Maeve's presence makes him, he is secretly relieved the nanny is here. The boys would be a handful without her. He would have to open a can of soup. He would have to bathe the twins himself, put them to bed on his own. Instead, Maeve sees to these chores. You don't have to do this, he keeps telling her, but she hears the helplessness in his voice.

I don't mind, she says.

After dinner they sit together in the living room and

watch TV. Rather, she watches TV; he watches her. She is intent on each program, eyes fixed on the screen. She likes game shows and nature documentaries. She races to come up with the answer before he does. She rises half out of her chair when the puma brings down the gazelle. The humor in sitcoms frequently eludes her. The accent puzzles her. She looks to him to explain, but despite or maybe because of all that has happened, he is embarrassed by the often crude puns and thinly veiled sexual innuendo. He moves his hand in emphasis, gently trying to make her understand. She observes his mouth closely as he talks. This somehow turns his words more real in the air. During the late news, she pelts him with questions: Why are so many Americans so heavy, is it really that easy to buy a gun, what do U.S. politicians have against immigrants. How come no one ever says hello.

When they retire for the evening, Martin lies in bed for a long while, unable to sleep. From the hall comes the creak of the floorboards, followed by the sound of the girl opening her bathroom door. She pees unabashedly, ringing loudly in the bowl.

Lily stays late at the office for the next four nights. Though the nanny's day off is Thursday, the girl works straight through.

I feel bad, Martin says.

Don't, Maeve tells him.

But I do. No cooking tonight, he announces. Let's take the twins out.

She brightens. Where should we go?

You pick.

The evening is chilly. They bundle the boys in their jackets and catch a cab to Canal Street, where she orders the Szechuan shrimp. Martin tries to demonstrate how to hold the chopsticks. In the end he has to take her hand in his own and crook her fingers just so. He is struck again by just how slight she is. Her bones feel like the hollow bones of a bird.

The heat of the dish makes her face flare. Meanwhile, his pork is tasteless. He shoves it aside after a few bites and orders a second beer. Then it occurs to him to ask, Would you like one?

She indicates her tea. This is fine.

For once the boys are quiet. They are mesmerized by the giant golden carp drifting in the large tank set into the wall.

The Irish au pair gives her whole face over to eating. Her jaw works with dense mastications. There is the small nicking sound of her chopsticks, the clank of her teacup on the saucer. She looks up to discover him watching her.

You must dine out all the time, she says.

It's true. Nights with friends, dinners with Lily, the occasional luncheon meeting at the office.

She slips a cashew into her mouth and chews slowly, closing her eyes as if the sight of the food gets in the way of the taste. She says, Tell me about this job.

I work for an investment firm.

She opens her eyes and asks, What is it you do at this firm?

It's a bit complicated.

You count money, she offers. It is not so complicated to her.

I buy and sell currency futures, he tells her. That is, I do statistical analysis so others can buy and sell futures.

You sell the future? She is teasing him.

Futures. It's not exactly the same.

The details of his job, he assures her, are unremittingly dry. They bore even him. His office is unassuming. His desk is a single sheet of acrylic two inches thick on which is mounted a computer console with an outsized screen. A second, smaller screen sits next to it. A phone sits next to that. The printer is behind him. His chair is crafted according to the latest ergonomic principles. There are no photos, no plants, no distractions of any kind. His focus must be total. The walls are white. The vaulted ceiling gives the room the austerity of an ancient temple.

Martin sips his beer and tells her how the lone window of his office opens onto another window across the alley, through which he can see part of a large computer array. Every seven days a man in a beige jumpsuit appears to service the mainframe. Martin rarely sees anyone else. Naturally, there is the weekly staff meeting, and on most days a delivery boy from the deli down the street brings him turkey on whole wheat for lunch. Otherwise, he spends his time watching numbers crawl past on a screen. He listens to disembodied telephone voices.

It sounds lonely, she says.

He admits that sometimes he imagines he is in a space capsule and has embarked on a long interstellar voyage.

And sometimes he imagines he is in prison, that he has been condemned to solitary confinement for unnamed crimes—though he does not mention this last.

Martin sits at his desk all day, every day, and tries to guess what effect the domestic output of soy or petroleum or timber will have on the dollar in a month or six months or a year. He checks these numbers against the British pound, the euro, the Mexican peso. He calibrates a series of twenty-seven different variables, ranging from the flooding in the Gulf states and reports of contamination in Vietnamese rice to an oil spill off the Aleutians. He charts the rise and fall of the yuan coupled with predictions of impending draught in the Zhengzhou region as well as projected austerity measures proposed by the new regime. He painstakingly inputs all the data into a battery of algorithms he has devised himself, each of which generates projections for the next two years at quarterly intervals.

And does that work? she asks.

He looks at her with new interest. No, he admits. The fact is, it doesn't.

❧

Studies show most brokers do little better than the random spin of a wheel. Yet the sums involved are staggering. For this reason, the field is dominated by superstitious types. His colleagues stuff their pockets with rabbits' feet, religious medals, and amber amulets. They keep ancient coins or polished chunks of quartz hidden in their desk drawers. They wear lucky socks. They stir their coffee exactly seven times. On the thirteenth of the month, the absentee rate soars.

He says, People don't realize just how fragile it all is, how many minute contingencies—any one of which could go wrong—have to line up for life as we know it to continue on. It isn't a house of cards; it's a palace of cards. The number of things that need to go right for you just to withdraw money from an ATM is shockingly huge. Brokers know this, of course, and so they cross their fingers and pretend they understand what's happening.

For whatever reason, Martin's predictions are more accurate than most. He has acquired a minor reputation for the precision of his projections. He spends all day, every day, collecting as much data as he can. It appears on three or four windows he puts up on his computer monitor. Three print-outs lie at his elbow. He's jotted a note to himself and stuck it to a corner of the screen. On the phone a voice is telling him what changes he can expect in the next fifteen minutes on the Börse Stuttgart.

It is far more data than any one person can assimilate. It is more than a dozen people can assimilate. But he takes in as much information as he can, and the next thing he knows, he is sending out an email instructing his firm's floor traders to dump the boliviano because the demand for copper is about to plummet.

You know what people want, Maeve says.

She points with a chopstick. You know what people want before they do.

Martin shakes his head. I know what people want, even if they don't want it.

She looks at him evenly, and with her eyes on his, she reaches for the hand that is holding his beer. They sit that way for an instant until she frees the bottle from his fingers and tilts it up and back and takes a long sip herself.

She gestures toward his plate: Are you going to eat that?

He finds himself telling her he sometimes imagines he has swapped his space capsule for a time machine. He feels like a traveler at the helm of a time machine, speeding away into the future to check on the exchange rate of the ruble. He returns to the present to make recommendations based upon these projections. In doing so he renders the projections obsolete. So then he has to generate a new series of projections, and on and on and on.

He tells her that hours, whole days pass in that room in the span of what sometimes feels like spare minutes. Weeks and even months flash by. He wishes he could slow it all down just once. He wishes he could freeze an instant and study it, turn it over in his hands. But it all tears past so quickly. Each second rises and breaks over you and is gone before you know it.

Gavin has fallen asleep, his head resting on his arms. Arnold has slid off his chair and wandered over to the fish tank to stare at the carp up close. Maeve finishes the last of his meal. She takes her cup of tea in both hands and downs that.

She asks if she can have some dessert.

Of course.

She wants the moon cakes with the five-kernel filling. When the dish comes she tucks in, elbows on the table. Here Martin admits to a crazy, private fear. He says, Listen to this. His tone is offhanded and breezy, but she detects an earnestness to his words. Every so often he is overcome by the idea that if he is not careful, he and those like him will bend and twist time so much that it breaks. This sounds silly, he knows. Time does not work like that. Life does not work like that. But whereas two generations ago trades were done by runners on the exchange floor, and took three or four seconds, today computer models manage such transactions in picoseconds—trades so fast no human can ever hope to keep up. You get cascading exchanges, an avalanche of trades that threaten to rush completely out of control.

Martin is troubled by the prospect that time itself might get pressed beyond its limits.

Martin is haunted by the notion that he and others like

him will so tinker with the hidden side of things that the very order of lived existence will be fatally compromised.

Martin is plagued by the idea that if they are not careful, they could end by blowing vast interdimensional holes through the very fabric of the universe.

He orders another beer and says he often thinks about what it must have felt like to be a shaman from ages past, one of those tribal prophets who cast bones to the ground or scrutinized animal entrails for omens. We dismiss such antics now, though he realizes he is not so different. He, too, peruses obscure signs for clues to the future, in a way that others think mysterious, though they follow his pronouncements with great interest, and even awe. The power he holds strikes even him as ridiculous. He feels like a temple elder, only without the crosier and the miter of office, a holy man contemplating the mysteries. But then he reminds himself how those long ago experienced a very different sense of chronology. Before and after once meant something else entirely, so much so that you have to ask how much, if anything, he and the ones who came millennia back have in common.

We're all human, of course. We must share all kinds of connections, deep and not so deep. Yet early man did not sit in an office alone all day, every day. These people did not peer into a computer. They did not talk to others ten or twelve or fifteen thousand miles away, to men and women on the other side of the world. They did not buy and sell the future. Martin has heard it said that oral speech began with counting. The very first piece of writing was an IOU. Money is really nothing more than a kind of social memory. Such innovations signaled staggering revolutions. Double-entry bookkeeping, the joint-stock company—history is replete with advances. Compound interest is to cash as the internal combustion engine is to the wheel. For eons, humans survived without ever bundling securities and investment products into a single financial instrument—two, three thousand mortgages, each representing the work of a lifetime, decades of hard labor—that is parceled and joined, then subdivided and rejoined once more, to be sold and resold time and again, all of it finally compressed into a single number flashing on his screen, a number that can at any second multiply exponentially—or vanish altogether, like the most sinister of magics.

These things wake me up at night, Martin explains. I lie there unable to fall back asleep. I lie there thinking of all that must have happened while I was snoozing, and of all that continues to happen. I will get up at two or three in the morning to check the price of the yen. I check the yuan, the rand, the shekel. I check options on wheat and natural gas and tungsten—wondering the whole while if time is about to get gnarled and bound up and tied into a hopeless tangle, and what will happen if it ever does, and what I would do if it did.

Even as he cautions himself that he has said too much already, he tells her how his reputation was burnished a few years back when he predicted a sharp rise in the Norwegian krone; everyone else called for a drop. The whole Street. His firm, following his lead, made a huge killing. Floor traders soon came to associate him with the Norwegian krone to such an extent that if the currency dipped, many of them grew cold and distant, but if it jumped, they greeted him with smiles and slaps on the back. It was as if the krone now wore his face. The krone has indeed continued to rise, with only the occasional misstep, owing in large part to the oil boom in the North Sea, and for this reason his own standing at the firm is now at an all-time high.

His first years on the job he was an outsider. People tended to ignore him. Of late, however, they have started to invite him out for lunch or for a drink after work. Several months back, he was asked to play poker. He has never been a very good poker player, which might be surprising if you think about his facility with numbers, but he is a wretched bluffer. Yet he went home that night some eight hundred dollars ahead. He was almost certain his success came because others around the table hoped to remain in his good graces. Those at the very top of the firm now seek him out for advice on matters relating to uranium or solar derivatives. Martin does not know anything about nuclear power or the sun, but he is flattered by the attention—so much so that when his subsequent models projected a slow but steady decline in kroner against dollars, he could not bring himself to disseminate the information, but instead altered the data to predict a further gentle rise. Deep down he knew that this was not only dishonorable but self-defeating, though he thought he might get lucky this once and so buy himself a little more time in which to sever the association between his name and Norwegian tender. The krone did stumble for several days but rallied eventually. This had the unfortunate effect of cementing the connection even further in the minds of others. Several months on his model again projected a decline, but at this point he felt he had no choice but to doctor the statistics once more. He enjoyed the minor celebrity and did not want to let it go. Sure enough, the currency spiked following a modest drop. Around the office they have started calling him "Martin the Red," in a riff on the Nordic explorer. It has gotten so his esteem on the job is now completely joined with the fate of the krone; he has been falsifying the data for some time now. A part of him even wants to believe that he somehow has played a hand, however tiny and indirect and unchartable, in the rising fortunes of the krone. It is as if he has this power he didn't know he had. He realizes this is utterly absurd and yes, dangerous, and that eventually the truth will catch up to him, yet he so enjoys being one of the frontrunners at the office he continues to dupe not only his colleagues but in a very real sense himself.

Here is what he does not tell her: Several years ago he happened upon the claim that some 50 percent of all web searches are for pornography. As soon as he read this he wished he hadn't. He does not tell her that he had never searched for pornography before—he really, really had not, if only because of his inordinate fear of viruses—but now that he knew half the world was doing so, he got to, too.

Since then, he will pause occasionally at a website that features pictures of naked women. If he phones this number he can talk to them. He doesn't. He won't. It is enough to know that he can. He checks the price of the euro instead. He checks the price of the New Zealand dollar and the Nicaraguan córdoba. Then he rewards himself by going back to the website to access another picture showing a man with two women. In the next picture, the woman is clothed and the man is naked. Here is a picture of two women together, and another of a woman atop a man. Meanwhile, the pound is falling. The dollar is on the rise. A woman runs naked on a beach. She runs along the sands, the waves foaming behind her. The pound keeps falling.

He does not tell Maeve about the website he discovered in which a couple has set up a camera in their bedroom. Several evenings a week, they webcast their lovemaking. They call themselves Day for Knight. The man always wears a knight's helmet complete with visor and cerise plume. She wears a Doris Day wig and sunglasses. They wear these disguises and nothing else. You cannot see their faces. You can see all the rest. He has broad shoulders and large arms and a powerful chest. She is a shapely woman with a fake all-over tan and labial piercings. The two make love for the camera, and when they are done, they lie side by side on the bed, utterly spent, the man's gear curling and pythonic against his thigh, the woman's sex glistening in the lights. They look back at you for a disconcertingly long time without saying a word, until the man in the helmet reaches over to turn off the camera.

He asks about Ireland instead. He worries he has prattled on too long. He wants her to repay him with a confidence or two of her own. His questions, however, make her reluctant. She says nothing really happens back home; there is not much to talk about. I'm interested, he tells her, I really am. Here her brogue stiffens with unexpected emotion. She says that her mother died a few years ago or her mother is dying or her mother practically died when her daughter left Ireland. She says she has never really been anywhere before except for Dublin, which is a seven-hour bus ride, or maybe she is saying she spent seven hours in Dublin once on a school trip. She says her hometown is a former fishing village founded in the fifth century with the arrival of Christianity—or perhaps she is saying hers is the fifth-oldest fishing village in Ireland. Still, he manages to glean a few spare facts, a quick glimpse of her life as it rears up suddenly in the telling, only to disappear back into the trickle of her words. She was raised on a failing dairy farm. Growing up, life was the weather. Life was simple meals. Younger brothers were always underfoot. Their house sat at the intersection of cow paths. There was the call of gulls in the air, the sight of linens drying on a line. She mentions an Aunt Clodagh, and in passing a cousin Rionach, strange sounds that belong not to people but to landscapes, whole topographies. She speaks of the broad sweep of the countryside, the cragged coastline, the drumming of the surf at the base of the overhang far below. The burning of peat is banned now, but when she was younger it got in your clothes, your hair, it seemed to invade even her dreams.

In the end these memories make her smile. She remembers the mists in the distance, the long curtain of rain, fields of winter wheat undulating in the wind. She presses her thumb into a lone sesame seed on her plate. He watches as she absently brings it to her mouth. She tells him about the old church, with the crumbling tower that has lost its bell. In the cemetery, the gravestones lean with great age. She remembers blood puddings and brined pig trotters. Looking at her, Martin is struck again by what a small, slender girl she is, a mere wisp—though the calves of her legs are large from dancing reels down at the common room on Saturday evenings.

CHAPTER THIRTEEN

THE AU PAIR WILL SPEND Thanksgiving with her relations, the street vendor and his wife, in Hoboken. The Tuesday before the holiday, the Fowlers board a flight for Indiana to be with Martin's family. They used to make the trip every November, but they missed last year when Lily had a large list of witnesses to depose, and they missed the year before that when Arnold had the croup. They can't not go this season. Yet the journey proves ill-fated from the beginning. Their car hire to the airport picks them up late, and they must rush down the long concourse at La Guardia, herding the kids like mustangs, to make their flight. When they arrive in Indianapolis, they learn two of their bags have continued on to San Diego. Their rental car reeks of cheroots. Because of holiday traffic amid a fresh fall of snow, they do not arrive at Nice until late. Though his parents have prepared the sofa bed in the living room for the twins, the boys, wound tight by the journey, refuse to sleep. At three in the morning Martin stands in nothing but his boxers, screaming dire but empty threats at his children.

Sitting across from his father at breakfast, Martin notices he has lost weight. The man looks haggard; a small cast appears in his left eye. He seems addled, his mind wandering off. Twice Martin draws his mother aside to inquire about his father's health, but both times she insists he has never been better. When Martin probes a third time, she begins to weep. His father made her swear not to tell. When pressed, however, she proves maddeningly vague on the details. They don't know what causes it; they don't know how to treat it. They don't know how long. That evening, the husband of Martin's youngest sister—the man is a part-time drama instructor and would-be playwright who once had a script workshopped at a YMCA in Ypsilanti, Michigan—seeks Martin out to ask if he can borrow five thousand dollars, which is two thousand more than he asked for last time.

The poet said you can't go home again, but the poet never lived in the American backwater. Less than forty-eight hours after arriving in Indiana, Martin wakes with the abiding impression that his two decades away have suddenly dwindled, each year no more substantial than a pleat on a collapsed accordion. Manhattan, meanwhile, feels not merely distant but galactically remote, as if not even a space-ship could bring him near. The stark intimacy of it all—the same dining room table, the food from a thousand meals grooved into the grain; the massive oak at the east edge of the lawn, the upper branches of which he used to scale with such abandon that the mere memory gives him vertigo; the dank reek of the basement, the odor of mildew creeping up into the den; the pull-down ladder to the attic, thunder clapping against the floor as it drops, bits of worn insulation sifting all around like a tepid snow; the same dishes propped faceup in the china cabinet, bordered in interwoven strands of fading blue and gold; the familiar spiderweb of fissures in the asphalt of the drive; the identical brand of orange juice on the second shelf of the refrigerator, its eternal taste in his life—generates in him the exact helplessness in the face of circumstance he experienced as a youth.

Still, there remain nagging differences. This point is driven home mercilessly that afternoon when Martin is descending the main staircase in the old house and hears a shuffling noise coming from the crawl space beneath the steps. He opens the door—its lintel follows the incline—to discover his father hunched inside, sitting amid the boxes of old tax records and family albums and books stored since Martin's graduate school days (Planck, Hawking, Feynman; also Aquinas, Bishop Berkeley, and Kierkegaard), books he used to devour, though he has not opened them in almost twenty years.

Dad?

Come in, his father says. He scoots over so his son can sit. I want to show you something.

Martin peers at his father bent low, the man's head grazing the undercarriage of the stairs. He says, Why don't we move out—

In here.

Martin wedges inside and sits on Newton's *Principia.* The old man closes the door. The only illumination comes from the thin line of light at the base. The effect is immediately claustrophobic.

See what I found, the old man says. He places a coin in Martin's palm.

From the size Martin guesses, A nickel?

Count the legs, the man urges.

When Martin starts to open the door, the man reaches past to slam it shut again. You can't do it out there, he says.

But I can't see in here.

His father leans close to explain. In the light it grows a fourth leg, he says.

Martin stares down at his father. His eyes have adjusted to the darkness, so he can just make out the man's shadowy visage, the same hooded brow and hatchet nose that populate so many of Martin's memories. He sits next to his father beneath the stairs in the house where he grew up, the house where all that fashioned him into the person he has become first happened.

His father pats his son on the leg and says, Let's let this be our secret for now.

Thanksgiving morning dawns gray and frigid. The front yard looks like a painting on a mirror you could shatter with a rock. As his family has lived in the area for generations, the crowd at dinner is thronging, the logistics worthy of a castle siege. Great-aunts, nephews, second cousins, any number of townspeople who have, over the years, phoned his father for a tow, along with the retired vicar, the new vice principal of the high school, and a wayward Japanese couple on their first visit to the States who believe they are touring an early Frank Lloyd Wright—all roam the rooms of the old house, and despite the cold spill out onto the front porch and down into the drive. An hour before the meal, Martin's mother decides she needs more mini marshmallows for the yam casserole and so dispatches him to the market. The only store open on this holiday is a small convenience mart at the other end of town. They don't have the minis. Martin purchases two bags of the large ones, but on the drive back he takes a wrong turn and finds himself moving deep into the countryside. While much about the view that passes by his window strikes him as alien, the occasional landmark leaps up in a flash of recollection. It is like watching frayed remnants from the tattered tapestry of his childhood. On past the water tower, the entrance to the limestone quarry, and the old baseball diamond. On past the falling-down Scottish Presbyterian church with its octagonal pillars. On past the Broadhurst farmhouse lying beside a fallow field, hoarfrost dusting the furrows. Six head of cattle stand motionless beneath a denuded ash. And then he is heading down to the river, pulled along by the magnet that is memory. He recalls once again the autumnal colors of the riverbank, and the sound of the flowing water in the distance, and the blue of the sky as it spun overhead through the trees and the crackle of dried leaves underfoot and traces of animal scat and the ancient sycamore scored by a twenty-year-old lightning strike with the birds skirting the lower branches and the giant millstone atilt of its axle shaft, all that remains of the old granary.

The scene has the character of a woodcut: stark and unsettling, the image made austere, and all the more beautiful for it. But in the next instant, Martin upbraids himself for such mawkishness. The Indiana of his childhood lies robed in myth. The state's history is replete with lynchings, forced sterilizations, and vicious labor strife in the steel mills up around Gary. Radioactive waste once flowed freely into the Wabash River. The Klan remains active. The state textbook commission had declared Robin Hood a Communist. If pressed, Martin could recall going with his father to watch one of the local farmers put a twelve-gauge slug into the forehead of each of his seventy-nine head of cattle following an outbreak of hoof-and-mouth disease. The group of men—they were all men—stood about quietly, sharing their helplessness before nature. He would remember the seasonal migrant workers who moved through town during the spring to harvest cabbage and pickling cucumbers, their children suddenly appearing in the hallways of his school for the next five or six weeks—the one named Asunción sat in front of him in American history; the day she smiled at him her smile blazed like a torch showing the way out of a subterranean shaft—and then just as unexpectedly disappearing.

He comes finally to the lot that he and Wendy Chalmers had such plans for, though he does not recognize the site at first because on it sit several small split-level homes gathered around a tight cul-de-sac. The houses are new. The sod has not yet been put down. You can no longer see the river for the rooftops. Across the street, where the meadow once lay, the earth has been ripped open. The concrete foundations for two more homes show their flat faces, and an unfinished network of underground pipes lies naked and exposed to the cold air. He parks at the curb and looks at the cars in the several drives. He looks at the mailboxes and the gutters already clogged with leaves, and the tricycle lying on its side in the mud. A dog yelps unseen in the distance. A figure moves behind one of the windows. It is like listening to a complete stranger casually rearrange in disarmingly intimate detail your most cherished dreams.

Driving back to his parents' house, Martin is delayed at a railroad crossing. He watches as freight gondolas from the Norfolk Southern rattle past. Sometimes a train whistle is enough to bring your head falling into your hands.

They return to New York to find the Christmas decorations have gone up. Bunting in the shop windows, giant red bows bound to the lampposts. The doorman of their building strings lights in the foyer and a bough of holly next to the mailboxes. The Fowlers hold off bedecking their own rooms, not out of any Scroogery on Martin's part but because he has always believed the premature rush to herald the Yule only diminishes its power. He is a purist in this regard. In spite of the protests of his wife and the impatience of the twins, he does not install the towering Douglas fir in the front room until the end of the third week of December. The evergreen is impressive. The star knuckles at the top, two of its points flattening against the ceiling. The lights blink on and off, the ornaments caught in their rainbows.

The tree's presence unleashes the full force of the holiday. Lily sets out festive saucers of homemade potpourri:

dried rose petals, ground cinnamon, crushed cloves. The boys hang their stockings—store-bought macramé fittings on loan from a giant—from the mantel. Wreaths appear in the windows. A long-dead crooner from the 1960s (a junkie and a wife-beater, a recent biography has it) blasts seasonal classics from the speakers. Maeve unpacks a small Nativity scene, the pieces roughly fashioned out of petrified wood from the Curraghchase Forest. The carvings are crude, almost featureless, save for a sparse line here and there to suggest the crook of an arm, a furrow of the forehead. This very spareness, along with their great age, confers on them a gravity that anchors the preparations. Later that evening, the girl accompanies the Fowlers to a performance of Handel at Trinity, the hallelujahs booming off the church's rafters.

One by one those in the crowd rise, and soon Martin himself is on his feet, singing for ever and ever.

Yet he approaches the holiday this year with battling sentiments. He enjoys the sound of sleigh bells and the scent of cedar, but the savage and pagan origins of Christmas manage to assert themselves as they never have before. Though it is the season of goodwill, he cannot ignore the way his nights have been given over to an unsavory intrigue. He and his wife have taken to lurking about their own bedroom like libertines. Their relations seem marked by a sexual cynicism from which he fears they may never entirely recover. He is not merely a man divided, but a man halved and quartered and quartered again.

Martin's tastes have always run to the modest, the unspectacular. Give him olive oil and Parmesan over a thick Bolognese; neckties knotted in half Windsors rather than Van Wijks or Merovingians; Rothko over Pollock. As his bedroom fare has also been fairly pedestrian, he is now shocked to discover he harbors such lurid libidinal propensities. He could not have been more surprised had he discovered he bore an unrecognized talent for the high-wire act in a circus, or had a special facility for defusing bombs in times of war.

The difficulty is made all the more pronounced by the obvious fact that Martin experiences an inordinate and wholly unanticipated degree of fun knowing another watches as he frolics with his wife. It is more fun than it has any right to be. While he has read bits and pieces of Freud, he still does not understand why this should be so. Maybe it is because the situation rouses in Lily an appetite about which he has been absolutely clueless all these years. Though this is to put the onus on his wife when he suspects it belongs on him. He worries that these episodes hint at an irredeemable flaw in his own character, some overarching indecency. For Martin, the marital bedroom has always been the arena in which his erotic bent served a higher purpose—namely, his love for his partner. Old-fashioned, perhaps, but it named his perspective exactly. Now, however, he feels dogged by baser impulses he cannot outrun. When set against the backdrop of the Yuletide, the contrasts strike him as contemptible and obscene.

Martin's rigorous approach to the rites of Christmas dates from his childhood. He was always the one who brought the ornaments down from the attic. It was Martin who roamed the woods in search of mistletoe sprigs. It was Martin who located the snowman's hat and scarf, and it was Martin who sought out the largest carrot in the crisper. And if he likes to wait until the last minute to erect the tree, growing up he refused to let anyone dismantle it until long after the holiday was done, though dried needles dotted the floor and a hot bulb anywhere in the area could have combusted the old Scotch pine. Christmas has always inspired in him the hope that somewhere out there peace and benevolence thrive, even if they do not do so on Earth.

The twins have magnified Martin's joy in the holiday. While barely able to walk, they were even then intoxicated by the colorful wrapping, the noels, the trays of powdered cookies stenciled with Santa Claus in green and white and red. This year for the first time, they have begun to grasp the full dimension of the festivities. Maeve helps them compose their letters to the Pole: I wunt a elektrk carr. Their excitement enlivens Martin's own appreciation. Their laughter is cleansing, even redemptive. It helps, too, that they regard him not as a deviant, but as their father. Yet this, he admits, is only because they have been lulled by delusions he himself has fostered. They do not know him. They do not know what he is capable of. When he considers his sons' well-being and then recalls the evening antics in which he and their mother are involved, he experiences

not so much a scalding shame—though there is that, certainly—but above all the low-grade throb of befuddlement.
This year such behavior threatens to gut Christmas of
much of its innocence. His mood in the coming days frequently echoes the druid tropes of cold and darkness, decay
and death. He worries that even the stockings stuffed with
sugary treats hanging from the walnut mantel will have, to
his nose, a whiff of the bituminous.

CHAPTER FOURTEEN

MARTIN'S OWN CHILDHOOD was benign and bucolic. He can count on one hand occasions of emotional turmoil or burning shame: He stole a candy bar from the Quiki-Mart on a dare, and was so consumed by guilt he threw it away rather than eat it; he lost a fistfight to Billy Kolchak in the fifth grade after Billy called Martin's mother a blimp; one of his sisters happened to walk in on him when he was in the bathroom not going to the bathroom. Yet despite the current vogue for memoirs in which the hero is brutalized from an early age, the truth is he faced few challenges to his esteem or well-being. One episode, however, deserves mention: At six he learned there is no Santa. All children come to this truth in time, but statistics show that Martin arrived at it almost two and a half years earlier than most, and in a manner that marked him keenly. At that age you think God wears a red sweater. The existential fallout was pronounced.

It came about this way: Mary Lou Rasmussen, a teen from down the street, would sit with the Fowler children on the occasional summer afternoon when their mother treated herself to a matinee at La Cinémathèque. This was well before the coming of the mall megaplex, back in the day when any number of small towns each had its own theater, usually with some old-world moniker—the Savoy, the Bijou, Il Teatro, the Roxy—and outfitted like a Reno cathouse, with a roped-off orchestra pit, a velveteen curtain, and viewing boxes embossed with cupids done up in faux gold leaf. Due to a scheduling error that went undetected for almost a full year, a major film distribution company sent a string of these hinterland cinemas subtitled flicks intended for art houses along the Boston–New York–Washington corridor. Every Thursday a reel arrived that explored the human condition in noirish hues. The shipping miscue spawned an unlikely audience of housewives from the hamlets, a demographic that traditionally opted for madcap comedies, romantic dramas, or tales of frontier justice to escape the domestic doldrums. Now, however, they found themselves transfixed by the French New Wave and Italian neorealism. These women sat through *The Bicycle Thief*, *À bout de souffle*, *The Battle of Algiers*, and *Belle de Jour* (three times). Who knew that the thickset homemaker with a damp ringlet of hair falling across her temple as she prepared sack lunches for her children and darned her husband's argyles dreamed the whole while of being wheelbarrowed across the floor of a pied-à-terre off the rue Saint-Jacques by Belmondo. If the distribution company had not duly corrected its error, one of those cultural upheavals—only this time with housewives at the vanguard—that unexpectedly rips through the social landscape might have imploded the America recorded in the history books. As it turned out, these theaters eventually shut down, only to be resurrected as mobile-phone outlets, frozen-yogurt franchises, and nail salons. In this way, the revolutionary conjuncture lapsed.

So Mary Lou Rasmussen would babysit the Fowler children while Mom went out for a bite of Godard. One afternoon a friend of Mary Lou's appeared at the door shortly after their mother had left. Martin remembers him vividly. The boy had long, unkempt hair and an unshaven chin, the stubble like iron filings beneath his skin. A cigarette dangled from his lips. He said, Call me Knuckles. Though Martin had ceased taking naps the previous year, Mary Lou sent the children to lie down in their bedrooms. The day was warm and flies buzzed at the screens. When he rose for a glass of water, he arrived on the stairwell just in time to see Knuckles dip his hands down Mary Lou's tube top. Martin gripped the balusters like an animal at the zoo.

Every Thursday for the next few months Martin crouched on the staircase. Because Mary Lou Rasmussen was a congregant at the Lutheran church, she would not allow her boyfriend to venture below the equator of her navel. But she permitted him full trespass of the north. She was one of those strapping midwestern gals of robust Scandinavian stock. Martin was overwhelmed by the shock and the size of her breasts. They were of an uncanny, almost porcelain whiteness, the left one lightly marbled by a raw blue vein. The vein was the river on which the full-masted schooner of his desire sailed. Her breasts seemed to have arrived from another place and time entirely, dedicated emissaries from a land of incalculable allure. Mary Lou Rasmussen never noticed Martin seated on the steps, but her nipples gazed up at him like purple-brown irises widened in surprise. Her boyfriend, meanwhile, pinched and nuzzled and slobbered over their pucker. The attention he devoted to them was feverish and prolonged. The expression on Knuckles's face was sweaty and racked by yearning. He was in agony. Never before had Martin witnessed such earnest and palpable devotion to anything or anyone. The prospect that he might himself one day arrive at such extremes of feeling—whether it be about a woman or a principle or an obsession or a way of life—made Martin sweat himself. Only at the sound of tires coming up the gravel drive would Knuckles hie out the back while Mary Lou covered herself up. This went on all through the summer and into the fall. Mary Lou Rasmussen's boyfriend rarely acknowledged the children, but when he arrived on the Thursday before Christmas and found the tree aglow in the living room, he turned to young Martin and mused, You know, Santa's dead.

The teen's tone was pensive, not malicious. Knuckles, if dim, was not mean-spirited. Still, it was a pronouncement worthy of Nietzsche. Not, There is no Santa Claus, or, Santa is a lie—either of which Martin could have weathered—but, Santa is dead. It left him with an image of Santa having crash-landed his sled out on Indiana State Road 168. He envisioned the staved-in red panels of the sleigh, the scattered toys, the reindeer lying broken and baying on the pavement. He pictured a splintered runner having skewered Santa through the heart. He eventually grasped that Saint Nick was a mere tale told to children, but Knuckles's words continued to haunt him. While Christmas remains for Martin a much-cherished holiday, even now he experiences some dark and not wholly fathomable linkage between Santa and mayhem, Santa and rent limbs.

In the opening months of the New Year, Mary Lou Rasmussen dropped out of school and moved to Cincinnati to attend a training program in massage therapy, which she dropped in turn. History has since lost track of her. Knuckles died several years later in one of the desert wars when a rocket-powered grenade pierced the armor of his M1 Abrams tank. With Mary Lou gone, Martin's mother retained the Widow Frackingham from across the street to sit with the children. The Widow Frackingham wore support stockings rolled to just below her knees and smelled of urinal cakes. Martin never saw Mary Lou Rasmussen again, though the episode proved to be a watershed in his development. Perhaps the confluence of her ample front with the archetypal refrain of the Absent Mother, along with the obliteration of the childhood pantheon—Martin reasoned that with Santa toppled the Easter Bunny, and the Tooth Fairy, and the Sandman must also be earmarked for extinction—inaugurated a seismic crisis in which his developing ego was fissured by Oedipal, psychosocial, and metaphysical tectonic shifts.

Especially scarring to Martin was the elaborate and thoroughgoing nature of the deception. Not only was the threat of a list-keeping Santa shamelessly employed to enforce draconian behavioral norms among toddlers, and to inflict enormous ecological damage on great masses of hewn conifers and butchered fowl, but vast quadrants of the economy relied on the dodge to garner upward of 40, even 50 percent or more of their annual receipts. Without this fiction, the gears of commerce would have been sheared smooth by spring. Santa dead was more powerful than Santa alive could ever be.

Such disillusionment is naturally a rite of passage endured by all, but in Martin's case there was a coda that compounded the trauma: The following autumn Warren Dewhurst, a schoolmate, asked if Martin thought there really was a Santa Claus. Warren asked him outright, and with such a searching concern Martin saw his friend would be crushed by the cruel facts. Martin lied and said of course there was. He did such a masterful job of maintaining the charade for the sake of his pal that he would at moments forget himself, and so experience once again, if only for a few passing seconds, the seasonal enchantment that comes with a fidelity to its myths and icons. Martin found these exchanges innocent and yet so doleful they left him with a bittersweet longing. In the right dosage nostalgia can bring us closer to an appreciation of the sublime, but in too great or coarse a quantity it has the consistency of bile. It was not until age ten that Martin discovered Warren had hit upon the truth years earlier as well. It turned out that each had maintained the facade for the sake of the other. You see, he and Warren Dewhurst were best best friends.

Despite the gentle irony of the situation and the tender concern of the principals for each other, Martin took from the incident a grim lesson. He saw in this heartfelt and well-intentioned subterfuge more sinister workings. If the might of the social engine could be used to power an illusion of this magnitude, then you had to ask which if any of civilization's totems was genuine. A fundamental and inescapable duplicity appeared to occupy the very heart of all things. Perhaps nothing was safe. He worried that God and country and freedom and self and the whole conceptual grab bag that fuels our sense of reality might be mere shibboleths we adopt out of fear or laziness or intellectual dereliction, the result of an atavistic herd instinct that manages to corral us all. Maybe we foment the charade on others so we can believe it ourselves. Say the real was what you got only when enough people acted as if they already had it.

Adolescent nihilism is among the most virulent. It can propel one down any number of soul-deadening paths, from glue sniffing or nonstop video gaming to compulsive onanism or student-council politics. Not Martin. Mathematics saved him in the end. He recalls the very instant. One second he was a listless kid who watched big-screen space operas, thumbed through comic books, and went swimming at the quarry. The next, he was head over heels for digits. Here was a world more real, more abiding than the familiar environs of tables and chairs. Numbers did not restore his faith in things. Numbers restored his faith in faith.

Up until that point, he had been a middling student. Teachers hardly noticed him. Yet his instructor that year was different. Her name was Miss Bucknell. Her approach to teaching was close to evangelical. She dutifully sat with him after class and talked him through Euclid. He struggled with the simplest of deductions, unable to see what was obvious to everyone else. Miss Bucknell couldn't understand what Martin couldn't understand. You can be so smart you're dumb.

She tried various approaches, lent him text after text. One happened to include an appendix that detailed the famous puzzles of mathematics. The four-color theorem, which avers that a map never needs more than a quartet of hues to ensure no like regions touch, caught his attention. Though formulated in the mid-1800s, the hypothesis took mathematicians over a century to vindicate. Martin solved it during the following Sunday's service. The answer arrived like a kind of grace, borne on the rays of the sun. Sitting in the pew, he saw the way the light struck through the stained glass, pouring into the transept, showering down on all those bowed heads. In the painted window, the Madonna held the Child. Joseph looked on. The nimbus above the Archangel Gabriel's head was maroon. Red and blue and green and gold also glinted in the pane. The solution came to him as if Martin were on Saul's highway: You didn't need the gold. The insight restored the world to its rightful place. He tackled Prince Rupert's problem next, then the infamous Tower of Hanoi, followed by Euler's notorious Seven Bridges of Königsberg. It can't be done, he told Miss Bucknell about this last, and he explained why.

She eyed him steadily. How did you do that? she asked. He shrugged. Beneath the planes and angles of the world he sighted hints of the sacred. He experienced the far-reaching inferences that are the stock-in-trade of the mathematician as wild leaps of faith.

I don't know, he admitted.

Dear Miss Bucknell. One waits all one's career for such a student. She died a quiet death several years later, as if her life's mission had been fulfilled. At the funeral were the priest and her nephew from Kokomo—who asked after the ceremony if Martin knew where he might score some weed.

But these puzzles were mere parlor tricks. The real work lay ahead. In college Martin immersed himself in differential equations, topology, harmonic analysis, fluid mechanics. You do not do math to make a lot of money or to gain the admiration of others or to get women. Everybody knows to get women, you play football or dress sharply. His clothes were either hand-me-downs from his father or arrived via mail-order catalogs. While he threw himself into athletic contests, on the fields and courts of his youth he struck out at the plate, dropped the pass, and fluffed the free throw. This may have been one of the reasons he took so readily to numbers. Here he felt in control in a way he did nowhere else. Give him a pencil and paper and an hour of undisturbed time to work and he plumbed to the core, seeing beyond the physical world to its very essence. Everything else in life seemed to involve a self-conscious display, a show he performed for a crowd of anonymous onlookers. Except math. When he did math it wasn't for other people. When he did math he had an audience of one. This audience was God.

⁓

That was all so long ago. It had been almost two decades since Martin abandoned his attempt in "A Stochastic Demonstration of the Principle of Sufficient Reason Using the Saperstein-Hideaki Conjecture" to substantiate the existence of the Almighty via the most advanced mathematical techniques and recent innovations in physics. If decades earlier the loss of Santa had been dispiriting, the loss of God in manhood threatened to sink him into a crippling despair. What proved most unnerving was that despite his failure, Martin could not avoid the gnawing suspicion that life isn't good enough for no God. Even to this day he cannot rise above the worry that in the absence of God the colors of existence are dominated by faded pastels instead of the rich, burning hues the human condition merits. Late at night, lying in his bed in the solitary darkness, he is convinced there ought to be someone or something out there who is a sympathetic witness to our most profound aspirations and desperate yearnings and unspoken terrors.

Such sentiments are complicated by Martin's abiding conviction that without God, competing attempts to explain the why and wherewithal of existence prove hopeless. It takes only the most cursory consideration to recognize the Big Bang—the idea that the entirety of being all somehow mushroomed in mere zeptoseconds from an impossibly small and impossibly dense pencil point of matter—as nothing more than a crude bit of imagery. The really interesting question is what came in the twinkling before the Big Bang, and about this we remain absolutely clueless.

⁓

His colleagues in the investment industry and his acquaintances in life remain untouched by such questions. The whys of the universe do not trouble them. Martin feels embarrassed by his own preoccupations. Naturally, there are some who like to insist that the pursuit of the big questions of existence stands at the vertex of human striving, but Martin has struggled to break free of their ranks. Indeed, there appears to be something sophomoric, if not downright pathological, about such concerns. Lily, for example, moves through her days unfazed by these worries. He admires this about her. She is a woman of imminent practicality. She would smile if she knew to what extent these other matters continue to exercise Martin. Yet he cannot escape the specter of anarchy that haunts all visions of a godless universe. Because if the proverbial void or near void lies beneath it all, then our ills and our successes are without rhyme. Having done as well as he has, Martin likes to believe he is to an appreciable extent the architect of his own luck. Through dint of hard work and native intelligence, he has had a role in his good fortune. Yet if a genuine lawlessness lies at the core of existence—and what is lawlessness but a confounding nothingness—then there is nothing to separate him from the urchins and mendicants and all other unfortunates who endure unbearable ignominy in this life; nothing but a hairsbreadth of chance and circumstance. And this frightens him. It would frighten anybody. It frightens him because if there is no reason to believe he merits what he has, then there is no reason to believe that at any second it cannot be stripped from him completely.

This realization infects even the most tender of his experiences. He can be sitting on a quiet evening drinking a twelve-year-old scotch or tucking the boys into bed or gazing upon the silhouette of his wife adoze beside him or watching the first day's light bathe the city's towers in honey, and remember in the very next second how fleeting and fragile and unearned each is. The only remaining explanation for why he has prospered and many have not is because for whatever reason the chaos of the cosmos falls disproportionately onto those others. He has somehow succeeded in placing their lives between him and catastrophe. In which case, his past is no longer the record of shrewd prudence and ordered effort he likes to think it is, but instead a litany of brigandage and outrage, to which he at any time could be subject in turn, without appeal or recourse. One-fifth of us can't dine on four-fifths of the food forever. In such a world Martin feels naked and exposed. His fortune could be pilfered out from under him, his home ransacked and torched. His wife could be violated in unspeakable ways and his children sold into slavery out of some Bedouin port. He could be murdered in his bed. And most horrible of all, such atrocities would go unremarked in the end, because in the absence of God, the only witnesses left would be either those party to the plunder or those others relieved it was not happening to them.

And so Martin waits. He waits for God to show Himself. He waits for his children to grow, for his annuities to mature, for his wife's disposition to soften, for his respect among his coworkers to flourish. At night he waits—he aches—for the girl to appear. Lying there in bed in the semidarkness, Martin experiences a curious kinship with the subatomic hyperon, wondering when the onlooker will show yet again, and so bring him into being.

Meanwhile, Lily waits, too. They listen to the wind moving through the eaves and hear the low grumble and beep of traffic from the street far below. He will see a plane cross the skylight or sometimes the moon itself hanging up there, looking ridiculously large.

It's funny, he whispers to his wife one evening.

It's funny, but you lie here and you hope and hope and hope, and then you go to sleep.

She considers him for a long time before saying, You know, life is like that.

CHAPTER FIFTEEN

LILY'S YOGA STUDIO is in the basement of a downtown fitness club. You walk through the keyed entryway and past the rowing machines and the treadmills and the free weights, the aroma of cleaning chemicals mixing with that of human sweat, to a windowless room with a drop ceiling, where an emaciated young man with a patchy beard and a shaved head lights several sticks of incense and puts on a recording of mantras set to sitar music. He leads them through a series of poses: Mountain, Downward-facing Dog, and Tree, pausing every so often to strike a large metallic gong with a rubber mallet.

Maeve wears one of Lily's old unitards. It bags in the hips and one of the straps won't stop slipping from her shoulder. The young man keeps stepping over to adjust the girl's position, and when he does so yet again, placing one hand on her diaphragm and the other on her thigh during the Warrior Two pose, she pushes his arm away and mutters, Get your gobby paws off me.

Afterward the two women go for a sauna. They sit wrapped in towels on wooden planks, their backs against the wall, along with several others. Twice Maeve reaches to ladle more hot water onto the dark rocks, harvested from the base of a volcano an hour outside Reykjavík, which sits atop the very fissure where the Eurasian and American tectonic plates meet. Coming from a land of pelting rain and chilled currents rushing in from the Norwegian Sea, she experiences the intense heat as a tonic. When she picks up the ladle a third time one of the other women says, I read somewhere that if you do it too much the rocks can explode. The diamond on her left hand is the size of an acorn. Maeve hesitates with the ladle in her hand, and looking the other woman squarely in the eye, she lets the water dribble over the stones once more, making them hiss and sputter. When Lily laughs, the woman who had spoken gets up and leaves, slamming the door of the sauna behind her. After another minute or so the other woman climbs down off the bench and escapes in turn. Lily and the girl are alone. They sit with their eyes closed. Maeve's normally wan pallor goes flush. Moisture beads on her long arms and thin shoulders. The Celtic cross sticks to the skin at the hollow of her throat.

I could sit here forever, the girl murmurs.

Lily looks over. So do.

Without opening her eyes, the au pair says, Right now my da is probably trying to herd the goats back into the shed before a freezing rain starts in, while one of the boys—Liam or Padraig—is out in the combine harvesting the winter rye. Finbar will be mending the fences. It is cold, and when they go back in, they will stoke the fire and then sit down to tea. You are cold all the time. Even when you are warm, there is the dread that the cold will come soon again.

Yet you miss it, Lily says.

I miss it.

Will you go back one day, do you think?

The girl's raises an eyebrow. Of course, she says. Of course I'll go back.

Lily nods slowly before saying, What's it like?

The girl looks at her out of the corner of her eye. What's it like?

What do you think of when you think of home? Lily says. She expects to hear about the girl's friends or school or her home life. She imagines talk of long, listless afternoons, lush, verdant vistas, farm animals nearby.

Instead, Maeve begins talking about an event that occurred long ago, though the memory isn't her own. It is the memory of a memory. There is a story they used to tell about her great-grandfather on her mother's side. She first heard it when she was only two or three, before she could begin to understand, and she has continued to hear it all her life. It is a permanent part of family lore. His name was Declán Duffy. As a young man, he couldn't enlist to fight the kaiser because of flat feet, but his dogs did not keep him from being hired as a letter carrier for the Royal Mail in Dublin. This was in 1916. He had been on the job only two or three months when he returned from his route the day after Easter to discover that the main post office had been occupied by the insurrectionary forces. Declán Duffy did not know anything about politics. Declán Duffy had no interest in politics. His passions were hurling and drink, and the pub where he ate and told stories and danced. He also liked a certain *cailín* in his life named Fionnuala ó Súilleabháin. Such matters took up all his time. But His Majesty's militia had cordoned off the building, and when they saw Maeve's great-grandfather passing by in his postal uniform, the commander demanded that Declán Duffy carry a dispatch to the rebels housed inside. The British gave the frightened mail carrier a white flag to wave and a sealed envelope. Terrified, Declán warily approached the post office and was shot at twice, but he eventually made them understand he was bearing a letter from the British. They ushered him past the barricades, where they learned the message demanded they abandon the building or immediately face prosecution and likely execution for sedition. Relieved at having survived, her great-grandfather wanted only to get home, but the insurrectionists insisted he return to the commander with a note explaining that as this was now Free Ireland, the British had no authority here. In this way and entirely against his wishes, Declán became the intermediary. For six days he scurried back and forth, bearing one communiqué after another. Having tired of the game on day seven, the royal commander outfitted Declán with a large satchel containing an explosive device sufficient to wipe out the entire leadership council of Sinn Féin ensconced in the dead-letters section of the PO. Maeve's great-grandfather knew nothing of the contents of the satchel, and, unaware that he was about to die himself, was dutifully making his way back to the rebel stronghold when he crossed paths with a pair of blackguards. At knifepoint, they liberated Declán of the bulky and expensive-looking satchel and promptly made their getaway. They were just the other side of the military cordon when the satchel went off, resulting in dozens of dead and dying among the British constabulary. When word of the explosion reached the rebels, her great-grandfather was immediately hailed as a hero in the cause of Irish independence. The

British stormed the building and ended the occupation the following day, but by then her great-grandfather's reputation was established. A price was put on his head. He was a boy of seventeen who had never been in trouble of any sort outside of the time he put carrageen—a local moss that acts as a natural laxative—in his English instructor's tea, but suddenly he was wanted dead or alive. He fled to the west countryside, and that is why many years later Maeve came to be born within sight of the great open sea. She understood the very first time she heard the story that her great-grandfather was something of a buffoon and a dupe, though his respect among the locals was enormous. Everything about his story was an accident, but if it hadn't happened in just that way, she would not be here now to tell about it.

And that, Maeve says, is what Ireland is like.

Lily nods, letting this sink in. She asks, Did they ever catch your great-grandfather?

Maeve says, Declán Duffy died sitting in the Harp & Red Lion Public House in Killarney, shot by a jealous husband. He was eighty-four years old.

Both women smile. Maeve rises to ladle more hot water onto the rocks. They spit and steam. When the au pair sits back down, she peers at the older woman, her face full of a question of her own.

What is it? Lily says.

I don't mean to pry.

You can ask me anything.

Have you and Mr. Fowler done this—

Never, Lily says. Never before.

The au pair sits for a time. And then she says, So he was your first?

The question makes Lily laugh, but then she catches herself. No, she finally says, and she shakes her head.

Maeve says nothing—waiting, the older woman realizes, to hear more.

Lily might have explained that her first lover had been a man in his forties named Stephen Bonaventure. He was a wine merchant who owned a shop on Houston Street that stocked rare vintages. As a girl she occasionally went with her father when he drove into the city to pick up a case. She followed the two men to the tasting room in the rear of the store. They would offer her sips from their glasses. She liked sitting between her father and the vintner amid the floral tones of this or that wine while bottles rose all about her, from floor to ceiling. The only illumination came from the back-lighting behind the display racks. The room had the feel of a cave housing an ancient oracle. The setting and a glass of good Burgundy always softened her father's demeanor. He seemed genuinely fond of her in a way he did at no other time.

The afternoon came when one of the men—she no longer recalls which—challenged her to a taste test. It began as a joke. Her father laughed as Stephen Bonaventure removed his tie to blindfold her—the merchant held her hand as he guided each glass into her fingers—but to both men's surprise she readily distinguished a cabernet sauvignon from a cabernet franc. This became a regular practice whenever she and her father went to the wine shop. She found it unnerving to sit in the dark behind the blindfold, but something about the experience seemed to focus her concentration. More often than not, she got the vintage right. Stephen Bonaventure told her father it was an extraordinary feat for a girl of fifteen.

On a weekend shortly after the New Year her father phoned from Ottawa, where he was giving a lecture, and asked her to run into town to Bonaventure's to pick up a brace of bottles of a good, good pinot noir that had just arrived. It was a blustery day, cold and sleeting, but she hopped on the train to do as her father asked. At the shop, Stephen Bonaventure uncrated the new wine and bagged the bottles, but before letting her go he said he had recently gotten in a most unusual varietal grown on the slopes of Mount Simonsberg, east of Cape Town; he wondered if she would be able to tell it apart from several domestics. While it was quite raw out and she wanted to get home, Stephen Bonaventure was already urging her toward the tasting room. He sat her down on a cask and blindfolded her before pouring several samples, maneuvering each into her grasp. She sipped two different vintages and while she was trying very hard to determine which was the South African, he said, One more, except this time when he took her hand, it was himself he placed in her fingers.

By the time she left the shop, it was dark and snowing hard. She slipped on the steps descending to the subway, breaking both bottles of the good, good pinot noir. When her father arrived home that evening and found his wine was not there, he turned away from her in wordless disgust. She did not deserve even language.

In the coming months whenever her father invited her to accompany him to the shop, she made her excuses. She went at other times on her own. The blindfold stayed on each time. She knew that what Stephen Bonaventure was doing was wrong, but she did not stop him. She suspected that if her father ever found out, he might kill Stephen Bonaventure. Despite his academic pretensions, he could be a man of unexpected violence. She once saw him slap a waitress when she spilled veal jus on his suit. But Lily also sensed that at some level this was her father's fault, that he had first exposed her to the situation. Maybe she never stopped Stephen Bonaventure because she thought in this way to punish her father. Or maybe it was something else. She did not know. She did not know if she wanted to know. This went on for over half a year and then the day came when she never again returned to the wine shop. She does not recall ever deciding to quit going. She just—something inside her just—did. When Stephen Bonaventure died of a stroke a decade later, he bequeathed her father two cases of very fine malbec.

But Lily has never told this to anyone, and she is not about to start now. Instead, she settles once more with her back to the wall of the sauna and says, I was once engaged to another man before I met Martin. This was a long time ago. The man's name was Ethan Gage. In all honesty, I hardly ever think about him anymore. I met him during my first year of law school. He was in my study group. He was bright. He hoped to one day teach constitutional law. I thought constitutional law a bore. A bunch of white men trying to design a society from the top down. But the week before the final exam, Ethan walked me through the entire course, explaining each legal precedent. His recall was extraordinary. He remembered the smallest of details. After I passed the class, he admitted he was in love with me. I don't know that I loved him back. I liked him—he was funny and unassuming and very kind—but I don't know that I was in love. Yet he was so obviously taken with me that I agreed to sleep with him. It seemed wrong not to. If someone felt that strongly about me, who was I deny him? That fall when school started again, we moved in together, into a one-bedroom in Morningside Heights. And by the spring we were engaged. I don't remember quite how it happened. I don't remember his asking. I don't remember saying yes. It was as if I woke one morning to suddenly find myself planning a wedding. The date was still a year and a half away, but the preparations took over my life. He wanted to be married at Christmas—I can't recall why now. His parents were wealthy and my parents were wealthy. They tried to outdo each other. Ethan and I were going to be married at the Church of the Transfiguration. This meant I would have to convert. I said, Okay, then I'll convert. The reception would be at the Pierre on the Upper East Side. The fitting for the dress alone took an entire day. His mother insisted on throwing a shower; I would have to travel down to Philly for a full weekend. It was to be at Le Bec-Fin, off Rittenhouse Square. So I agreed to travel to Philly. I kept agreeing to everything. It was as if I had lost the capacity to do anything else. After the ceremony, we were going to honeymoon in Patmos, a tiny island in the Aegean—the site of the Cave of the Apocalypse, where John the Apostle received his visions in the Book of Revelations. I agreed to that, too.

At the end of the school year, I worked as a summer associate for a firm downtown. The subway took almost an hour each way, sometimes longer. I woke when it was still dark and walked through the early-morning light to the station. The neighborhood is perfectly safe now, but back then at that hour, I had to step over drunks and watch for people suddenly emerging from doorways or lunging for my purse. I was assigned to a partner named Abby Fleischman. She was tall and immaculately dressed and stunningly beautiful. She let me sit in on client meetings—I remember because at these meetings there were always the most extraordinary pastries from a bakery next to City Hall—and asked me to compose the first drafts of briefs. I was lucky. Most summer associates spend their time at the copy machine or proofreading memos, but Abby let me do real work. I wanted to be Abby Fleischman.

When fall came I started my third and final year of law school, but there was one big case that I had been working on that Abby Fleischman said I should see through to the end. Whenever there was a meeting she would let me know, and if I did not have a class I would go. Sometimes I would go even if I did have a class, if only to see Abby Fleischman and eat fantastic rugelach. I was just sitting down with half a dozen others at a conference table inside the South Tower when there came the sound of a distant plane. You hear aircraft all the time in Lower Manhattan, but this sounded different somehow. It grew louder and louder and then louder still, louder than it had any right to be. We all looked at one another and this was when the first plane struck. It caused a terrific, ear-shattering boom. The window facing north immediately filled with an immense fireball. It was as though the whole planet had burst into flames. We looked at one another once more and then we all jumped up and made for the stairs. The stairwell was packed and it seemed to take forever. The second plane hit just as we arrived at the lobby. It seemed the very sky over our heads had split open. The lobby filled with smoke. It felt like we were witnessing the end of the world. We raced out into the street. It was chaos. There was smoke everywhere and people running. The smell of diesel fuel was overwhelming. It was very difficult to breathe. The noise kept going on and on. You couldn't tell where the screams stopped and the sirens started. I tried to reach Ethan on my cell, but of course everything was down. Police and firemen were tearing every which way and there were groups of people wandering about stunned. Then there was another explosion and a huge billowing cloud of smoke shot down the alley. It chased us down the alley. This was the first tower coming down. We all ran as fast as we could the other way. I came upon one woman collapsed against a fire hydrant with a gash in her leg. The ash covered her face and her hair. She was an albino save for the blood coming from her leg. I helped her up and together we hobbled over to a makeshift first-aid station that had been set up out in front of the stock exchange. The trains weren't running, the phones were down, and the streets were clogged with cars that had been abandoned. Another woman was crying, and though she appeared unhurt, she was hysterical. I talked to her for a while and helped calm her. People kept saying, We're under attack. We've been attacked. I somehow got it into my head that they meant not humans, but aliens. Humans couldn't do something on this scale. It had to be space aliens that had landed and were attacking us. This seemed suddenly and eminently plausible, as plausible as anything else. I wondered if I would see an alien. I tried to picture what it might look like. Then someone shoved a milk crate full of water bottles into my arms and I walked around handing out those. It was raining ash and the smell was awful. I tried calling Ethan again, but I still couldn't get through. This was when the second tower came down. I heard it before I saw it. I turned just in time to see the top floors slump and then the whole thing fell like an old man collapsing to his knees. The utter enormity of it all hit me. I was thinking how a whole way of life was coming to an end. For all we knew, this was only the beginning and maybe buildings everywhere around the country would start falling. We'd already heard about the Pentagon and there was talk the State Department had been hit as well and you could not help but think that this was the first in a series of catastrophes that would strike the country and its buildings and the people in the coming hours and days and weeks and maybe forever. Maybe this was our new life now. And then I was thinking about the sheer beauty of it. It sounds horrible to say, but the World Trade Center's coming down had the power almost of a kind of terrible poetry. I remember seeing photos once of the Buddhist monks who immolated themselves during the Vietnam War.

It was ghastly to see the shape burning there, squatting in a meditation pose but absolutely aflame. But what I remember too was how the flame looked like the head of a rose, one of those burnt orange antique autumn roses. It was ghastly but stunningly breathtaking as well. To attack the heart of the financial world with human missiles. It seemed absolutely apocalyptic and yet so perfectly apt. Also terrifying. I was terrified for myself, of course, and for Ethan and for my family, but most of all I was terrified for a way of life. I was terrified for the world as I knew it because I saw it was coming to an end.

A man now came staggering along the sidewalk. I saw he was bleeding from the head. I ran over to help him sit. He was covered in ash, too. He told me his name was Louis Ferrante. He was dressed in worker's overalls like a mechanic or repairman wears, with *Lou* stenciled on his breast pocket. He wore work boots, but he had lost one of them. I remember because he had a hole in his sock and his big toe poked through. It is funny that I remember that. All sorts of things were happening that day, but this is the one thing that stands out more clearly than most: his big toe showing through the hole in his sock. We sat side by side and watched Armageddon while I dabbed at the wound on his head with some tissues from my purse. Reality seemed to be tearing apart right in front of us. It was as though the very truth of things was coming undone. When Lou Ferrante took my hand, I let him take it. When he kissed me, I kissed him back. I told myself I couldn't do this to Ethan. Ethan and I were going to be married. Ethan and I had something really real. But I did it anyway. This was out in the open, sitting at a curb on Water Street, down at the southern tip of the island, but people were too busy running for their lives to notice. When he opened the front of my blouse, I wanted him. I wanted some human connection before it was all over. The world was ending, and this did not seem to be asking too much. No one would ever know because we would all be dead. Those were my actual thoughts on that day. But then I had another, a second thought. I had this idea that if I did something with this man then that would mean the world would have to end, because if the world did not end then I never would have done such a thing with a complete and total stranger. Which meant if I didn't do anything, maybe the world would survive. And still I considered letting him do whatever he wanted to do. I am ashamed to say I actually debated whether the world deserved to continue on. His hand felt so good. But at this instant, a police cruiser came through and an officer leaped out and said we had to clear the area because there was a gas leak and the whole street could blow. So Lou Ferrante and I jumped up and began running. We held hands while we ran. We looked at each other like we knew we had some unfinished business. But there were a lot of other people running, and in the rush his hand slipped from mine and I lost him in the crowd. I never saw him again. And so the world survived. I saved the world. I didn't get back home until late that evening. Ethan was waiting in the lobby of our building. Thank God, he said when he saw me. I've been so worried. He tried to take me in his arms, but I pushed him away and said, I never want to see you again. The words came out of my mouth as if they were being said by someone else. I had not planned on saying any such thing. But I said it again. I heard myself say, I never, ever want to see you again.

Somehow after what I had been through, the thought of marrying Ethan seemed preposterous, like a very bad joke on the part of the universe. Who was Ethan Gage? I didn't know, not really. Most of all, I did not want to know. He stared at me and said, Why? I said, Why? Because the towers came down. He said, But that's not an answer. He didn't understand. But I understood. After what had just happened, I could not go on living my life as if nothing had happened. Something had to change. I said, It's the only answer, and I went upstairs and started packing my things.

Ever since then, I occasionally stop whatever I am doing to look up phone numbers. Last time I checked, there were seven Lou Ferrantes in Manhattan alone. I phone one of the numbers and whenever anybody answers, I hang up. I don't talk. If I talked the world would vanish.

The two women are quiet for a while. They seem to be inhabiting Lily's story, trying it on for size. In the end, the au pair rises once more and reaches for the ladle and again filters water over the rocks. A great tower of steam fills the small room so thickly it is hard to make out the walls and the ceiling. The two women look at each other and then they look at the pile of volcanic rocks, waiting for the explosion.

On one of those evenings when the girl doesn't appear, Martin again stays awake until far into the night, unable to nod off. He rises finally to tiptoe down the hall to the study to check the foreign exchanges. The British pound holds steady, the U.S. dollar has rallied, while the Albanian lek, of all things, has plummeted. Though the fate of the lek is of little concern, even to a currency analyst, Martin enjoys seeking out the underlying dynamics of anomalous patterns. It takes him over an hour to chart the causal flows: Albania is one of the largest exporters of nickel and chromite, both of which are essential in chromium electroplating, used to coat plastic and metal surfaces in an aesthetic sheen impervious to corrosion, such as you find in engine casings—think of the gleaming bulge of a motorcycle fuel tank—decorative jewelry, and machine parts. Such plating minimizes friction while enhancing tensile strength and durability. Electroplating is also used in the production of a certain action figure out of Seoul popular among boys between the ages of ten and twelve—which is unfortunate, because the coating happens to leach a highly carcinogenic alloy. The presence of chromite in these toys has only recently come to light, following a consumer product–safety investigation, precipitating a dizzying decline in the fortunes of the Albanian economy—and with it, the lek.

Satisfied that he has traced the cause down to its very germ, Martin pauses to peer out the window at the vast honeycomb of light that is a skyscraper rising against the black sky, and then rewards himself by going to a website where he watches a woman by herself.

Then there are two men with a woman.

Next, two women undress a third woman.

Martin comes upon Day for Knight. Knight takes her

from behind. His palms look large on her buttocks. Day is on her hands and knees, her hair swinging in her eyes.

When Martin realizes Maeve is standing in the doorway, he shuts off the computer.

                                 ✍

I'm sorry, he says. He says it again: I'm sorry. Did I wake you?

I couldn't sleep, Maeve says. The illumination from the desk lamp casts the lower half of her body in full light. The hem of her flannel nightgown brushes the tops of her worn slippers, though her face remains draped in shadow.

Me, neither.

She indicates the computer. Am I disturb—

No.

You can turn it back on, if you want.

That's okay.

She goes to the cage and removes the cover. The bird hunkers on its bar, its wings gathered closely around it. Looking in on the bird, Maeve says, So I can watch you, but I can't watch you watching.

Martin considers for a moment before saying, That's right.

She nods slowly, then reaches through the bars to stroke the feathers beneath the creature's neck with her thumb. Its pupils dilate suddenly, swelling like miniature saucers.

Martin says, It likes you.

I like him.

Does it ever fly? he asks.

Not so much, I think. No.

On impulse, Martin reaches past the girl to unlatch the cage. The hinges cry out. The bird peers back through the open door without moving.

Maybe he is shy, Maeve says.

It doesn't talk. It doesn't fly. Martin shakes his head. Maybe it's just stupid. He means to make a joke, but it comes out sounding harsh, even cruel.

Her look is quick. He is not stupid, she says. Perhaps he is afraid.

Martin, still trying to get her to smile, says, Three squares a day and a place to sleep. What's there to be afraid of?

But she doesn't smile. Instead, she says, And what are you afraid of?

His head comes up. Who says I'm afraid?

She does not answer, but reaches through the open door and runs her finger from the bird's pate all the way down to its tail feathers in one long slide. Aristotle bobs twice on his perch, emitting a high-pitched rumble, like a cat's purr.

Only now does Maeve say, She loves you, you know.

He looks at her, but she does not look back. All her attention is focused on the bird. Martin starts to respond but then thinks better of it. They both watch as the parrot bends into her finger, its wings arching and easing, until Maeve reaches over to close the cage door.

CHAPTER SIXTEEN

C HRISTMAS DAY. Maeve gives the Fowlers a set of decorative tea towels she has sewn herself. She gives each of the twins a wooden whistle carved from elderberry. The Fowlers give Maeve the latest-model cellular phone, just out. They give her a purse, the clasp a legendary monogram in gold plate. They give her a gift certificate to an online retailer, and two weeks' pay in crisp one-hundred-dollar bills tucked into an envelope.

Martin gives Lily a set of crystal champagne flutes, their necks long, like a woman's. He gives her a full day at a famed spa up in Mamaroneck. He gives her a cutaway stole of Canadian lynx. When she tries it on, the snowy fur announces the freckles along her décolletage. Lily gives Martin a pocket watch 150 years old, save for the fob, which is fashioned from titanium and captures the light in a retina-searing flash.

The twins receive, in no set order, a toy football and toy telephones and clothes. They receive miniature stock cars and a loop-the-loop track, which will take their father three hours to assemble, or two hours and thirty minutes more than promised in the instructions. They get new sneakers.

The older one receives a stuffed lion and the younger one receives a stuffed tiger. Arnold unwraps a Pee Wee first baseman's glove; Gavin, a catcher's mitt. They get picture books and chapter books and pop-up books. They get a pair of wooden ducks that quack from one grandmother and toy AK-47s from the other. Gavin receives a radio-controlled 787; Arnold, a helicopter. They each receive a computer tablet. They get bow and arrow sets with suction-cup tips. They get a video of classic fairy tales sanitized for modern times. Aunt Gwyneth gives them twelve hours of introductory ski lessons at Camelback Mountain. Grammy Van Slyke also sends each a five-hundred-dollar U.S. savings bond that matures in twenty years. Uncle Archie makes a gift of five shares of Apple Inc. They get stockings engorged with candy (caramels, chocolate bars, striped canes, fudge drops, yogurt-covered raisins, mints, nuggets of taffy, lumpy moons of divinity). They get battery-powered cars—Arnold's is a Lexus; Gavin's is an Audi—big enough for them to ride up and down the long hallway.

There's one more thing, Lily says. She pulls a hat box out from behind the sofa and places it in the girl's lap. The previous Christmas, each of Maeve's brothers received a new wallet fashioned from calfskin with a ten-euro note inside. She gave her father a satin pouch filled with Danish pipe tobacco. She received a new pair of low-cut pumps, the same ones that now sit in her closet.

The girl shakes her head. This is too much, Ms. Fowler.

It's Lily, she says. Go on, open it.

The au pair carefully undoes the tape so as not to rip the paper. Inside, a field of cream-colored silk. The girl holds it up to the light.

Put it on, Lily says.

Maeve reappears wearing the dress, a single sleeveless sheath with vertical and bust darts. The effect is electric. Her normally lifeless complexion now stands out against the shimmering fabric with a coruscating luster all its own. The material clings to her thin features. Her slender shoulders appear disconcertingly naked above it.

Lily looks at her.

Martin looks at her.

Even the twins pause in their playing to stare.

I don't know how I can ever repay you, the girl says.

You repay us every day, Lily says.

She takes the nanny by the arm to lead her to the master bathroom, where she spends the next twenty minutes making up the girl's face. When Maeve reappears, her blemishes are gone and her normally ashen pallor is now the color of buffed ivory, save for the smallest hint of blush at her cheeks that reflects the tint of her lips. Her eyes, meanwhile, are lined in the way of an Egyptian goddess. Sitting in the recliner, Martin half-rises out of his seat. Lily goes back down the hall and returns with a pair of pointy-toed mules in one hand, the heels as narrow as straws, and her sapphire earrings streaming from the fingers of the other. Borrow these for today, she says. They're perfect.

The girl totters gamely about in the shoes—Martin thinks of a fawn the first time it stands—pausing only so

Lily can affix the jewelry. The stones bring out the color of Maeve's eyes, as if they were shifting views of the same cloudless and eternally blue sky.

For Christmas dinner, they take the Long Island Expressway out to a house in Friday Harbor. The Van Slykes arrived almost four hundred years ago, fleeing the collapse of the tulip bubble just ahead of creditors. They made some money in shipbuilding—their vessels were among the first to bring slaves to New Amsterdam—and later set up a small textile factory at Peck Slip, just off the seaport. Though there are certainly larger homes in the neighborhood, and the family fortune is one of the smaller in the village, Lily grew up in circumstances the very far side of comfortable. She and Martin take Maeve for a tour. If the nanny was surprised at the expense of the Fowlers' furnishings and the size of their quarters, she is unprepared for this. Forty-eight hundred square feet on three and a half acres hard to the Sound, an English garden out back. The Great Room reminds you of a museum. A portrait above the fireplace, a bust in the corner, a three-hundred-gallon saltwater aquarium set into the far wall, the pump humming as neon tangs and queen angelfish hold steady in the flow. In the library, they come upon wall-to-ceiling bookshelves fashioned from Australian cedar. Three, four thousand volumes, with another ten thousand in storage. Lily opens a volume to show Maeve her father's photo. The author is a handsome man with sweptback hair, a pipe in his hand, and the same nose, though there is a slight curl to his upper lip, as if he has just had a disagreeable thought.

He looks sad, Maeve says. She touches the photo with a finger, as if she might somehow be able to soften the features.

Lily says, He used to say the only time he felt truly happy was when he was alone.

For dinner, four generations gather around the table. Though it is not quite two in the afternoon, her mother is already deep in her cups. The meal is subdued. Lily's eldest brother keeps calling her husband Marty. When someone directs a question Maeve's way, she responds shyly, her eyes on her hands in her lap, her cheeks filling with color. For that moment, the sounds of eating stop so everyone can hear. As one course follows another, she watches Lily for a clue about which fork to use, how to rest the knife on her plate. She softly declines the offer of another serving of goose, but when Lily's mother insists—youth achingly reminds her, as it does all aging drunks, of fond kingdoms cruelly lost—the girl attacks a second helping. For dessert, she eats a massive wedge of pumpkin pie with salted dark chocolate ganache. After the meal, a dozen of the guests go for a walk around the grounds. Maeve's small ears stand out red in the cold. Along the western track, some of the elms have been cleared because of the fungus. The party wander among the stumps and watch in the distance as the wind chases whitecaps along the surface of the water. That was the afternoon Maeve sat so still on a slender granite promontory, a finch perched on the toe of her shoe.

Later Martin comes upon the girl on a bench in the mudroom at the back of the house with his brother-in-law's son. The young man sits cross-legged at her feet. He leans toward her intently, his talk animated. His eyes drift to her naked arms and then back to her face. He lights his cigarette from the dying ember of the previous one. Old tack hangs from the wall.

Martin nods at his nephew and asks if Maeve isn't chilly. Inside, the fires roar in the chimneys. They're having coffee in the parlor. Maybe she wants to go back in, he suggests.

The boy—Henry, Martin remembers—says, She's all right. He has sullen good looks, his blond hair a bit long at the collar. He puffs on his cigarette. He was expelled from Dartmouth for cheating. Days he plays tennis. He owes money in town.

The boy turns to Maeve and says, You're all right, right?

Maeve stands. The sapphires shudder like droplets. Would only that they never stopped moving.

She says, Maybe I should go in after all.

They don't arrive back in Manhattan until late. Upstairs, Arnold drifts off within seconds, though Gavin throws a tantrum, one of those increasingly frequent episodes where he hurls himself about the nursery as if his body were a missile aimed at the heart of the family. It takes Maeve half an hour to calm him down. Out in the living room Lily tells Martin, It's no wonder, given all the sweets he ate today. When the girl finally comes back up the hallway, she finds the Fowlers waiting for her with a glass of wine.

Unless you're too tired, Martin says.

It's Christmas, Lily says. She's not that tired.

In their bedroom, the au pair watches in frozen fascination as Martin kneels before his standing wife and gently traces the chiaroscuro of her sex with a teasing finger. Before it is over, Lily starts to buck.

He can never decide where to put his eyes during these episodes. They have too many places to go. There is his wife aflutter above him, the sudden flush at her sternum. And there is Maeve, her lips slightly parted. A moan from Lily makes the girl's eyes swell. A swift intake of breath on the part of the nanny will cause his wife to cry out. These sighs and gestures serve as ciphers in some secret correspondence between the two women, a communication more profound than words. He comes away from these exploits feeling curiously unmoored. He finds it impossible to go about his day acting as if nothing has happened. He begins to worry that perhaps other people sense this as well. Maybe they detect something awkward about his demeanor, some miscue to the way he appears or the things he says. He fears that whenever he buys a newspaper from a street vendor or sits across from a priest on the subway or drinks a cup of coffee in a diner, the vendor or the cleric or the waitress might manage to spot the fact that only eight hours earlier Martin lay supine while his wife straddled his face and rattled the headboard in her hands for an audience of one.

In truth, several of his colleagues have indeed noticed just how preoccupied and inattentive Martin has been of late.

None can put his finger on exactly why this is, and most are too discreet or too professional to talk of it openly. But several younger staff members short on compunction did discuss among themselves—the dress code had been relaxed in the days leading up to the holiday; they stood about the coffee cart in loafers and khakis—how Martin Fowler not only failed to see the coming default of the Bank of Zambia, in Lusaka, and so did not predict the collapse of the Zambian kwacha but how he also wore the same tie two days running. These staffers are relatively new to the firm and hungry to scrabble their way to the top. They are impatient with the likes of Martin Fowler and wish only that he and others of his ilk would get out of the way. Such scuttlebutt is not uncommon, of course, and is generally ignored by wiser heads, but in this instance it reaches the higher echelons of the firm. And so while Martin is surprised to discover two days after Christmas one of the firm's three executive vice presidents—a man named Pierce; not his boss, but his boss's boss—outside his door, no one else in the office is.

Can I come in?

Of course, Martin says. He indicates a seat, but instead of sitting, Pierce pauses to make a slow pan all the way around the room. He is not a tall man—he is, in fact, pretty short, though he has a low, booming voice that he aims like a howitzer—but he carries himself as if he ought to be.

You could do with a picture in here, or a plant. Some color, Pierce says. And then he settles a buttock onto the corner of the desk and adds, I'm here to talk about your upcoming projections.

Martin pivots in his seat. Okay.

The man pulls out a phone and pecks at it before saying, You forecast a three percent rise in the Norwegian krone for the first quarter. He leans to display the screen, but Martin doesn't need it.

That's right.

And another five percent in the next two quarters, Pierce says.

Five and an eighth.

Pierce spends another thirty seconds tapping the screen before saying, Five and an eighth. He slips the phone back into his pocket. His eyes make another tour of the office.

Not even a photo of the family, he says. It's like a monk's cell.

Here the executive vice president crosses his arms and leans back—there is an instant where Martin fears the man is going to tumble off the side of his desk altogether—and says, Pfaffenhauser is calling for a drop.

Pfaffenhauser, another of the analysts, is also in contention to one day be named head of the currency desk. He is a nondescript man save for his tanning-bed skin. He lives in a loft in Park Slope with a wife who is a curator of Native American textiles. Martin's memories of her, on the other hand, are graphic. He and Lily went there once for a retirement party for one of the senior partners. She was a deep-breasted woman with a towering white chignon. Not blond, but white. He remembers she was oddly barefoot, her toenails painted an eye-catching turquoise. She was so pale and angular and finely featured she looked not to have a drop of indigenous blood in her, but somehow standing before a Lakota war blanket, the color springing from the walls, she seemed a picture of arctic abandon. She looked like the kind of woman who will take her time coaxing you right up to the very edge, only to make you beg. She served chilled vodka in small tumblers that were themselves fashioned from ice and so required you to handle them with a chamois mitt you collected from a dispenser at the edge of the bar. The stunt struck him as contrived, but Lily insisted on trying it at their next dinner party. There must have been some defect in the mold or in their freezer, because their tumblers leaked. The Fowlers' sofa still smells like a czar's distillery.

Pfaffenhauser is calling for a drop, Pierce repeats, and I wanted to see that you're certain of your numbers.

As certain as I can be, Martin says.

I want certain certain, the executive vice president says.

But nobody is certain certain.

Pierce gets up to move around the room. He stops before Martin's window to look out onto the mainframe across the way. He says, Pfaffenhauser is.

Pierce was there back in the days of runners on the trading floor, the ubiquitous sound of the ticker tape. They used to gather up boxloads of the stuff for parades along Broadway. He saw Armstrong and Aldrin drifting in a convertible down the Canyon of Heroes.

Pfaffenhauser is sure, he says again, and when Martin doesn't respond he asks, Everything all right with you?

Martin nods. Fine.

You sure?

I'm sure.

As sure as you can be, anyway, Pierce says.

The older man turns avuncular. He puts his hands flat on Martin's desk and leans close, the hash marks in his forehead standing out. He says, You ever want to talk, we can talk. It doesn't matter what. You lost the kid's first two years at Yale playing cards, you're doing the babysitter, ass cancer—anything, you hear me?

Thanks, but I—

Meantime, if you're wrong, we'll be caught with our pants down.

Martin regards the other man. I don't think I'm wrong.

He doesn't think he's wrong.

Just what is it you want me to say?

Pierce shrugs. Tell me you're right. Tell me like you mean it.

All right. I'm right.

Pierce says, You're right and Pfaffenhauser is wrong.

I'm right, Martin says. Pfaffenhauser is wrong.

Tell me Pfaffenhauser can go to hell.

Martin says, Pfaffenhauser can go fuck himself.

Pierce smiles for the second time that day, his enormous teeth once more exploding in the center of his mug. It is as though he keeps the smile in reserve, husbanding it, saving it for those moments where it can do the most good.

At the door he turns back to say, Or maybe a ficus. I'll have Supply bring one up.

That evening Martin has trouble falling asleep. He keeps hearing Pierce's imperious voice. He keeps seeing the man's face. When he does finally sleep, he dreams. He dreams he is at the base of a large hole. A sun-drenched sky shines at the aperture overhead. In his dream he has been in the hole for a very long time. He waits for the passage of a cloud or a jet, anything to break the monotony, but the sky above is empty and profoundly, eerily blue. Standing in his hole, he is just about to drop off to sleep— he has the curious impression that he ought to fall asleep in his dream so he can then wake in real life, though the hunch is so ill-formed, he senses he shouldn't trust it—when a rock comes flinging down the hole to strike him in the head. The blow hurts. The second rock hurts even more. It seems someone above is pelting him with stones. It is only when he looks down at the gathering collection of projectiles that he sees they are not stones at all, but Norwegian one-krone coins, with the hole in the middle and the puffin on the obverse. They continue to come tumbling down the hole, bouncing against the sides and deflecting off his head with such force he fears he may suffer some mortal injury. He curls up against the curved wall of the hole, protecting his face and his head and his eyes with his hands and his arms, but the coins continue to accumulate. He soon realizes the danger won't come from getting beaned by a coin, but from being swamped by the flood of them. In no time, he is in money up past his knees. The mound of specie is already so high he can no longer move. He crouches as the sea of coins continues to rise all around, screaming for help, though the acoustics of the hole—the acoustics of his dream—are such that it sounds as if someone is on the outside, screaming in.

CHAPTER SEVENTEEN

BETWEEN CHRISTMAS AND NEW YEAR'S, Martin and Lily always fly to a tiny isle in the Caribbean. They began the ritual before they married and have maintained it throughout. Nothing—not the winter a blizzard closed every airport within 120 miles, requiring a trip on the Metroliner down to Dulles; not even the birth of the twins, whom the Fowlers usually deposit with Lily's sister up in New Rochelle—has kept them from making the trip. The couple escapes the cold and the snow to lie on the beach and gorge themselves with snapper in salsa verde. These journeys serve as an oasis to which they return again and again in the desert that any marriage can sometimes be. They stay at the Hotel Quetzal. In the lobby, potted bird-of-paradise plants grow from massive urns decorated with Toltec glyphs. Hammocks hang in the bar. The Fowlers always reserve the same room, its door not twenty stepping-stones of polished obsidian from the beach. The sand has the consistency of confectioner's sugar.

This season, however, when Martin wonders aloud if they shouldn't cancel the trip, it is Maeve herself who insists they go. She will stay behind and tend to the boys.

You don't want to look back on this year as the year you didn't go, the girl reminds them.

I'm positive that's not how we'll look back on this year, Lily says.

And so the Fowlers find themselves hugging the twins and bidding the au pair good-bye just as the doorman buzzes to say their car to the airport is waiting downstairs. They hustle a golf bag, tennis rackets, a laptop, a large hatbox containing a straw sunbonnet wreathed in a chartreuse ribbon, a carry-on packed with three mystery novels and a tome on copyright law, and four other pieces of luggage into the trunk and drive through a freezing rain. They reach JFK, only to learn that because of overbooking he has been assigned 22C, while she will be in 6A. He is seated in coach between a large, flatulent man who spars the whole trip long with elbow and knee, and an elderly biddy with a hacking cough, the phlegm in her chest crackling. The faceless passenger in the row ahead reclines fully, causing the seat back to rest on Martin's knees and making it impossible for him to lower his own tray. Lily, on the other hand, is placed in business class beside a younger fellow with two days' growth of beard and oil in his very dark hair. He resembles one of those *compañeros* in a sepia photograph who rode with Zapata. When Martin goes up to check on her, he finds the two sitting arm to arm, eating the sole on real china, conversing in her high school Spanish and laughing for reasons about which he remains clueless. He returns to his own seat to eat a ham sandwich with squeeze-packet mayonnaise out of a cardboard box.

The Fowlers arrive at the hotel and discover their usual suite is unavailable because of ongoing refurbishing. Instead, they are given a room off the elevators. Yet the sun coming through the windows is bright and the bed large. Above it hangs a painting that details almost exactly the view of the surf as it appears through the window opposite, as if it had been composed by an artist propped against this very headboard. The bed, meanwhile, has been turned down. Standing in the middle of the room, looking at the sheets made startlingly plush and white in the fierce light, Martin imagines how it will be to lie with her amid such softness. But dinner that first evening turns out to be marked by awkward, often painful silences, and when they do finally return to the room they are so weary and jet-lagged both drop off to sleep almost instantly, only to be awakened at five the next morning by the sound of hammering and the whir of a power drill from the floor above. Lily and Martin spend the early part of the day on the beach, though when she begins to gather up her things and he asks what's the matter, she says the sun has given her a migraine.

I'm going back to the room to lie down. Maybe take a nap.

I'll come with you, he says.

But when he begins to nuzzle her on the too-white, almost virginal sheets, Lily says, No, I meant a nap nap, and he says, Why didn't you say so in the first place?

He goes exploring instead. He walks down to the *mercado* and through the Jardín de la Revolución, with toucans housed in great corrugated iron cages hanging from the limbs of the jacaranda tree, and on past the *teatro* and the ancient *iglesia* to a falling-down *museo*, the rooms of which are filled with huge *molcajetes* fashioned from volcanic rock and jaguar masks of gold and blow darts with tips poisoned by secretions from indigenous toads. Next door sits a building with narrow columns and a plaque out front that tells the story of a group of slaves who, having been freed by the proclamation of 1838, appeared on these very steps to beseech their former master to take them back into bondage. When the man refused, he and his family were massacred.

That evening Lily, following a phone call to the boys, allows Martin to undress her before the open window with the muted light of innumerable stars filtering into the room. They climb onto the large, firm bed, where Martin begins to caress his wife. He caresses her for upward of ten minutes and still she does not respond. It feels odd to make love to her without an audience. They are strangely shy with each other, as if the coupling of two people alone somehow constitutes a bizarre deviation, a perversion. But when he eases into her, she sighs thinly. Desire falls over her features like a shadow. He rocks above her and groans, and she sighs again. His movements quicken. She begins to whimper. She runs her hands up and down his back. She gazes up at him through narrowed lids. He seems to experience once more the first powerful stirrings of love that always overtook him in the earliest years of their relationship. Her eyes open wide suddenly, as if perhaps she at that very instant has unexpectedly experienced these exact same stirrings. And then they open wider still.

Here she begins to scream. She screams again. The shadow turns out to be not desire, but a bat. Though the creature is not large, in Martin's field of vision its visage seems especially vivid, pointed ears attached to a creepily human face like you see on shrunken heads. Lily screams a third time and heaves her husband off with uncommon force. The bat flutters up near the ceiling and then dive-bombs the bed. Lily screams once more. Martin leaps up and stands starkers in the middle of the room, his erection disproportionate and absurd. He grabs the first thing he can lay his hands on and proceeds to beat the overhead fan to death with his nine iron. He flails away for a good ten seconds, bleating with the effort, until Lily, her voice now calm, says, Martin.

He stands gripping the golf club, eyes darting madly about the room for the carcass. Lily sits up in bed, clutching the bedsheet to her throat.

She says, Martin, it's gone.

She dreams of bats. He doesn't, but only because the incident has been so unsettling he hardly manages to sleep. Though she does not say so, he knows she blames him. The following morning, they wait out in the hallway while a repairman replaces the fan. Upon finishing, he informs Martin in tortured English that fifteen hundred pesos will be added to his hotel bill. After lunch Martin suggests a nap, but Lily says, No, I want to go for a stroll along the promenade. He is not invited. He tries to take in a round of golf instead, but by the third hole he is so parched and drenched with sweat he goes back inside. And that night when he tries to take her in his arms, she shrugs out from under them and says the ceviche—raw white fish and octopi cured in a lime marinade—she had for dinner has not agreed with her. He suspects she is making excuses, but a short while later she locks herself in the bathroom. The noise is detonative. When Martin knocks on the door to ask if she is all right, she yells, Leave me alone.

He takes a brooding walk down the beach, with the surf foaming silver in the moonlight. The sheer number of constellations overhead recalls Indiana nights from long, long ago. At the curving edge of the coastline, guitar music drifts up from a tiny cantina. Two men sit at the lone table. Bamboo blinds obscure a back room. Martin takes one of three cane stools lined at a bar fashioned from a single plank of driftwood. He orders a *cerveza* and then another. The men at the table have unkempt facial hair and soiled shirts and blackened nubs of teeth. He guesses they are common laborers or perhaps fishermen. He is reminded of a documentary he once saw on the pearl divers of Mexico. They lived in shacks with sporadic electricity, downwind from open sewers, and yet their women in the film loved them deeply, you could tell. They looked like women who made it all worthwhile, women who took pleasure in the pleasure they could give a man.

Martin enters into a reverie in which he does not return to the hotel. He does not return to his wife. He imagines how Lily might react. She would wait and wait for him and perhaps even work at offering a word of amends for when he walked through the door. But say he did not. Say she fell asleep and woke to discover he was still gone. Of course she would be furious. She would simmer the whole day waiting for him to show, no longer in the mood for reconciliation but instead practicing a speech censuring him for his selfishness. Abandoning your wife without a word for a night and half of a day is the act of a selfish man. Yet as the afternoon wore into evening and she spent a second night alone, and then a third, and when he still had not appeared for the day of their departure, she would panic. She would convince herself the very worst had happened, that he had fallen off a seaside cliff or been set upon by banditos or swept away by the undertow or torn apart by some unfamiliar Caribbean marine life, *el tiburón loco*. She would make her way to the airport in case he showed at the final moment, but he would not show. He would not show because he would have traded his ticket and his clothes and all his belongings for a loincloth knotted at the waist and a life in which he flings himself time and again fathoms deep beneath the water, emerging with a pearl the size of a ball bearing between his teeth, an apt gift for the dusky woman who evenings would greet him at the door of their shack wearing nothing but a Carmen Miranda headpiece.

Martin has started on his fourth beer when a girl appears from behind the bamboo blinds and walks straight up to

him. She says, For fifty pesos I for you dance. Her skin
is bronzed and her hair the same shade as a newly black-
topped drive. *Tú vienes conmigo* and for fifty pesos only I for
you dance. Martin stares at the girl. Fifty pesos is not even
five dollars. She can't be more than thirteen or fourteen,
but her blouse hangs off a naked shoulder in a way that he
finds unconscionably captivating. His thinking cartwheels.
But when she tries to take his hand to lead him into the
back, something about her touch—her palm is so small; her
wrist disconcertingly narrow—fires warning shots across
the bow of his scruples. He wiggles free and murmurs, No,
gracias. Instead of giving up, the girl begins to move her
feet. The men seated at the table eye the girl and then Martin. They all wait to see what he will do. Martin waits, too.
She snaps her fingers and spins slowly around. Her hips go
cha-cha-cha. In the end Martin makes her understand he
will pay her fifty pesos, but only if she stops dancing. The
girl goes away happy. He leaves before her sister can come
out and offer not to dance for a hundred.

He wakes the next morning with a jungly taste in his mouth
and his shoes beside the bed, streaked with dried salt. He is
struck once more by the intense whiteness of the sheets in
the light from the window. Lily sits in the chair opposite in
a hotel bathrobe, her hair wet from the shower.

How are you feeling? he asks.

Better, I guess. I'm sorry about last night.

It's all right, he says. Should we dress and get some breakfast?

Let me phone home first.

He listens as she talks to Maeve, and then to each of the twins. When Lily hands Martin the phone, Arnold tells him a long story about how Maeve killed a spider in the kitchen. When Gavin comes on, the boy starts to cry; the Irish nanny is in the background, trying to calm his son down. She goes on to explain that she caught him again playing with the control knobs on the stove. She made him sit in the corner and now he is furious with her.

After Martin hangs up, he turns to find Lily staring at him.

I feel like pancakes, he says.

She continues to gaze at him for a while before saying, What do you think she thinks of us?

She thinks we're fine.

Maybe she laughs at us.

She isn't laughing at us. Or waffles. With bacon.

Or maybe she feels sorry for us.

This hasn't occurred to him, but Martin shakes his head as if he has thought it all through. He does not want his wife to get upset or to stew over such matters so he says, I think Maeve feels lucky to have this job and fortunate to be with such a nice family and happy to find that we are so welcoming. That's what I think.

Do you think she's pretty? Lily asks.

He hesitates before saying, Not particularly. This feels and sounds true to him. And though there has been a time or three when he has looked up and something about the combination of the light and his mood and the girl's expression has made him think she is particularly striking, this is the exception more than the rule, and so he does not say this now.

Lily looks out the window. She keeps looking out the window.

He says, If you'd rather go for a swim now, we could eat breakfast after . . .

Lily takes her time before saying, Do you think about being with her?

Martin can hear his heart going in his chest. No, he finally says. No, I don't.

She nods at this and turns once more to the window. Gazing out on the foaming surf in the distance, she says, Do you think about me being with her?

He settles back against the pillow. He watches the new ceiling fan rotating lazily overhead.

I do now, he admits.

Following an awkward silence, Martin jumps up and again says, Let's get changed. He goes into the bathroom and brushes his teeth and puts on his swimming trunks, but when he comes back out, he finds her still in her bathrobe, standing before the mirror. She turns to look at her reflection from over her shoulder. She lifts the hem of the robe.

Tell me the truth: My ass, it's getting heavy.

No, he says. No, it's not. It's perfect.

He means it. She has a large rear and thick thighs—a

legacy, he imagines, from all those years of equestrian training, perched atop half a ton of horseflesh—and when paired
with her long torso and narrow shoulders, the contrast is
especially marked. Yet he has always found the combination of her small breasts and surging buttocks electrifying.

Anyway, he adds, I like it big.

She squares her body. She puts her hands on her hips.

Did you just say what you said?

Martin waits before saying, No.

She pulls on a pair of slacks and a cotton blouse. Swimming
is no longer an option. She stands before the mirror, brushing her mane with vigorous strokes. Martin has counted to
twenty-three when she says, Men are lucky.

He waits to hear why he is lucky.

They don't have to worry about these things.

This strikes him as unfair, and he says so. I worry. I
worry plenty. I worry if the boys are going to grow up nor-
mal, and if we've set aside enough for retirement. I worry
about heart disease, and about greenhouse gases. I worry if
you're happy.

It's not the same, she tells him. Not at all. It would be
like if you worried all the time whether it's big enough. But
you don't. You don't have to worry about wrinkles in your
face or if your hips are going flabby. You don't spend half an
hour in front of the mirror trying to get everything perfect
and then go out in the street and realize men have stopped
looking at you. They used to look at you all the time. You'd

get on the subway or step into an elevator and you could feel their eyes on you. They wanted you, you could tell. Not that you would ever act upon it, but simply the knowledge that half the species found you instantly desirable made this huge difference in your life. Now they don't even see you. It's like you've disappeared. You're no longer there. Some oaf steps on your foot and you say, Excuse me, and he looks up shocked to discover you even exist.

The largest praying mantis—it must be half a foot long— Martin has ever seen suddenly emerges from the bathroom and moves with disconcerting speed across the floor, only to disappear into a gap between the baseboard and the tile. They both watch it go. He once read that it sees the world through five eyes.

So is it? Martin asks after a time.

Is what?

Is it big enough?

She leaves the mirror and comes now to settle once more in the chair. Husband and wife look at each other. Though his own size is rather modest, he has always regarded his erections as unquestionably sincere and well meaning. But he admits now that whenever he looks down, his member seems to be in retreat beneath his growing belly. He says, These days all I see is stomach and a little more. I tell myself it's not getting smaller, everything else is getting bigger. I know this on the conscious level of ideas, of course, but I have this weird notion that it is shrinking.

What if it shrinks so much that I no longer see it? I'll need you to report on whether it is even there. So when you talk about whether it's big enough, I admit that, okay, this makes me think.

She lifts her chin and regards him from a distance, like one trying to read the small entries on a menu.

So, is it?

It's perfect, she says.

CHAPTER EIGHTEEN

THE REST OF THEIR STAY is like that. Lily goes to the beach every morning and Martin tags along, though he senses that she does not care whether he comes or not. One afternoon he walks into town and purchases a pair of leather huaraches as a peace offering. The ties crisscross halfway up her calves, making her look like an Etruscan goddess. She is momentarily appeased, but when the supposedly hand-sewn stitching comes undone later that evening to reveal a MADE IN INDONESIA sticker, she deposits them in the trash. The next day he works at convincing her to accompany him on a whale-watching tour, but she refuses. Gawking at a barnacled mammal doesn't sound like fun to me, she says, looking at him like he's a barnacled mammal. He says, So maybe I'll go by myself, and she says, I wish you would. Whereupon he pays thirty dollars for a two-hour quest for the mighty humpback. He boards a battered outboard captained by a man with one arm. They see no whales, but forty-five minutes into the trip the boat springs a leak and Martin and the other passengers—a very old couple and two sorority sisters in their late teens, something omega something emblazoned on their shirtfronts—must bail using their hands while the boat limps to a nearby reef. The atoll is deserted, but there is an abundance of coconut and breadfruit trees, as well as a freshwater spring fed by a fall gunning from a rocky summit. The heat is intense, and while trying to relax in the shade, he has a fever dream in which the rest of the Earth suffers some unspecified ecological convulsion and for reasons about which he is not entirely clear the burden of repopulating the planet falls to Martin and the sorority sisters. He imagines them decked out in nothing but palm fronds while he makes do with a codpiece fashioned from a scallop shell. A big scallop shell. He is on the point of plucking the most strategically placed frond from the taller sorority sister when a boat from the Armada del País motors up and rescues them all. Though Martin will live for another thirty-nine years, this is the closest he will ever come to seeing the mighty humpback or any other kind of whale.

The final night, he and Lily go to dinner at a new restaurant that is on the other side of the island, because the *conserje* at the front desk insists it is not to be missed. The hotel arranges for a local cab to take them down the coast road. Along the way, they can hear the surf thundering against the seawall. They arrive at a large boardwalk milling with people. There is a Ferris wheel and booths featuring games of chance, as well as a fire-eater. The music is thumping. Sweating couples gyrate in the muted glare of Chinese lanterns strung beachside. While outside it is steamy, the night sweltering, inside the restaurant everything is cool, table surfaces fine-edged and gleaming. The air-conditioning whispers as if it is in on some secrets.

When Lily removes her wrap, a thin silk shawl, Martin is reminded once more of just why and how much he adores his wife. He is reminded not because she is an unparalleled beauty, but by the very blemishes inherent in her looks and her person that might put off another. They do not put off Martin. For example, this evening she has donned a long gown she bought especially for the trip, one with a dipping neckline. The truth is, she really does not have the figure for such an outfit. While she does for the most part dress quite well, she will every so often enter into a miscalculation of unsettling proportions. She will wear a top that she cannot fill or a ballooning skirt that showcases the girth of her hips or a vest in which her waist vanishes altogether. She will wear harem pants. But it is precisely these small miscues where the world catches her unawares that endear her forever in Martin's eyes.

Indeed, the women at the other tables tend to be curvaceous and dark. Their tops are hoisted and bunched. By contrast Lily appears lean as a shoot, her face wan and shiny. Yet Martin's affections for his wife at this instant gape wide. The point perhaps is this: Be there a thousand million females more comely or gentle or winning, Martin has not seen any of them sitting on the sofa with her legs curled beneath her, tweezing a few minor hairs from her chin. He has not heard these others break wind after a meal that includes garbanzo beans, and it is not they who occasionally lie tethered by a small thread of drool to their pillows in their sleep. If from time to time they also papier-mâché their upper lips as Lily does, he does not know about it. He does not want to know about it. For it is in these moments, caught as she is in the midst of her war against aging and decline, that he observes most pointedly the little girl from three decades earlier, desperate to steer her father's attention to her, if only briefly. Here she appears most genuine and naked and unpracticed of all. His outlook on his wife's foibles is oddly proprietary, if only because he is privy to them when no one else is. In these moments when she is perhaps less attractive and more unbecoming, she is most his.

During dinner, the floor show features a magician who makes a pigeon appear and then a rabbit and then a woman in a nude-colored body stocking. The magician next positions the woman in a coffinlike box and proceeds to saw her in half. When he is about two-thirds of the way through, he stops to cover the woman and the box with a long shawl. He goes back to sawing, and when the woman screams beneath the shawl, everyone laughs. She emerges later from the wings with her body intact, and the audience claps.

For dessert they agree to share the *pastel de tres leches*, but after a single bite Martin puts down his fork and says, Have we made a mistake? Have we made a huge, huge mistake?

You wanted the flan?

I wasn't talking about the flan, he tells her. He settles deeper into his seat and hears himself say, Let's go away.

Lily looks at the room around them and says, But we have.

He shakes his head. It seems suddenly impossible to

explain, though it is all so clear in his mind. You and me and the boys.

You want to take a vacation with the boys?

I don't mean a vacation. I mean a fresh start. You've always liked Boston. Or the West Coast.

She stares at him as if he is not her husband, but an acquaintance from long ago she is still trying to place. You mean leave New York?

I'm afraid it's all turned a little sour.

She pauses a very long time before continuing. Let me get this straight—you think if we up and move to Oxnard, everything will be sweet once more.

I didn't say Oxnard, he says a little more sharply than he meant to. The man at the next table looks over.

And what about her? Will she come with us to Oxnard?

Nobody's talking about Oxnard, he says.

What is it, exactly, that you want, Martin?

He looks down at his hands, as if the answer might lie in his palms.

Because I don't know, she goes on. She gestures with her fork and says, I don't know anymore.

Like you ever did, he says, and immediately wishes he hadn't.

God, I hate it when you whine.

He scoots his chair back from the table and stands, reaching for his wallet. I want to leave, that's what, he says. He wants to go back to the hotel and go to sleep and wake in the morning so this night will be over. But when they step out of the restaurant, the heat seems to mirror their anger. The night is sultry. It is like trying to breathe through a wet blanket. The carnival has shut down. The square is strangely empty. The Ferris wheel lies unmoving. They have to step over a drunk passed out on the sidewalk. They make their way to a street corner where the ALTO sign lies on its side and try to hail a cab, though the traffic is sparse. The hum of the air-conditioning has been replaced by the buzz of jungle insects, by the small sounds of critters scurrying away into the darkness. After several minutes, the shirt beneath Martin's jacket is soaked through. Her hair, which began the evening pinned high, has come undone, stray strands bunching at her nape and hanging down in her face. It takes almost half an hour before they manage to flag down a very small green car with a red passenger door and a busted headlight. It is a vehicle some fifty years old, shipped from a former people's republic in Eastern Europe. Martin leans in the window to dicker as his guidebook suggested, explaining that he will pay eighty pesos for a ride back to the Hotel Quetzal. The driver nods. They take a different route than the one they took earlier in the evening. Previously, they moved down past the shore, but now they cut deep into the heart of the rain forest, the canopy of trees joining overhead to make the dark even darker. Soon they leave the pavement and go tracking along a dirt path through the underbrush, the tires sifting back and forth amid the sweet aroma of rotting fronds. The lone headlight offers a perplexingly Cyclopean perspective on the maze of vegetation. They seem to be driving through a giant salad. The car bounces over a small boulder, sending grit knocking against the rocker panels. When Martin asks if there are no seat belts in the back, the man glances at the rearview mirror and nods.

They have been on the road maybe ten minutes when the driver swerves to avoid a steep ditch but fails. The impact is jarring, the front of the vehicle slamming into the earth, then popping back up again as the cab clears the trough. The shocks are spent and the Fowlers come down hard against the seats. The driver swears softly and jerks from the car to inspect the damage. After some moments he pokes his head above the passenger window and, looking past Lily, performs a pantomime to make them understand they should get out of the car. When they do, the cabbie loosens the nuts on the front driver's side tire, hands Martin the lug wrench, and then with his back to the grille strains mightily to lift the front of the small vehicle. Martin says, Don't you have a jack? But the man only nods and with trembling arms indicates that Martin should hurry. Once the flat tire is off, the man gingerly lowers the vehicle, hitches up his pants, and begins rolling the wheel down the path. Don't you have a spare? Martin calls after him. The man pauses to look back and nod, then continues to coax the tire along. By this point, Martin's pants are filthy from kneeling and his jacket is streaked with grease. His face is misshapen by bug bites. Mud flecks the hem of Lily's dress. They stand next to the car, bewildered, and watch as the man disappears over a small ridge. They are suddenly, terribly alone. The air is so humid it seems to press down upon them from all sides. Swarms of tiny gnats hover before their noses. Martin casts about for something familiar about the setting that might prove reassuring, but it feels as if they have been delivered to another planet. He smoked for a period of three and a half months during his second year of graduate school while enduring a particularly brutal course sequence ("Heckle

Operators, Poisson Summation, and Theta Functions of Lattices") and gave it up once his final exam was finished, though now for the first time in twenty years he finds himself craving a cigarette. They try their phones, but neither can get a signal. After almost an hour of waiting—they have climbed back into the car to avoid the mosquitoes—Lily says, For all we know, he's gone back home and is at this moment asleep in bed.

He's not going to leave his car, Martin says.

Apparently, he has.

What do you suggest we do?

She doesn't answer. The darkness seems to condense and thicken around them, as if infused by their moods.

I was looking forward to this trip, he says now.

She turns his way, though he cannot quite make out her face. I know, she murmurs.

I thought it would give us a chance to—

I know, she says again.

They sit for so long he has the uncanny sense that perhaps the chronicle of their memories is merely someone else's dream, until she says, Maybe one of us should wander back up the path and see if we can find a house and get some help. Maybe someone will have a phone.

Martin turns to peer at the jungle outside the window, and then back to her.

Maybe we should both go.

She shakes her head. He could return and leave without us.

I'll go, he says.

You don't speak Spanish.

He opens the door and steps out. He removes his jacket

and lays it on the seat next to her. While he doesn't look forward to traipsing through the dark, that seems more inviting than sitting alone in the car and wondering if something has happened to his wife. He says, I'll just follow the path for fifteen or twenty minutes and see if I can find anything.

He reaches over to lock the car door.

Be careful, she says.

Martin heads toward the ridge, in the same direction taken by the driver, but he soon finds the landscape all but impossible to navigate in the dark. He falls twice, glancing around both times to see if Lily is watching. Lily is watching, her face small but distinct through the car window. He forces himself to go some way farther without looking back, struggling to climb the rise. From up here, the cab melts into the graying darkness. He shambles down the opposite side of the incline, where the tree cover thickens. It is like entering a dank tunnel. The odor of decay deepens. Though it has not rained in all the time they have been here, everything is wet and dripping. Mud squelches beneath his feet. He seems to be descending into some sort of netherworld. He goes another twenty yards, the mud clutching and sucking at his ankles, until it rips his right shoe clean off. The pair cost him six hundred dollars at a shop in SoHo—Italian leather, hand-tooled. He gropes about for the wing tip but manages only to cake his forearms. He hobbles along on one shoe, though the scene ahead is construction-paper black, tree branches and shoots rearing up at the last second to lash his face. Civilization seems something that cannot be expected to happen for millennia yet. He considers returning the way he came but decides not to, if only so he doesn't have to listen to Lily repeat her bromide about how if you want something done right.

He continues to pick his way down the path. It descends for another hundred yards and then tilts sharply, rising once more. He gropes for shrubbery and hanging vines, hoisting himself up, as if the vegetation were the rungs of a ladder. The jungle canopy overhead parts unexpectedly, delivering him to a clearing atop a small abutment. He is met by a palpable cleansing of the air that carries a light, crisp aroma, as with berries. To the south there is nothing but more rolling jungle, an endless covering of fronds spilling away toward the horizon. But to the north the crescent of the coastline, the water gleaming, appears in the distance, laid out beneath more stars overhead than he has ever seen in his life. They crowd the sky as if it were a sieve through which a powerful light shines. He stands in the middle of the clearing and slowly rotates a full 360 degrees, taking in the full panorama. It is lustrous, phantasmagoric. The silence is absolute. He could be the last person on Earth, absolutely alone among the trees and the rocks and the clouds and the sea. But he is not alone. The realization is surging. He wants to race back and fetch his wife, to drag her up from the depths of her mood, to show her the staggering splendor that stretches before him, convinced the experience will not only salvage their vacation but bring them both to one of those moments of unspoken joy out of which the very best marriages are forged.

Remember this, he thinks, and it takes him a moment to realize he has spoken the words out loud. It is like overhearing a prayer said by a stranger.

Now he spies, squatting among the lowlands, a small shed of some sort, walls that resolve themselves into a tin roof that reflects the starlight. He quickly hurries down to the hut. The setting is derelict. A stack of nail-ridden lumber lies to one side, and next to it a pile of broken roofing tiles. Several lengths of PVC pipe lean against the wall. As he comes nearer, he sees it is a single room with glassless windows, bars over the windows, and a door of paneled wood with iron hinges the size of old Bibles. He knocks twice on the door and then goes to one of the windows. Inside it remains dark, though as his eyes adjust he can make out a hammock and a small woodstove, a chair and a table. The habitat of a hermit, an outcast.

Hello, he calls. Hello.

He continues to circle the house, but when he arrives at the opposite side the sight draws him up short. A bulking shadow looms into view, in what at first seems an incomprehensible choreography. You don't always see what you see. It takes several seconds more before he realizes he is watching a pair of rutting dogs. The one on the bottom remains obscured in the shadows, but the other one stands out clearly: large, scabrous, plagued by mange, broad swaths of its hindquarters stripped of all fur. Martin freezes, yet this only causes the one on top to turn toward him. The gesture is unsettlingly human, almost accusatory. Starlight seizes its eyes, as if its cranium were packed with diamonds. Yet its tongue hangs long out of its mouth, debauched and monstrous. The scene seems nakedly primitive, as if Martin has arrived at a timeless place beyond the reach of all calendars, a place where he has no right to be. Very slowly he begins backing away, but even as he does so the eyes of the dog follow him, searchlights that pick him out in the darkness. Once Martin clears the corner of the house, he begins to run. He charges back up the incline, pursued by the thought that the dogs have lit out after him, that they are even now closing in. He scrambles along, groping at weeds and small branches to keep his balance, and having gained the clearing he does not stop, but roars down the other side, the noise of his wheezing large in his ears, so loud that it overtakes the sound of the breeze as it moves through the trees.

He arrives back at the car to find Lily kneeling in the mud, working to tighten the lug nuts on the new tire while the cabbie strains to lift the front of the vehicle. She looks up in both fury and relief as Martin takes the wrench from her.

When they are again on their way, the driver's smile comes once more through the rearview mirror. Martin cannot tell if it is a sheepish smile because the man feels contrite about his unreliable auto, or a collegial smile because the two of them have managed the repairs, or a gloating smile because the cabbie has succeeded in duping two tourists into taking a ride in his death trap. The vehicle ascends a small knoll where the vegetation parts, and the stars appear once more, though weakly now, as if they are spent. The Fowlers sit in silence for the rest of the way until they arrive at the door of the hotel, where the driver turns with a profile like one of those large Olmec statues carved from basalt and says, One fifty.

Martin says, One fifty?

The driver nods, and Martin pays it.

CHAPTER NINETEEN

THE FOWLERS RETURN from the Caribbean just in time for the annual New Year's Eve party at the Davenport-Finkelmeyers. The Davenport-Finkelmeyers occupy eleven rooms in the East Seventies. A sushi chef offers made-to-order selections from the butcher-block island in the kitchen. Tzipporah Davenport-Finkelmeyer, now eight, plays "I Have a Little Dreidel" on the viola before being sent to bed. Two dozen champagne coupes form a pyramid in front of the living room window. Seated before the coffee table, Naomi Woodbine holds forth. She and her husband have had to let their Sri Lankan maid go. It is the third in eight months.

She was a thief, Naomi Woodbine explains. She stole two pairs of shoes from my closet and four hundred dollars from my dresser drawer and who knows what else. It was at least four hundred dollars, maybe more. And her feet have to be at least two sizes bigger than mine. I don't know what she was thinking. But when I finally confronted her, she seemed amazed that I was making such a big deal about it, as if stealing is just something everybody does.

Naomi Woodbine pauses to shake the ice in her glass and say, Harold, honey, get me another. Her husband is a small man, smaller with his wife. But Harold is on the board of one of the largest private equity firms in the city.

People come over here and look what they do, she continues. I'm desperate to find someone I can trust for once.

We've found someone new ourselves, Martin says. An au pair.

Lily listens as he talks about the girl, about how good she is with the boys.

I'd like to meet her, Naomi Woodbine says. She casts about the room.

She's home with the twins.

You make her work on New Year's Eve?

Maeve volunteered to, Martin explains.

Naomi Woodbine grows more interested. May?

Maeve. It's Irish.

Why, that's hardly a color at all, she says. She presses forward. How much do you pay her?

We— Martin begins, but his wife kicks him under the coffee table.

On their way home, Lily explains. Any of half a dozen women in that room would love to have Maeve.

She wouldn't do that, Martin says. He is certain. She wouldn't in a million years do that.

His wife puffs in dismay. Naomi Woodbine would murder to get her.

Martin gazes out the window as block after block streams past. He has had three glasses of champagne. Lily has had three herself. Or maybe five.

I wasn't talking about Naomi Woodbine, he says.

᷍

In January a fierce cold seizes the island. It lasts for much of the month. The earth feels like iron underfoot. Ice glints on the sidewalks. The sky is brittle overhead. A water-main break on Broadway turns Liberty Plaza into a skating rink. White floes drift down the East River. There is talk it could freeze over completely for the first time in two generations. Buildings rise in the twilight like the bulking hulls of arctic shipwrecks.

Maeve has never known such chill. She cannot get warm. Lily keeps raising the thermostat. Still the nanny wears two pairs of socks and long underwear beneath her jeans. She puts on a cardigan, and then a sweatshirt over that. For dinner she prepares rich stews: leek and oatmeal, cheddar and ale, stinging nettle soup. Your spoon stands upright on its own.

The cold causes rolling blackouts over several days. On an evening shortly after the girl has entered their bedroom, the lamp winks out. The numbers on the end table clock disappear. The skyline outside the window vanishes. The hush is sudden. They will read in the morning how everything below Nineteenth Street plunged into darkness. The only light comes from the thin chain of traffic moving out on the Westside Highway. At this hour, it is hardly enough.

I like the dark, Maeve admits, her voice emerging out of the night. She gestures toward the window and says, It never gets dark here. Not really. Even now with the lights out, it isn't completely dark.

They all turn to look. There is the glow from the

headlights on the roadway and the windows of New York–Presbyterian Hospital lit by emergency generators and in the distance the lights of directional beams from ships in the harbor.

It never gets dark here, the au pair says again. Back home on moonless nights when the sky is overcast, you cannot see your feet on the ground in front of you. But then when the stars are out, there are so many you cast a shadow.

It sounds lovely, Lily murmurs.

Maeve looks at her before shrugging. It is lovely, she admits, until you trip over a drunk lying in the street at evening's end, or the mother who lives two doors down doesn't come out of the house before dusk so as to hide her black eyes.

Martin finds himself explaining how a huge portion of the universe is composed of dark matter. They call it dark matter because there is no direct observational evidence for its existence, he says. Scientists can only infer its presence from the rotational velocities of stars as they orbit galactic cores. The stars don't always behave as they ought to—

Like people, the girl says.

He looks at her for a moment before going on. Like people. They don't behave as you would expect. The only way to account for this discrepancy is to posit the existence of massive gravitational energies that we cannot see. The upshot is that no more than a twentieth of the universe remains visible. There are immense celestial volumes and far-reaching causes at work that we can only guess at. We like to think we know what is out there and what sorts of factors shape our lives, but the fact is we remain literally in the dark about the real nature of things.

His voice suddenly sounds very far away, as if it were coming from the impossibly distant reaches of space itself.

I don't buy it, Lily says. Her tone is simple and direct and unimpeachable.

He looks at her. Most physicists—

You make it sound as if we are these lost, helpless beings with no hope of finding our way. I refuse to accept that. Some things work in this life and others don't. You look long and hard at the world and try to make sense of it. When you do you succeed, and when you don't you fail. Those who suggest otherwise are just inventing excuses.

But I'm talking about stars, Martin says.

He turns now toward the skylight. With the lower half of the island cloaked in shadow, the view through the glass is powdered with unexpected pinpoints of illumination, each shimmering through the glass.

I'm talking about the cosmos, he says.

You're talking about us, his wife tells him. This idea that we are absolutely clueless ignores the fact of human progress. There is rising life expectancy and spectacular technological development and unprecedented material abundance. Somebody, somewhere, must be doing something right.

Maeve looks from her to Martin and then back again.

You speak of progress, her husband replies. But I don't know that a man hanging from a subway strap in an overheated car at the end of the day, fretting about office intrigues and tax woes, weighed down by triglycerides while a jingle for breath mints courses in an endless loop through his brain, is better off than an Anatolian goatherd from two thousand years earlier filled with awe by the bowl overhead of a star-filled sky. I don't know that he is any braver or wiser or happier in the end. You make it all sound so simple and straightforward and unmysterious and uncomplicated, when I think it is none of those things.

This is the difference between you and me, Lily says. I can't imagine your goatherd is better off. Night after night he is besieged by mosquitoes or subject to sustained bouts of dysentery from eating tainted meat or huddled in the freezing cold. He loses all of his teeth by the time he is thirty, and five years later he is dead.

They are all quiet for a time, turning the issue over, when Maeve says, Or maybe his time on this Earth is so rich and free of the million and one little details that nag at modern life that his thirty-five years are far, far richer than seventy or eighty or even a hundred years are to us

The other two stop to stare at her. But when she turns again to gaze up through the skylight, they turn, too.

It is complicated, Lily admits. But it is not mysterious.

You never surprise yourself? the girl asks Lily. You never have doubts?

My wife hasn't surprised herself since 2008, Martin says, and they all laugh.

⤳

Of course I have doubts, Lily says. She has stopped laughing.

Name one, Martin says. He smiles still. He wants the joke to last.

Lily shrugs. I worry about the boys. I worry whether I spend enough time with them. She looks at Maeve. Understand: You are perfect with them. I couldn't ask for anyone better. But I worry that I am away so much. When they are older, will they look back and decide I was a neglectful mother who could not be bothered?

No, Maeve says.

I worry about Gavin in particular. Arnold, I think somehow that Arnold will be okay. Arnold will find his way. But when I look at Gavin, I see my face in his face, only different. I see my nose and my eyes and the forehead before life has done its work, an absolutely helpless face. I want to protect him from what's ahead. I want to keep the world at arm's length from him.

But you can't, Martin says softly.

I can't, but that doesn't stop me from being terrified for him. You have met my mother and seen what a mess she is. What's funny is my grandparents, my mother's parents, were wonderful. They would visit every summer and take me upstate to a cabin in the Adirondacks. Just me. We would leave my brothers and my parents behind and for six weeks in June and July I was in heaven. The finest memories of my childhood come from the time I spent with Nana and Grandpa. But my mother was a complete and total wreck as a mother and as a human being. I suppose it is inevitable that I occasionally worry whether I am a fit mother myself. My one rule of thumb is to ask myself what my mother would have done in any given situation and then do the exact opposite.

Listen, Martin says now, you're a fantastic mother.

His wife's look is rueful. What do you know about motherhood?

He tries again. Everyone has doubts from time to time.

I did not know you were the expert on doubt.

I am, he says slowly. I am the all-time expert on doubt.

I doubt that, Lily says.

CHAPTER TWENTY

THE LIGHTS COME ON ALL AT ONCE, making them start. Beyond the window the skyline leaps up. They continue talking softly, their eyes staring off into empty space, like people seated at the screen of the confessional behind which the priest listens, himself hardly moving. They joke about the lovemaking noises that come from the couple who live below them—they must be in their seventies—they debate whether it is time to retile the kitchen floor, and if they should upgrade to an even larger TV. They seek out the girl's opinion. She is one of them now.

They talk until far into the night, even though it is a Tuesday and both Lily and Martin have to work in the morning. In the coming weeks there will be more such evenings, evenings where the girl appears, but instead of making love they will find themselves talking until three, four in the morning. Sometimes they sit in a tight circle on the bed and play three-handed games of whist or pinochle, or switch—this last a game from back home Maeve teaches them. On another evening Martin throws on his coat and runs down to the twenty-four-hour bakery six blocks over, returning with half a dozen almond bear claws and a trio of flavored coffees. They talk without ever getting around to the sex.

Yet if an unexpected and welcome tenderness has come to characterize many of these evenings, there are still moments of such raw prurience they leave not only the girl but the Fowlers reeling.

One night toward the end of the month, Martin and Lily go out for dinner and drinks with several colleagues from her office. The conversation is wide-ranging—these are hardworking, educated people with an abiding commitment to their own convictions—and the drinking spirited. The evening is well oiled. Martin and Lily arrive home in a state. They ricochet gently off the walls as they make their way down the hall, clinging to each other. They come upon Maeve in the living room. She has built a fire. She sits with her legs beneath her on the love seat, a mug of tea steeping in her hands. On TV they are debating the advisability of extending the wall along the southern border.

The Fowlers collapse on the sofa opposite. They ask about the boys, about her evening. The girl looks snug in her robe, the one they gave her for Christmas. Maeve wants to know if it was a nice dinner.

He flirted shamelessly, Lily says. She pulls off her shoes.

Martin shakes his head, but he is grinning. That's not true.

Lily doesn't hear. I couldn't blame a woman, she goes on, and she reaches out to lay the back of her hand along his cheek. Martin takes her fingers and wraps them in his.

You're drunk, he says.

Outside, it has started to snow. They can see the way the flakes dart past the glass. It feels good to sit inside with the fire going across the way. The flames jerk and crouch and leap again.

I used to go riding in the snow, Lily says now. She stares off in the corner of the room as if her memories roost there. She leans suddenly to kiss her husband. Still kissing him, she begins to undo his shirt buttons. When she has unfastened three, she stops and says, You finish.

Martin hesitates, glancing at the girl.

Go on, Lily says.

He pauses once more before standing. He continues unbuttoning the shirt. Maeve sits with both hands around her mug.

Meanwhile, Lily is talking. I would ride in the snow. I loved the feel of it hitting your face with the horse so huge and warm beneath you and the smoke steaming from his nostrils. It would be freezing out and you heard the sound of his hooves cracking the ice and you could feel the beating of his heart in your thighs. He was such a big animal, and I used to think how if he ever threw me or took a tumble, he could kill me. Half a ton of horseflesh coming down on top of you can crack your pelvis like a twig. It happened to a girl I knew. She never walked right again. But he never threw me, and despite whatever dangers there might have been, I never felt safer than when I was atop my horse. No one said you could stop.

She is speaking to Martin.

He looks down at Lily and then quickly over at Maeve once more before bending to pull off his left sock, and then the right, and then all the rest. Maeve sets her mug on the coffee table. She sits up straight.

Lily leans forward to touch him. She weighs him thoughtfully in her palm. She releases him and settles deeper into the sofa. The two women watch as it looms and rears on its own, steered by a secret tropism, as if their gazes have acquired the power of levitation.

To Maeve, she says, Have you seen many?

The nanny does not answer. She sits with her back very straight.

But when Martin reaches to undo the zipper at the side of his wife's skirt, she stays his hand.

Be my pony, she says.

Lil—

Be my pony.

He hesitates, then lumbers awkwardly down onto all fours. His wife stands, the material hissing against her stockings as she hikes up her hem. She sits astride his back, her ankles locking at his torso. She clutches his hair like reins. When she clicks her tongue, he begins to shamble slowly across the floor. Rider and mount turn down the hall. Maeve moves to the doorway to watch. Lily rocks from side to side like an Indian mahout.

Just outside the kitchen, Lily stops to wet her thumb in her mouth. She looks back at the girl. Still looking at her,

Lily reaches behind to work it in gently, only as far as the first joint. A noise sounds low in his throat.

In the middle of the next circuit, her thumb suddenly disappears altogether. He roars like a bull elephant. The excitement between his legs continues to aim high. You think somehow you shouldn't look at it, but you look at it.

Stopping in front of Maeve, Lily asks, Do you want a ride?

Martin glances quickly at the au pair, and then, craning his head to look at his wife, he says, You're drunk.

Ponies don't talk, Lily tells him. She makes a slow ceremony of wagging the four visible fingers of her hand. His eyes broaden in his head.

She turns once more to the girl. I give you my permission.

Maeve stands with her arms crossed. She stands for a long moment, leaning with one shoulder against the jamb of the entryway. He can hear from the living room the faint ticking of the grandfather clock. It takes Martin a moment to realize he is holding his breath.

It would change things, Maeve says softly. It is not an objection; it is a warning.

But we want you to, Lily says.

The girl shakes her head. You want me to want to, which is not the same.

Before Lily can respond, there comes a noise Martin cannot place at first. It sounds for a moment like the call of a bird in a wood. Gavin again yells, Maeve? Maeve! This is followed by the soft but unmistakable plod of footsteps moving from the twins' bedroom. Martin's understanding of the situation seems to take a long time in arriving. He glances back at his wife for some hint of what to do, but he is met with a look of unmistakable panic blooming on her face. He tells himself he should struggle to his knees, rear to his feet and cover himself up somehow, but the crushing awareness that it is far, far too late paralyzes him. Lily, too, sits stock-still, as if the future is rushing up so fast they are helpless in the face of it.

The girl, on the other hand, braces suddenly, the whole of her body contracting, gathering itself together, her limbs drawing close. It all takes a split second, no more, but Martin can sense a series of microadjustments on her part, muscle memories forged over the millennia. And then she uncoils, flying past the Fowlers like a hurled lance. Martin, his eyes tracking her, turns just in time to see the left sole of the boy's footed pajama poking around the far corner of the hall. With a sinking feeling, he understands Gavin is about to endure a trauma of unspoken magnitude, a trauma his son will revisit again and again in the decades ahead as he struggles to make sense of his history. But before the toddler can fully materialize, Maeve, without breaking stride, reaches the end of the hall and bends to scoop him up in a motion so fluid and precise it is as if she has spent her whole life rescuing children from the primal scene. Martin glimpses nothing more than a flash of the boy's tousled hair from over her shoulder as she spirits him back down the hall and out of sight.

The girl's soothing tone now emerges from the twins' bedroom, intonations of immense feeling in the rolling tide of her voice—Peekaboo, they hear her say, followed by Gavin's laughter—as she coaxes him back to sleep.

Only then does Lily move to climb off her husband's back.

PART III

CHAPTER TWENTY-ONE

For Valentine's Day, Lily receives a box of Belgian chocolates and brunch at the Calvert Room. But she has a special request: Can she have a few hours to herself, a few hours alone? That is what she wants most of all. And so Maeve returns from Mass to take the twins to an animated film featuring singing rodents—the boys will talk like that the rest of the week—whereas Martin leaves shortly thereafter to accompany George Davenport to watch the Knicks at Madison Square Garden. Lily has the afternoon apart from the others, the shocking serenity of quiet rooms. She can count on one hand such moments since the birth of the twins.

Opposing counsel is maneuvering for yet another delay in the start of the Schlüsser-Bonhoeffer trial. The details are exhausting. They overrun her thinking. Lily wants to empty her mind, if only for a while. She pours herself a glass of wine and takes her time at the kitchen table, reading the Sunday *Times* as it ought to be read. She fixes herself a lunch of Brie on water crackers. Afterward, she runs a scalding bath. She lies back in the water and begins a book she has always meant to read. The pages curl in the steam.

In this tale, an eighteenth-century woman on the New York frontier is abducted by the Huron and lives with them for nine years. In that time, she learns how to cure an elk hide. She learns how to fire a clay pot and build a birch-bark wigwam. She marries a Huron warrior. She bears three Huron children. She becomes a medicine woman, proficient in the healing powers of herbs and the casting of spells. Fifty pages in, Lily puts down the book. She knows already how it will end. During a raid, the woman will be taken prisoner by colonial troops. Her identity will be discovered and she will be returned to her family. Though her children will be teenagers and her husband middle-aged, they will welcome her back with open arms. But she will refuse to wear a corset. She will insist on sleeping on the bedroom floor. She will tenderize venison by chewing it raw. One night she will stab her husband in his sleep and escape. But her tribe will have been slaughtered by the soldiers. She has nowhere to return to.

We leave her standing on the banks of Lake Champlain, the snow slanting down, while wolves howl in the great distance.

Lily is still in her bathrobe, her hair up in a towel, when the bell rings. She opens the door to an older woman standing on the other side, her skin the texture of an old brown brogan about to crack.

Señora.

Paloma. My God.

The two embrace. The older woman has aged. Lines have come into her face and throat, into her hands. Lily excuses herself to dress and then reappears with a tray of coffee and scones. They sit in the living room while Paloma talks about her new home. It is always sunny. There is always so much to do. She and her merchant marine spend all day on the beach. He has taught her how to fish, how to golf. Nights, they go dancing. They spent New Year's Eve in Miami, blazing crossettes showering down over Biscayne Bay.

Paloma asks about the boys. She asks about Señor Fowler.

Couldn't be better, Lily says.

Paloma gazes around the room. It is exactly the same, she says. It is as if I never left.

Lily sips her coffee. The clock says 2:15.

Paloma holds her saucer in both hands. I feel bad about how I went away like that.

No, Lily says. It's fine.

Then you found someone, Paloma says.

We did, yes.

Paloma waits to hear more. Lily responds by picking up a scone and considering it, only to return it to the plate.

The old woman looks out the window. She looks at the buildings, looming immensities that puncture the sky, not a cloud in sight. It is one of those cold, clear days, any promise of spring still far, far away. She says, I bet the boys are big.

They grow so fast.

I miss them.

I'm sure they miss you, Lily says. And then she asks, How long are you here for?

Paloma smooths her skirt twice over her thighs before saying, I have a ticket for a flight out on Tuesday.

Lily brushes the wet hair back from her forehead. She

wishes she had had time to dry it. She says, If you want to come by tomorrow, I'll make sure the boys are here.

The older woman nods vaguely. Her eyes make another tour of the room, only to settle once more on the other woman. I don't have to leave on Tuesday, she says quietly, so quietly that Lily is not sure she has heard.

Pardon?

I could delay my flight, if you needed the help.

Lily looks at her carefully. That's kind of you, she says, but you don't have to do that.

Paloma nods slowly.

I would like to see Aristóteles.

In the study, Lily watches as Paloma removes the cover from the cage. The bird blinks against the sudden light and then gives a quick shake to its head.

He is just as I remember him, the older woman says. She leans close, trying to catch the parrot's eye, but it regards her blankly. When she opens the cage door, the bird presses back into the corner.

Come here, *niño*, Paloma says.

Aristotle ruffles it feathers, and when the woman reaches in to gather the animal in her palm, it rears back and strikes, strikes twice, quickly, beak boring down, bringing a pair of bright red nail heads to the meat at the base of the thumb of her hand. The woman emits a strangled cry and jerks back and away, leaving the bird to huddle on its bar, its feathers wrapped tightly. It squawks loudly now, a barking, disagreeable sound.

Paloma—

It is nothing, the woman says. But Lily insists on leading her out to the sofa. The afternoon light comes through the window and bathes Paloma in harsh light. Lily returns from the kitchen with the first-aid kit, first dabbing at the wound with antibiotic cream and then laying sterile gauze over it. Paloma watches as she tears off two strips of adhesive to hold the gauze in place.

Aristóteles has never acted so before, the older woman mutters. Her look is narrow, full of reproach. Never, she says again.

Lily finishes securing the bandage in place and says, I am so sorry, though she feels more irritated than sorry. The former nanny watches her stow everything back into the kit before saying, I want to come home.

You want to go home? I can call you a cab.

Paloma shakes her head. This is not what she meant. I—

They are interrupted by the sound of the elevator. The front door opens and the room fills with sound, the nanny and the twins spilling inside. The boys are halfway down the hall, but they stop when they see Paloma. They look at her unsurely, and then back at Maeve. Paloma looks at Maeve, too, before rising to reach for her purse and edge past the trio. They all watch her go. At the door, the old woman pauses.

She is just a *niña* herself, she says.

Two evenings later, when Maeve appears, Lily plants herself astride her husband's middle. She realizes after a few moments that she can see their reflection in the dresser mirror. She watches for a while—she watches Maeve watching them—before she discovers that if she crouches a little lower, she can see this same reflection doubled and redoubled in the second, smaller mirror hanging from the closet door. In this way their lovemaking is replicated time after time, funneling down to a distant point on the flat surface, as if each of them is nothing more than a loose chorus of moods.

Can you see it? she asks the girl.

I see it.

I can't, Martin says.

Tilt your head this way.

I see, he says after a moment. It makes me think of your machine, the one in the lawsuit. But which one is me?

He is joking, but Lily points. The first one, she says. Or maybe that one. She shakes her head. You know, none of them looks like us, not really.

He glances once more at the telescoping images in the mirror. They don't?

They look happy, she realizes, and this makes her happy.

But later that night, after the girl has left and he is lying in the darkness, leaking into the night, he says, Do you ever ask yourself when you do something in bed if you would have done it anyway?

What do you mean?

I mean say you do something in the bedroom that surprises you. You think back later and are curious about where it came from. So the next time, you watch yourself. You watch her watching you. When it's over, you can't say for sure if what you did came from you or if it came from the fact she was watching you.

He looks over and says, Haven't you ever asked yourself that?

No, I don't believe I have, Lily says. That sounds to me like you're overthinking it. If someone came to me and said what you just said, I would tell him, Just act naturally.

You're probably right, he says.

A few minutes later he says, But what if after a while you're no longer quite sure what natural is? You thought you knew, but ever since you started thinking about it, the idea of what comes naturally doesn't come naturally. Maybe you notice that I act a little different in bed, too. I do and say things I don't normally do and say, and so you wonder if what I do comes from me or if I am just doing it because the girl is there.

He says, Don't you ever do that?

No, to be honest, I don't think I do, Lily says. But I would say to this person that he needs to quit worrying about it so much and just be himself.

That's good advice, Martin says.

She is almost asleep when he says, But isn't that just what we're talking about? I could see someone waking up in the morning after one of these nights and feeling altogether new, like he was this entirely new person. There is no going back to being himself.

Maybe, Lily says. Or maybe this person is finally waking up. Maybe he is just waking up for the first time to who he really is.

Right, Martin says.

And then he says, Though say it doesn't stop there. You start to think about what you say and do other places, too. You think about how you appear when you are at work and on the subway and eating in restaurants and just walking down the street. You get this idea that maybe you are acting there, too. Before you know it, you are so far into this way of thinking that you start scrutinizing your whole life. You begin to worry you might be nothing more than this big reaction machine responding to the fact that people are watching you, parroting what you think people think you should think. Maybe the you when you stand in the mirror is just the sum total of all the ways you think you look to others. Like if you could go all the way down to the bottom of you, you would never get there, because there is no bottom.

You really never have thought anything like that?

Lily yawns. She turns and plumps her pillow. No, I really haven't.

Martin looks back at her. Me, neither, he says.

CHAPTER TWENTY-TWO

THE CARD COMES THE FIRST WEEK of spring. Padraig, Maeve's brother, is getting married. He is not yet eighteen, but he has been out of school for a year. His name is on the list for a job as a bagger at Tesco. Because of a postal strike, the announcement has been delayed. It turns out the wedding is only ten days away.

Lily makes the plane reservation. She arranges for a bus ticket to be waiting for Maeve in Dublin that will take her the rest of the way.

I can never repay you, you know.

You owe us nothing, Lily says.

They hear the girl's laughter from the kitchen as she phones her father, the quick ripening of her inflection, the unfamiliar lilt of rich intimacy.

You tell Paddy to get his suit pressed, Da. I'm feckin' serious.

She leaves on a blustery day late in the month. She will be gone for a week, no more. Mrs. Nagorsky from downstairs has agreed to watch the twins. Lily's mother has also promised to help out. A strange quiet overtakes their rooms. Even the boys are subdued. When Martin offers to read them a story at bedtime, Arnold says he does not want a story. He wants Maeve.

She'll be home soon, Martin says.

But what if she isn't? Gavin asks.

The days stumble like losers in a three-legged race. One afternoon, Mrs. Nagorsky has a doctor's appointment and Martin has to leave the office early. On another morning Lily's mother does not show as promised, and Lily tries to get some work done at the desktop in the study while Arnold and Gavin beg for her attention. By the middle of the week, the tub drains halfheartedly. They forget to buy milk.

Saturday morning, Lily wakes at dawn and announces that she absolutely has to go into her office and spend all day catching up. She hands Martin a list of errands and leaves. He wrestles with the double buggy for twenty minutes before announcing they will walk. They stroll along, a boy in each hand, the pair tugging and jerking like an unruly team of oxen. At the post office, Arnold shreds a pack of bubble wrap from the display case and Martin has to pay for it. After leaving, they stop for doughnuts and hot cocoa at the bakery. From there, they head to the dry cleaner's to pick up Lily's two silk blouses and her blue suit. While waiting, Gavin knocks over the take-a-number dispenser. Leaving the cleaner's, they get three pretzels from a cart. They deposit the laundry at home and set out for the library, where Martin's list tells him he is to check out five fiction and five nonfiction books from the toddlers' section. Martin spends forty-five minutes reading about talking trains, a bighearted robot, and a chest full of lonely toys. He spends another forty-five minutes reading about the life cycle of the honeybee, it takes a community, and our friend the kilowatt. Meanwhile, the boys methodically dismantle the two shelves of hardcover mysteries. On the way home, they stop for three banana-strawberry-kiwi smoothies from a street stand. They deposit the library books on the coffee table in the living room and then head out to the supermarket, their final errand of the day.

The truth is, Martin does not spend all that much time alone with the twins. He never realizes how little time it is until he finds himself with them once again, and a curious awkwardness ensues. At such moments, he will recall how his father used to pick him up and pitch him in the air and then catch him. Martin remembers vividly this early taste of flight, the surge in his heart as he saw for the first time just how different the world looks from up there. So whenever he is with the boys and is at a loss about what to do, he will grab one of his sons and throw the boy in the air. Lily murmurs, Be careful, which is exactly what Martin's own mother used to say to his father many years ago, and he will experience a sublime minute of validation that confirms, if only temporarily, his role in the lives of his sons. At other times when he confronts doubts about his abilities as a father, he will hoist one or the other of the twins up and run piggyback through their rooms, catching sight of himself in a passing mirror in order to note his resemblance to a real father. Or the few times when he takes the boys to the park, he will think, I am tossing a ball with my sons like fathers everywhere, as fathers—American fathers especially—have done for generations and even centuries.

Yet Martin never feels more like a father should feel—or at least how he imagines a father should feel—than when he takes the boys to the market. The three of them race to nab a green shopping cart. When they cannot get a green shopping cart, the experience is diminished. They will groan with disappointment in the entryway of the store and look with undisguised envy upon the young mother and her son or her daughter who have, in fact, snared one of the green shopping carts. The green shopping carts have a plastic casing mounted in the front where the twins can sit, each behind his own toy steering wheel. When they do manage to get the cart, Martin moves contentedly around the store, stopping to pick up celery in the produce section, sea bass from the fish counter.

Sometimes Martin will call out, Do not go too fast or you will hit someone. He will say, Watch in the turns or you could flip the car over. The twins lean forward in their seats, steering carefully so that they do not roll the vehicle or hurt passersby or take down the display case of avocados in aisle seven. They drive as if everything depends on it.

Occasionally, people pause to smile at the three of them. These smiles contain worlds of meaning. These smiles are affirming. They are like applause. They say, You love as a parent should. You prepare them for not only the universe of commerce and civil society but also of the roadway, inculcating them in the rules, mores, and customs that are the very stitch and sinew of the social fabric. Because of your efforts, your children will one day know how to vote and drive and shop. These smiles say, We, the people of New York, of the clan of Manhattan, of the tribe of America, we salute you. And sometimes the face behind the smile is a comely face, a face of surpassing beauty. These smiles are special. They are like a benediction. They say, You are not only a good parent and a watchful steward of a hallowed legacy but also a man capable of, not afraid of, expressing tenderness and care. These smiles say, Who knows, if things had been a little different, if the proverbial butterfly eons past had died in the pupal stage instead of fluttering away, maybe you and I would have met long ago. Maybe I would be waiting for you at home. These would be our kids. These would be our groceries. Tonight I would be the one mashing the potatoes and washing your greens and deboning the fish that is in your cart. These smiles say, Maybe, maybe, maybe. You are not dead yet.

His sons make engine noises as they drive along. And Martin, with his hands at the bar of the shopping cart behind them, makes engine noises, too.

He and the boys arrive home laden with bags. After Martin stows all the groceries, he sits with the twins and plays a board game where you climb a maze of ladders, though at any step a trapdoor might open and plummet you back to the beginning. He lets Arnold win and then he makes sure Gavin wins and then he wins just so they don't conclude early their father is a dope. Later, he parks them in front of the TV and tries his hand at unclogging the tub. He partially succeeds, but by then the tub needs a good scouring. He finishes only when bleach dots the front of his sweatshirt and he has used all the paper towels. He makes the twins a late lunch and afterward lies down with them so they will nap. The last thing he remembers is Arnold suddenly standing on the bed and saying, Reach for the skies, hombre! and the three of them all throwing their hands in the air. He wakes alone, drooling into Gavin's pillow. The boys are in the kitchen, having shared two half-pound bars of semidark baking chocolate. Arnold throws up and Martin cleans it up. Gavin throws up and Martin cleans up again. Lily arrives early in the evening, exhausted from her day. All she wants is a bath. Martin feels underappreciated, but he dutifully feeds the boys and puts them to bed while Lily bathes. He tosses half a pound of linguini with oil and shallots. He shaves three transparent curls of Parmesan over each plate. He and Lily eat sitting on the sofa. She is still in her bathrobe, her hair damp. The hibiscus smell of her soap fills the room. When they finish and he rises to take her plate, she says, Just put it in the sink; I'll clean up in a minute, and he says, No, you rest; I'll do it.

In the kitchen, he scrapes the plates and loads the dishwasher. He dispenses the powdery white tablet into the depression in the door, but when he goes to turn the machine on, nothing happens. He pushes the START button and the RESET button and he turns the cycle dial all the way around and nothing happens. He opens the dishwasher door and closes it and repeats the entire process another three times, not as one who has any genuine understanding of what machinery will do, but as someone who is reduced to faith in the power of what ritual repetition might do. Miraculously enough, and for reasons about which he remains clueless, the mechanism finally begins to churn, followed by the gurgling rush of water. He proceeds to wipe down the counters, but there is a pinkish smear that does not want to come up, whether jelly or catsup or hot sauce, he is not sure—it looks fungoid, almost extraterrestrial—so he roots around in the utility cabinet beneath the sink for a squirt bottle of something and then sprays the entire counter again and wipes it down once more, bending into the stain. He bundles the trash in the kitchen and goes out into the hall and listens as it tumbles down the fourteen flights to the dumpster in the basement of the building. He comes back in and sweeps the kitchen floor. By this time he feels happy with his efforts and pleased with himself, and when he goes into the living room to enumerate all the good deeds he has done on this evening, he discovers Lily sprawled on the sofa fast asleep, her legs parted. With a finger he carefully edges the robe wider, gazing down at the tiny blond corkscrews that peek out from the edge of the elastic band of her panties.

He thinks about what he will say should she suddenly open her eyes.

Midweek, Maeve phones. The connection is bad, a slight lag, their voices echoing faintly. Yes, everyone is well. Her father sends his regards. She has shown him photos. He refers to them as her "American family." But she will have to stay a little longer.

Lily holds the phone to her ear. How long? she asks.

Four, no more than five days. How are the boys?

The boys are fine. They miss you.

What? Maeve asks through the fizzing line.

We miss you.

I have to go, the girl says.

Her absence proves disorienting. Their rooms, their routines feel oddly unfamiliar, as if she has taken some part of their days with her that renders all the rest unrecognizable. Martin stands before the bathroom mirror, trying to recall what he looked like before the girl came into his life, before he had the mirror of her eyes in which to find himself.

She has been gone ten days when the Norwegian krone falters. It falters badly. Martin never saw it coming. No one did. It catches the futures markets unprepared. The currency embarks on a death spiral, one of those declines so sharp and precipitous that you could go to bed living in one of the most solvent economies in the world, only to wake and learn you inhabit an impoverished financial fiefdom, the rating agencies and bonds traders and the IMF lining up like griffin vultures.

At work people make a point of ignoring him. He finally seeks out Paul Bogdasarian, his best friend among his colleagues, hoping for a word of reassurance, but after thirty seconds even Paul Bogdasarian excuses himself, suddenly remembering someplace he has to be. Martin has become the office pariah. There follows a string of days in which he feels listless, his thinking slow. Yet he sits at his desk, determined to focus. Perhaps the darkest hour calls for the most decisive action. He stays up very late one evening, immersed in numbers in the study, and in the morning puts out a memo in which he urges the investment firm to redouble its commitment to the Norwegian krone. His is clearly the minority voice. A flurry of opposing memos appear, issued by other analysts, warning management off the venture. Martin makes the mistake of sending out a second memo, adamantly reiterating his position. But before the afternoon is out, the krone goes from twenty on the dollar to twenty-four. By nightfall, it is up to thirty. It rallies briefly the following morning but then plummets once again. Throughout the day, the currency operates on the principle of the yo-yo. By the close of business, it has lost almost half its value. Word soon spreads that Martin's recommendation has been so ill-advised and unthinkable in light of the cold statistics that the Securities and Exchange Commission may initiate an inquiry. Whispers circulate regarding possible fiduciary hanky-panky. While Martin is confident of his innocence, at the same time he is not sure innocence is the sort of thing you can be confident about. Guilt—despite his constant self-reminders that it is groundless—starts to permeate the reaches of his mind. He begins to contemplate what he will do should he have to go to jail. He does not think he can survive jail. Though he is troubled by the usual worries regarding the loneliness and the violence and the boredom, he fixes instead on the loss of those minor luxuries that make his life bearable. It is funny what happens when the mind is trapped. Yet it may be that only the electric toothbrush, the single-cup espresso machine, and the loofah distinguish us from the savages.

One morning very early he wakes terrified, as if the walls of the world are closing in. Feeling trapped and desperate, he is pricked by the thought that maybe he should either flee or kill himself. He has no idea where he would go if he fled or what he would do. At the same time, he cannot imagine stringing a noose around his neck or putting a gun in his mouth or leaping from a building to smash horrifically into the hard pavement below. He lies awake until dawn, his dread mounting. Dressing for work, he realizes he could load himself down with weights and hurl himself from the Staten Island Ferry. Though his dumbbells are in storage and it is impossible to locate sizable rocks in Lower Manhattan. Such is the unbalanced state of his thinking that he goes to the cupboard to count the soup cans. He will die with his coat pockets stuffed with mulligatawny, oxtail, and Italian wedding.

Meanwhile, the krone continues to plummet. He puts off mentioning the matter to Lily for as long as he can, not wanting to worry her, but following a particularly gruesome afternoon in which the Norwegian currency hits a thirteen-year low, he finally confesses his fears.

What does this mean, concretely? she asks.

Concretely, he repeats.

I mean, will they reduce your bonus?

He shakes his head. Lil, understand: This could mean no bonus. If it's bad enough, it could mean even worse.

His wife gazes at him for the longest minute, as if he is a stranger who has just entered the room unannounced. What could be worse than no bonus?

It means we might have to tighten our belts.

How tight?

Well, we'll have your salary.

She looks to see if he is kidding. We can't possibly live on my salary.

Most people live on a lot less.

Do you want to be most people, Martin? Because I don't want to be most people.

Chapter Twenty-three

ANOTHER WEEK PASSES with no additional word from the girl. Their living conditions continue to deteriorate, as if the Norwegian krone conveys their existential state. Lily tries phoning Ireland, but the number she has keeps ringing a Niall O'Kerrigan outside Slieve Aughty Bog, who says the only Maeve he knows is eighty-seven years old with sixteen grandchildren. Meanwhile, Martin begins to worry that in the girl's absence his life might unravel completely. The prospect that she won't return inspires in him something approaching panic.

Matters are made only worse when Paavo Kuusik chooses this time to knock. The super enters their rooms in his sweat-stained T-shirt, toolbox in hand. His shirt rides up, exposing a large, hairy belly, the hair kinked and matted. The man carries with him the odor of garlic and tobacco. He has finally come about the bedroom door. After a cursory examination, he announces that he will need to pull it off its hinges, reset the lock, sand and repaint the door, add another coat of varnish, and then hang it once again. Martin tries to tell him never mind, but the super is already standing before the frame, tapping the butt of a screwdriver to free up the hinge pins. He works for a while, then leaves to tend to some other emergency in the building, only to return and work until the next emergency. It takes him the rest of Friday, all of Saturday, and into Sunday, ruining the Fowlers' weekend with the bang of his tools. The super has a small radio that blasts zither music. When he isn't playing the radio, he is whistling a mournful tune in a key that even to the untrained ear sounds all wrong. Mornings, Martin's eggs taste of turpentine.

Your Ukrainian, Paavo says when he is halfway through the job. She's gone?

She's Irish. She'll be back.

What?

She'll be back, Martin says again. He is in the study, trying to work. The super has set up his sawhorses in the hallway, not six feet away.

Paavo hovers over the door laid flat. He runs the sander along the edge in long, practiced strokes. Narrow ribbons of pine drop to the floor. Some ten minutes pass before he looks up and says, How old a girl like that?

Martin hesitates before answering. I believe she's twenty. Or maybe twenty-one.

That's young. The Fogartys, in Twelve B? They had a young girl in to clean three times a week. Turns out when they were away, she'd take their car joyriding. A brand-new Jaguar. Mr. Fogarty would come out and see scratches in the paint, dings in the fender, then go back in and yell at his wife for being a crap driver.

Our nanny doesn't drive, Martin tells him.

Paavo Kuusik shakes his head. Says her.

At midday the super spreads his meal out, using the door

as a table. The aromas of sausage and brined sardines are sharp. He eats a raw onion as if it were an apple.

You want some?

No, Martin says. Thanks.

The man eats with a gnashing of his teeth, followed by long drafts from a thermos. He takes a bite, tilts back and chews methodically, his eyes ranging toward the ceiling, and then leans forward and takes another bite. Crumbs dot his mustache; they sprinkle to the floor. He belches twice, very softly, and then murmurs something in a language Martin doesn't recognize. Martin is thinking about how he cannot think when he hears the super say, You want she should keep you warm at night?

Martin looks up to see Paavo Kuusik in the hallway, the remains of his repast all around him. Martin stands, bumping his desktop as he does, making the screen quiver. His tongue feels curiously thick in his mouth.

Why in the world would you say such a thing? he asks.

The super, stooped over his lunch, peers up at Martin. His features narrow, especially around the eyes, where wrinkles pop into view like fissures through which a brewing anger might erupt. He gestures with his sandwich toward the ceiling and says, You want we should change the burned-out light?

He and Lily eat a subdued dinner. She has prepared pot roast. The meat is underdone and the gravy is thin and the entire dish is oversalted; otherwise, it is fine. Even the twins appear listless. Martin puts them to bed, telling them the story about the troll beneath the bridge, but it only makes Gavin cry. Once the boys are down Martin and Lily try watching a movie, but fifteen minutes in the narrative has descended to such a level of imbecility that they switch to the news, which consists of a bleak and unremitting litany of outrages and horrors. His mood deepens even further. Tomorrow will be a brutal day unless the krone makes a dramatic U-turn. There are moments when it seems your life is slowly being torn apart as you look on. They go to bed where Martin, contrary to form, falls asleep almost instantly. It is one of those deep, dreamless sleeps that feel upon recollection like a brief rehearsal for death. In the middle of the night, he rouses and finds Lily's side of the bed empty. He lies there for some minutes waiting for her to come back, but when she still has not returned he enters into a waking reverie where he imagines that something has happened to her. Something has happened and she has been taken from his life. If he were to go down the hallway he would find his wife lying in a heap before the open refrigerator door, leaving him to raise two young boys. People would talk about him as he and his sons came and went, pointing to the three of them and whispering, Poor guy, his wife keeled over while going for some left-over pot roast at three in the morning. Word would get around and friends and families would converge, bringing him casseroles in glass dishes and picture books for the boys with titles such as *When Mommy Is Gone.* When Lily still has not returned, Martin finally climbs from bed himself and tiptoes out into the hall, suddenly worried he may indeed come upon her sprawled on the kitchen linoleum. Instead, he discovers a thin bar of illumination at the base of Maeve's door. There is a moment in his befuddled, half-awake state when it seems the au pair has, in fact, returned. But when he throws open the door, he comes upon Lily standing at the girl's dresser in the harsh light. She glances up at his entrance. Laid out on the bedspread he sees the nanny's New York State Frommer's, the vial of holy water, her flat cap, a Bible bound in stiff boards. The white silk dress dangles from a hanger hooked over a nail in the wall.

Pausing in the doorway, he says, What are you doing?

Nothing, Lily says.

She turns back to the open drawer. She moves her hand around inside. She takes out a roll of socks, an I heart NY T-shirt, and a map of the subway system.

I don't know that we should be in here.

This is our home, his wife reminds him.

No, he tells her. This is her room. These are her things. He frowns and says, You can't just—

I didn't find anything anyway.

He cannot imagine what—a repository of shoplifted panties, a brick of hashish, or a cache of assault rifles destined for the Provos—his wife expected to come across. He watches now as she returns everything to the dresser and settles on the bed. She smooths the quilt with her hand. There is a fog rolling in from the harbor. The lights beyond the window are nested in eerie halos.

Martin eases down next to her. The room feels all wrong somehow in the girl's absence. Lily surprises him by suddenly taking his hand. She'll come back, she tells him—though he cannot say whether this is for his benefit or her own.

They sit that way for a moment, her fingers warm in his palm. They sit on Maeve's bed with the dresser across the way, the dresser with the missing drawer handle, the worn threads of the quilt beneath them, the scuff marks on the floor from where they used to store the old furniture. A light draft comes through a small gap below the window.

She needs us more than we need her, Lily says.

Indeed, when Maeve returns the following week, it feels unthinkable that she ever wouldn't. She appears rested, the color high in her cheeks. She gives Martin a long hug in greeting. He feels the small bones in her back and shoulders. The boys will not leave her alone. They follow her everywhere, demand her attention. She must see the pictures they have drawn, a new toy in their bedroom.

Watch how I can almost tie my shoe, Arnold says. When he gets no further than a big clumsy knot, she kneels before him to finish, praising him for what a good job he's done. The boy reaches out to touch her hair.

After dinner, once the twins have been put to bed—they make her read them three different stories as well as promise them she will still be there in the morning—she and the Fowlers sit in the living room drinking wine. You must be exhausted, Lily says.

I am tired, the girl admits. But I missed this, she says, and she looks around the room. I missed the twins.

As you can probably tell, they didn't miss you at all, Martin says.

They hardly knew you were gone, Lily says.

They want to know all about the wedding. Father Foley performed the ceremony. Father Foley is eighty-two years old and cannot hear and can barely see. He called Padraig Colm at one point and then Liam at another, until he had run through the complete roster of her brothers. The church was filled with the townspeople; they clogged the pews and were standing along the sides of the nave. Her brother wore his old suit, which was too short in the legs and needed pressing. His one concession to the day was a dove gray hat with an oriole's feather in the band that he had ordered from London. After the ceremony, they went to the common house, where her father had set up a barrel of stout and a giant kettle of skirts and kidneys. It rained the whole while; you could hear it drumming against the windows. It leaked through the holes in the ceiling and mixed with the spilled stout on the floor. They all danced for an hour and then stopped to drink and eat and rest, and then someone would get up and start dancing again, and soon everyone would be out on the floor once more. The band consisted of a Celtic harp and a fiddle and a bodhrán, the small frame drum that you beat with a cipín, along, of course, with the Irish warpipes. Father Foley passed out and had to be carried upstairs. Her own father tried to make a speech, but he blubbered so through most of it that he finally sat down in embarrassment, though everyone cheered. The bride's name was Saoirse and her hair was the red of the whiskey produced at the distillery up in Connacht. Her gown had been handed down by her mother and her grandmother before her, and though she was already five months along, you could hardly see the bump for the lace.

With Maeve away, they had put off doing a number of things. They'd put off having the car serviced, they'd put off bringing in the carpet shampooers, they'd put off Martin's dentist appointment and the boys' annual physicals. But when the au pair takes them in, she returns with the news: The pediatrician wants to speak to you.

You mean he wants us to phone?

He wants you to go in. And take Gavin.

In the doctor's waiting room, Martin watches his son coax a wooden train around a set of tracks. The train climbs a plastic mountain pass and crosses a trestle suspended over a river of blue crepe, moving finally through a town lined by storefronts: a bakery, a dress shop, the feed & seed. It looks like a frontier town from eighty, a hundred years ago, a town built out of vestigial memories. At a level crossing, lights flash as inch-tall figures line the railway, arms frozen in greeting. The boy makes the circuit again and again, pausing to move the figures onto the track and mow them down one by one with the cowcatcher at the front of the locomotive, quietly mimicking the screams and agonies of the victims. Sitting opposite, a mother and her young daughter look on, the girl regarding first Martin, then his son, and then Martin once more. You shouldn't stare, Martin wants to tell her.

After forty-five minutes, a nurse appears to show Martin and his son to an examination room, where they wait another twenty minutes, Martin having to move first a glass receptacle containing tongue depressors and then another filled with cotton swabs out of the boy's reach. Dr. Kaplan is a short, balding man with three chins and a sleepy demeanor. Martin listens to the doctor while Gavin fiddles with the corner of a wall chart that displays the horrors of streptococcal infection.

Ten minutes later, Martin admits, I still don't understand.

Watch, Dr. Kaplan says. He kneels before the boy and moves his finger back and forth before Gavin's face. See? His eyes aren't tracking.

Martin takes in this news with obvious alarm. Does that mean he doesn't see?

Oh, he sees, the doctor says. He just doesn't see what he sees. He lacks object permanence. When the object isn't right before him, he has no sense that it remains in his absence. Let me guess: He still likes to play peekaboo.

Martin stares at the doctor before shifting in his seat. But he can see people, he asks.

The doctor shrugs. The shrug makes Martin want to punch the man. The doctor says, He looks at people and he doesn't see a face. He sees a nose and ears and a mouth, but they don't always add up to a face.

The doctor will refer them to a specialist, a pediatric

neurologist. He hands Martin a brochure and says, Take this with you and read it. And here, take this one, too.

Martin returns home with Gavin, where Maeve is waiting to take the boys to the park. But instead of going into the office as he had planned, Martin phones to say he'll be working remotely today. He retreats to the study where he tries to make sense of the unexpected climb of the Macanese pataca, but his focus keeps drifting. He tells himself that this latest news is merely one among many obstacles life throws your way, though he cannot escape the sense that unless he manages to summon all his powers of concentration, something deep within him may come irrevocably undone. He shifts his attention to the Guernsey pound and then to the Mongolian tugrik, but in each instance he keeps coming back to the soft yowls his son made as he plowed the train through the toy pedestrians. The sounds make him want to flee his own mind. In the end, Martin returns to a familiar bookmark on his desktop discretely labeled "Directional Qualities of Overbought Denominations." The link takes him not to a virtual currency desk, but to a screen where Day is clad as always only in wig and high heels. She lies alone and absolutely still for a full minute before Knight materializes in a corner of the screen to join her. Their lovemaking begins as usual, but instead of the jackhammer rhythms that characterize their usual fare, this time they move slowly, pressing, grinding right up against each other. They fuck like weight lifters. Soon the sweat stands out on Knight's shoulder, his back glistening with the effort. At one point Day takes Knight's ear between her teeth, and Martin can hardly watch. He

keeps waiting for her to bite clean through it, to spit the
flesh onto the floor. When Knight finishes, he collapses
on top of Day, sprawling across her in exhaustion. She lies
beneath him, trapped by the weight of the man, though her
expression has taken on an unexpected serenity. She looks
past Knight's shoulder directly into the camera. Directly
at Martin. Her gaze appears by turns victorious, accusatory, and finally beseeching. Martin peers back, waiting for
Knight to sit up and reach as he always does to turn off
the camera, but Knight continues to lie atop the woman,
his only movement the rise and fall of his breathing. And
still Day continues to look at Martin with a look so intent
and unadorned, it seems she is somehow seeing clear
through to the very thoughts behind his own eyes, reaching thoughts behind the thoughts, thoughts about which
even he remains clueless. Martin gazes back for what feels
like an intolerably long time, waiting for Knight to rouse.
Martin stares until he is sure he can stare no longer, but
then he does, one more moment, and then another moment
more, moments crawling over one another to reach him,
until he hears the front door open, followed by Lily's call,
Lily saying, I'm home, and he reaches up himself to shut
the computer down, watching as the screen flashes to black.

They wait until after dinner to talk. In the bedroom he
says, They don't know why it happens. They're not even
sure of the diagnosis. We might have to send him to a special school.

She says, Is Arnold—

It's just Gavin.

But why—

I told you. They don't know.

We'll get a second opinion, Lily says.

Dr. Kaplan wants to send him to a specialist.

We'll find our own specialist, she says. She sounds more angry than sad.

He shakes his head. What do we know about specialists?

At least he'll be ours.

Understand, you can't fix everything on your own, he says. The world doesn't work that way. Only then does he realize he is shouting.

Watch me, Lily shouts back. And I don't need you, of all people, to explain to me how the world works.

Maeve appears in the doorway. She looks from Martin to Lily and then back again, a frown knitting her features.

Quiet, the au pair says.

The older woman puffs indignantly. You don't tell us to be quiet.

No, her husband agrees. It is nice for a change to direct their anger toward someone besides each other.

But when the girl says, The boys can hear, the Fowlers both go quiet.

Beyond the windows the sun is just setting. The days are lengthening. The cityscape spikes up through the thin red band of light on the horizon. A lone star appears far to the west, the first one in the evening sky. Later still, he hears Maeve putting the boys down for the night. She sings to them as she always does. He has heard her sing this tune countless times, though he has never listened to the lyrics before. Now, however, they come to him clearly, as if he needed life to prepare him before he could understand them:

> I see the moon, and the moon sees me,
> God bless the moon, and God bless me.

CHAPTER TWENTY-FOUR

IN MARCH THE GIRL MEETS THE BOY named Iqbal. It takes Martin and Lily by surprise. As Maeve explains later, she had gone with her girlfriend from Dublin to a party in Jackson Heights. Iqbal is only an inch or so taller than Maeve, and just as slender. You would not call him handsome. He is slightly goggle-eyed and his right canine is gone. He nurtures a patchy, underperforming goatee. His laugh has something of the jackal about it. Yet his voice is surprisingly deep and full-bodied. It has the rounded tones of the bassoon. Close your eyes and that voice takes you away from here. Close your eyes and you think of wind, sand, and cool green visions of springs of water.

He saw her first. He saw her from across the room. She stood out, a tulip in a sea of poppies. She could feel his eyes on her from the start, as if his vision were a beam that warmed the very spot on which she stood. It seemed if she were not strong, she might wither in its glare. He must have stared at her for a good twenty minutes, but when she finally glanced over, he was gone. She wandered around the party aimlessly, vaguely looking for him. In the next instant he materialized at her side; he arrived out of nowhere, pushing right up against her without ever actually touching her, as if his personality were an undiminished force, a power that hung over that half of the room.

He asked if she was thirsty. She could not hear for the music, so he leaned close and shouted, Thirsty? She blushed shyly. He did not wait for an answer. The blush was the answer. He was like that. He vanished and then reappeared not thirty seconds later with a soda in a paper cup. It turned out he did not drink. He did not smoke. *Al-hamdulillah.*

They sat in a corner and talked. This Iqbal seethed with plans. He was a member of a sometime band. Twice he had enrolled for classes at Queensborough Community College, but both semesters he dropped out. He liked the idea of learning more than he liked learning. When he sat in a classroom, his mind shut down. The cramped desks with the stiff backs, the teacher's drone—they put him in a coma. Still, he was thinking of enrolling yet again. He was not so stupid he didn't know you had to be smart. He thought he might want to take a film course, or maybe become an architect. His life was too small for his ambition. He burned with a vast desire, sprawling, nameless, without direction. In the meantime, he worked in his uncle's shop. The man sold everything from cell phones to hijabs, condoms to dried dates.

Somewhere during the evening, her friend from Dublin left with two brothers from Long Island. She phoned Maeve the next morning and told her they were funny. They did everything together. The first began a sentence that the second would finish. They passed a cigarette back and forth.

When one paid, the other received the change. Later, she sat between them in the back of a car with a kerchief in her lap and used both hands.

What about you?

I went home early, the au pair said.

This was a lie. After the party, Iqbal took her out for dessert. It was past midnight, but he knew a place where bitter coffee was softened by the taste of honey. Three men were smoking a hookah in the corner. The phyllo dough flaked onto the front of her blouse. He kept brushing it off until, grinning, she made him stop. Twice he rose to wander over to other tables to talk with people. He knew everybody. Each time he came back a short while later, saying, Miss me? When he tried to kiss her, she said, Not yet. There came that laugh again, undisciplined, a weird cackle. At one point, he gently lifted the cross hanging from her neck—she felt his fingers lightly brush her throat; they seemed to linger, though she wasn't sure—and held it in his palm, looking down at it thoughtfully, and then back up at her with a gaze so impenetrable she had to tear her eyes away. He insisted on riding home with her on the subway. He refused to let her go by herself, not at this time of night, not in a city full of creeps. True, it would take him over half an hour each way, but that was all right—he wasn't ready for morning to come. He would go straight to the shop to work for his uncle, the bastard, falling asleep on his feet, but he didn't care.

Better to stay up with his Viking princess, as he called her.

Standing on the street before her building, they shook hands good-bye. His eyes ranged back and forth, taking in the whole edifice looming behind her. He was revising his opinion of her, adjusting her possible role in his life.

You live here?

I work here, she said.

A change overtakes her. Following dinner, she will put on her coat and call good-bye. They hear her arrive home late, the creak of the floorboards rousing them at one, two in the morning. On her days off, Maeve leaves early and returns even later. She continues to come to their bedroom some nights, though her visits are less frequent. She does not stay as long. One evening in the middle of their lovemaking, she falls asleep in her chair.

We're losing her, Lily says.

Watch, Martin says. She'll grow tired of the boy.

Then there will be another boy.

And she'll grow tired of him. It's just a phase.

Wake up, Martin. Existence is just a phase.

We don't see you so much anymore, he mentions the next time.

I know, the girl says. I'm sorry. It's just that . . .

You could have your friend over, Lily says. Martin and I would like to meet him.

It takes another three weeks—he is busy; he always has someplace he has to be—but on a cool day in April, Maeve greets Iqbal in their doorway. Martin has fired up the gas grill on the rooftop. He waits for the sear marks on the porterhouses to set. Lily bought the girl another dress for the occasion, this one a maroon-and-white print—the hem is short; it shows off her legs—and insisted she wear the sapphire earrings once more. Dangling from the sides of her head, they make her throat look profoundly naked. Iqbal, meanwhile, has gone to surprising lengths of his own: He wears a button-down shirt and a tie, and a pair of pants that, while faded at the knees, have a fresh, stark crease. For all that, the boy is cheerfully sockless beneath his sneakers. While the steaks are resting, the girl leaves the two men sitting in the living room—when she says, Be nice, Iqbal promises, Oh, I will, but Martin says, Actually, I think she meant me—to join Lily in the kitchen. Soon Iqbal is back on his feet, looking closely at the furnishings. The crystal vase on the mantel, the bowl of fruit on the coffee table—he helps himself to a pear, polishing it on his shirt—the books on the shelves. He rubs the titles on the spines as if he remembers with his fingertips. He stands at the window. The lights of the bridge are strung along the night sky like a jeweled necklace on a field of black satin. To live at such a height, he admits, with this view . . . He shakes his head. The twins appear and in no time they have wrestled the stranger over to the sofa; they are climbing up and on top of him, touching his face and nose, tugging at his ears, squealing with laughter. He is good with them. They will talk about him for days after.

Ickball, Ickball, they will remember.

At dinner he refuses the offer of wine. He eats the corn, a bit of the salad.

You won't have any of the meat? Lily asks.

Not this meat, no. I am sorry.

She looks stricken. I didn't realize.

I should have mentioned, Maeve says.

It's fine, Iqbal says.

But that's hardly enough, Lily tells him.

This is quite all right, Iqbal assures her. I go for two, three days without eating. I am so busy. There is no time. And then I will go out and eat a grand feast. I will eat a whole roast chicken, a plate of rice. A pie. Two pies.

Like a camel, one of the twins offers.

Arnold, Martin says.

No, he is right, Iqbal says. His cheer is tireless. His humor is headstrong. He reaches for a roll, shows it to the table, and eats it in two bites. His joy in his chewing is prolonged and immense. It stands out in his face. Life, it is written, is a sport and a pastime.

Just like a camel, he says.

Later, they sit before the fire and talk. He asks the Fowlers about their professions. He listens closely, respectfully, his attention focused. They live, he thinks, the lives found in stories. They ask about his own plans. He has given up on dreams of architecture; he thinks music may be the way he wants to go, or maybe drawing. It is so hard to know; he wants to strike out in all directions at once. Talk eventually turns to the Middle East, to Israel, the ongoing and unceasing war. What is on the news, the boy explains, is so simple as to be a lie. Martin asks about sharia banking, the prohibition on interest; he has never understood how it works. It is a different way of living, of thinking, Iqbal says.

If time itself has a price, then the entire kingdom of being is cheapened.

That view would put me out of business, Martin says.

The twins fall asleep on the floor beside the sofa. Iqbal helps Maeve carry them to bed. From out in the hallway Lily hears him say to the girl, Years from now we will have twice as many ourselves, big and strong.

Are you being careful? Lily asks her the next morning.

The girl is folding laundry. The basket sits on the sofa in the den. Knots of socks form a small pyramid like Civil War cannonballs. Careful?

I could make you an appointment with my gynecologist.

Maeve pauses, a pair of Lily's yoga pants in her hands. I grew up on a farm. I don't need a gynecologist, Ms. Fowler.

It's Lily. And one has to think about these things.

The girl suspends a pair of Martin's khakis from a hanger on the doorknob. She fits one of his polo shirts onto the wings. Thank you, but I'm not a child.

With you being so far from home, Martin and I feel a certain responsibility.

Is that what you call it? the Irish au pair says.

⮑

The relationship lasts another six weeks, through most of the spring, but then ends without warning. Maeve takes to her bed and refuses to leave her room. They stand outside her door, tapping gently. Please, she tells them, go away.

They learn the story gradually, in bits and pieces, over several days. She had been spending more and more time with Iqbal. She had never known anyone remotely like him before. He went out at night with a set of spray cans to paint stencils beneath subway underpasses, along pedestrian walkways. The Semitic script wound and curled up the side of an office building. She watched from a distance in case the police came. He made her his accomplice. She did not mind. She would have done it again. She would do it still. Later, he took her to small clubs, after-hours gatherings to listen to music, a woman with dense eye shadow and markings on her hands ululating in the corner. He took her into a market and said, Stand over there. As she watched, he stuffed a tin of pork sausage into one pocket and a quart of beer into another. He somehow managed to hide a whole watermelon in his pants. She stood over there, terrified, her heart beating. Two blocks down the street, he gave the sausage and the beer to a beggar. The melon they took back to Iqbal's room to eat. He split it by putting his fist through the middle. They each sat with a half, spitting seeds at each other, their faces glistening.

He talked about going away, she says. He mentioned Berlin, or Barcelona, or Algiers. He said you could not do anything any longer of significance in America. He said America is dead. He wanted to go somewhere new. Somewhere alive.

Maeve—

We were going to go together, she says.

The twins camp outside her room. Their parents have warned them to leave her alone, to give her some privacy. They sit watchfully, waiting. They inhabit a respectful silence. Even at that age, they understand. They are like mourners at the wake of first love.

But as more days pass, and the weather warms, and there comes through the windows the sun striking against the glass, and the greenery of the park visible from the street, Maeve ventures out.

Forgive me, she says. I have not been doing my job.

These things take time, Martin says.

To cheer her up, Lily buys her a leather jacket, brown as a coffee bean. It cuts away at the waist.

It's grand, Maeve says. She stands in front of the mirror. She turns around. She peers over her shoulder to see. But this is too much, she says, and she starts to take it off.

Nonsense, Lily says, and she comes up from behind to reach both arms around to zip the jacket closed, pulling the girl tight against her, her face almost a full head taller in the reflection.

It is another few days before Maeve again takes her seat at the foot of the bed and watches as the Fowlers make slow, leisurely love. The final moment of excitement arrives not all at once, but like a gradual submersion in calming waters, after which Maeve quickly leans in to kiss them both good night, and they listen to her footsteps wane down the hall.

How much? Martin asks when she is gone.

Turns out he didn't need Berlin or Algiers, Lily says. He was happy to go to Chicago.

How much?

She names a sum.

He sits up. Is that all?

I know. I was prepared to offer him three times that.

CHAPTER TWENTY-FIVE

THE GIRL MOVES THROUGH a swelling melancholy. Her silences grow longer. She inhabits them like a friar inhabits his cell. She turns brooding. On her days off, she stays in. She will sleep until eleven o'clock, until noon. The Fowlers come upon her some nights late, sitting at the kitchen counter and eating the leftover chicken from dinner, or from a pint of ice cream. Twice now—once in the middle of a weekday breakfast and another time on a rainy Saturday afternoon—she has suddenly risen and fled. They hear her crying softly through the walls. But later she will smile and bend once more to adjust the cap on one of the twins, or she will laugh at something on TV, or they will overhear her telling her friend from Dublin on the phone how she is determined to make it true tick and tin.

The late-afternoon light now lingers bravely on into the early evenings, in muted hues that anticipate the brash golds and greens of a coming summer morning. Despite the beauty burgeoning out the window, the girl takes to watching TV. She plants herself on the living room sofa and powers through all seven hundred channels in search of soap operas, talk shows, reality TV.

There is one film in particular she likes. It features a couple destined to fall in love, though whenever they come close to meeting, some miscue prevents it. They are destined to sit next to each other on the red-eye from New York to Seattle, but her cab gets stuck in traffic and she misses the plane. They are destined to dance with each other at a wedding reception (he is the groom's old college roommate; she was on the bride's high school soccer squad), but instead he makes a failed play for the maid of honor. His Siberian husky is destined to fight with her poodle at a dog park, but on the way over her animal is hit by a laundry truck. Time and again, the inevitable stumbles. The plot is absurd, but an air of inevitability hangs over it all. Still more misadventures— misplaced phone numbers, missing parcels, not one but two cases of mistaken identity—hound the couple before fate manages to overcome the forces of entropy and chaos. At the close, the couple clench and kiss. They swirl around and around in a sun-drenched park to a violin pizzicato.

They're acting the maggots, the girl says as the credits roll. But the cable package allows her to view it again and again and again.

They arrive at one of those periods in which the details of life seem to come at them all at once, a flurry of concerns that must be seen to. They talk about the boys, of course; there are always the boys. They are learning more about Gavin's diagnosis; they are slowly coming to terms with it. And Martin speaks at length about the latest turmoil that has gripped the markets. It is not just the krone that is in trouble. He can feel an unease among the traders that is new. It is serious this time, he tells them. It is different.

For her part, Lily is more preoccupied than ever with Schlüsser-Bonhoeffer. The German giant has resorted to a new round of delays, filing motion after motion in an attempt to put off the trial date, a common tactic when you realize you are on the losing side. Anything to defer the inescapable. This makes her own clients, owners of the small firm, anxious to settle. They have reached the limits on their credit cards, remortgaged their homes, borrowed from families and friends and borrowed again, all in an attempt to stay afloat. They push her to accept the latest offer, and she has to remind them that this is exactly what the other side hopes for; they want to wear them down. The resources of Schlüsser-Bonhoeffer are near to inexhaustible, yet if her clients can hold out for another three or six months—okay, maybe a year, a year at the outside—she thinks they can settle for four, five times what is now on the table.

One morning Lily takes Maeve to the orthodontist. Though ceramic braces are far less obvious than the metal ones, they still appear to emphasize her adolescence. On the cab ride home, Lily asks if she has thought about enrolling in classes. She finished high school in Ireland, but maybe she could register here. There is City College, and Pace is just up the street. And then there is NYU.

You mean go to uni?

You could study nursing if you wanted. You could become a paralegal.

I would like to teach, the girl says. She lowers her eyes as she says this, like one confessing to an indiscretion. I think I would be good at teaching first or second grade.

We could help you out with tuition, Lily says. You could go on living with us.

When Maeve doesn't say anything—she covers her mouth to hide her smile, though her eyes start to mist over—Lily reminds her: You're like family.

That evening Maeve asks, Is there anything you haven't done that you would like to do?

The Fowlers look at each other. It's funny you should ask, Martin admits, because he was just thinking the other day about how he would like to retire early, certainly no later than fifty-five, maybe even fifty, if they work it right. That may sound premature, particularly given the state of the economy and his own difficulties, but if his luck should turn and a strong, sustained rally begins sometime within the next year, it is not out of the question. He would like to retire and move to a place in the Berkshires—

Or out on the Vineyard, Lily says.

In the Berkshires or out on the Vineyard, he agrees, either would be fine, a place away from it all, though not so far away that they cannot come back to the city for a weekend. The boys will be going to college themselves at some point, and Martin imagines a cabin set back from the road amid a broad run of conifers or else—he nods at his wife—maybe a seaside cottage propped up on stilts with a view of the east, the sun rising over the surf and launching its broad rays through the windows. Lily mentions here how she would like to travel some more. Yes, we can have the cabin or the cottage or whatever you want, but there are half a dozen places I want to see yet, and another half dozen I have seen and hope to see at least one more time. I would like to see the gardens of Kyoto and the Prado. I would like to attend a service at Westminster Abbey. . . . He says, You know what I would like? I would like to visit the place where that tribe lived in the Southwest, the ones who lived in the caves, the Antanasi or Anasazi or Atanzazi, or whatever you call it. That tribe of cliff dwellers who disappeared, Lily says. Yeah, the cliff dwellers, he says. I like the idea of waking up in the morning and walking to your front door and looking out over the heights of a sheer expanse. Just like here, Maeve says, and he laughs and says, Just like here, I guess so. And while we are there, we can go back to that little shop in Taos. . . . Lily jumps in here to say, The little shop with the pre-Columbian figurines? That's the one, he says. This was maybe ten or twelve years ago, and you could buy a jade jaguar statue for under fifty dollars, which must be worth hundreds now. It is probably illegal, but back then we didn't know about such things, and if you cashed it in today you could make a tidy profit. I would also like to sail a ketch to the Florida Keys and see the northern lights from a berg in the Bering Strait. And I would like to hike the Appalachian Trail, he says.

Lily looks at him. You would like to hike the Appalachian Trail.

I have heard you can do it in some five to seven months.

Send me a postcard, Lily says. But someday I want to take out a month—one month, not seven—and go on a yoga retreat. Gina Cummings went to one in Delhi. She says you meditate with your own personal guru four hours a day and eat a diet of filberts and dragon fruit to purge your body of toxins. Gina Cummings came back a new woman.

Sounds expensive, Martin says.

Lily shrugs. It costs twelve thousand, but you know what they say: You cannot put a price on genuine happiness.

He says, Apparently, you can.

They turn to Maeve. How about you? Martin asks.

Me?

What do you hope to do?

I don't know, Maeve says. She shakes her head.

Do you want to travel? Lily asks. Do you want to live on a beach?

Maeve does not speak for a time, but when she does, she says she wants a man she loves and who loves her.

She wants four children, two boys and two girls.

She wants a home she can call her own, with rosemary growing in the garden and a four-hob electric cooker.

She wants to live close to her brothers and her father, and to the grave of her mother.

I would like to learn to play the piano, she says.

She thinks a bit more. And I want to walk barefoot in the rain and eat potted hare and dance one night all night until the sun comes up.

Lily and Martin look at each other. That's all? he says.

That is everything, she tells them.

But anyway, the girl explains after they have talked much of the evening away, that is not what I meant.

She says, That is not what I meant when I asked if there was something you wanted to do that you have never done.

They both look at her.

Oh, Lily says.

Oh, Martin says.

Maybe you should go first, Martin says.

You first, and then me, Lily says. And then it occurs to her: Scared?

It is not that he is scared. It is only that he has never really considered it. He has never given it serious thought because, living with Lily, he simply assumed there was no real chance it would ever come up. Far more likely he might one day scale Everest or plumb the depths of the Marianas Trench. While he would admittedly be intrigued by the prospect of descending in a bathysphere to where light never reaches, he would prefer to weigh the opportunity in his head before embarking, just as he wishes now he had the leisure to weigh the opportunity of being hog-tied in bed well before the first half-hitch knot is tightened. But as both women are looking at him and waiting for an answer, and since he does not want to feel diminished in their eyes, he hears himself say, Of course I'm not scared.

Yet as soon as he agrees, it all happens with unnerving

speed. When Lily goes to her closet to select a few scarves—wool, silk, alpaca—his breathing turns ragged. A tightness sets up in his chest. As she ties one around each of his wrists and the other end to a bedpost, his mouth goes very dry. When she does the same with his ankles, his heart beats like a bongo. She steps back from the bed and stands with her hands on the hips of her nightgown, surveying her work. The girl hovers off to the side, her look circling from Lily to Martin.

He has never felt so naked in his life.

Are they too tight? his wife asks.

They are kind of tight, he admits.

Good, she says in a voice that has turned suddenly guttural. The two women smile at each other.

Lily reaches into the closet again and brings out his $150 silk Harrods signature cravat with the nautical theme—anchors, sextants, lobster traps, and the compass rose all stamped into the material—covers his eyes, and knots it at the back of his head.

I didn't know you were going to do that, he says. His voice sounds calm, but his heart feels as if it could tear from his chest. I was thinking I would get to see.

No, is all his wife says.

He hears her step away. He senses them out there, though neither says anything. He feels the seconds pass. He says, What are you doing?

No one answers at first. He waits and waits. Time in his head slows. He worries that what seems like twenty seconds in here is really two seconds out there. Or maybe two hours. Eternity must feel like this.

We are looking at you, Lily says.

When Maeve whispers, It isn't very big, it gets big.

Watch this, Lily whispers back.
    No whispering, he calls.
    Lily ignores him and instead says, Make it jump.
    There is a protracted silence all around, as if time itself has gone into hiding.
    Now do it again.

Lily says, Maeve and I are going to have a glass of wine.
    He uselessly inclines his head as if to see them, but from behind the blindfold, there is nothing to see. What about me?
    You want a glass of wine?
    No. I mean, are you going to just leave me here?
    Yes.
    This strikes him as unfair. And just what am I supposed to do?
    There is another stretch of silence before Lily says, again in that voice, You can think about what we are going to do to you when we get back.

CHAPTER TWENTY-SIX

NOW WHAT, EXACTLY, does a man dwell on in such circumstances? Rarely have Martin's expectations for the coming moments felt so disjointed. His immediate reaction is to ask himself if the women have really left. He heard the door open and close, though maybe the door closing was a ruse and even now his wife and Maeve stand at the foot of the bed, laughing behind their hands. Maybe they think once he believes himself alone, he will whimper or thrash about, demonstrating beyond all doubt that he is a sensual milquetoast. Instead, he works at conveying a certain breeziness, which is hard to do when you are the only one naked and fettered. But as the minutes pass, he feels his focus drifting; the light from the bulb overhead, filtering through the edges of the tie around his eyes, appears to wane, yielding to a darkness that comes from within. The texture of the darkness continues to deepen with such inexorability he can't decide if this is a trick of his vision or his mind or if perhaps he has fallen asleep. Maybe he fell asleep and just now woke. If he did, he has no idea for how long.

He tests the bindings, straining against them. He had assumed he would be able extricate himself easily enough if he really wanted, that this was all a bit of theater, though now he is not so sure. Lily has done a job worthy of an Eagle

Scout. His vulnerability feels total; his state, abject. Yet the experience is accompanied by a curious and entirely unexpected tendril of relief. Whatever happens in the next hour is not up to him. Though trussed and hobbled, he is suddenly liberated from the lifelong responsibility of playing at being the being he is supposed to be.

Lying there pinioned to the four corners of the bed, Martin turns to the question of what lies in store for him once the women reappear. They are at this very instant sitting at the kitchen table, imbibing repeated glasses of wine. In due course they will trundle back down the hall—he sees the two weaving, bumping shoulders, faces made feverish by alcohol—and through the door, at which point he supposes Lily will take the lead, touching and tickling him in all the likely places. Say they take turns, making it into a game. What if one touches him and then one or the other says, Guess who, and he guesses and she says, Wrong, and admonishes him by lightly pinching him or gently pulling his hairs. What if one says, Guess again, and so he guesses the other but she says, You were right the first time, and she pinches him once more. He pictures the women smiling at his confusion in lighthearted fun. The thought makes him smile beneath his blindfold. Yet he can well imagine the two continuing to go back and forth like this, each pinch occasioning a growing round of giggles, which is itself matched by increasingly substantial tugs, until gales of laughter accompany a general wringing of his genitals.

He reminds himself: This is his wife, a learned woman, decorous and thoughtful, and the au pair, a gentle soul thoroughly imbued with old-world virtues. But what if his rising objections—Hey, no, wait, ouch—coupled with the sight of him writhing and spread-eagled like a spatchcocked chicken, only unhinge the women still further. What if they duct-tape his balls to his asshole and take pictures. In a matter of hours, he could be an Internet sensation. What if they raid the refrigerator of the leftover Parma ham and make of him a *jambon-beurre*. Or what if they lead him to the living room, where they bend him over the back of the davenport and spank him with the commercial-grade pizza paddle his wife got him last Father's Day and which he has yet to use. What if they bring out the portable dust buster to hoover his cock up the suction tube. What if they escort him all the way down in the elevator and push him into the middle of foot traffic on Broadway. Martin will be arrested, have a record as a sexual predator, and be censured by the condo association. Or what if they break out the set of felt-tip pens from the kitchen junk drawer and barber-pole his shaft in alternating ribbons of Raspberry Glacé and Wild Blue Yonder, so that he arrives at work in the morning to find the image on everyone's screensaver. What if they lure the nuns from the Buddhist soup kitchen up on West Thirty-fourth for a visit with promises of a charitable donation, half a dozen of them lining up in their saffron robes at the foot of the bed, shocked faces beneath their shaved craniums, yet being ever mindful of the relentless cycles of samsara they dutifully pray that he be reincarnated with a larger penis.

⤳

He once read somewhere you should always have a safe word so when things get out of hand, you say it and everybody knows to back off. He wishes he had remembered this earlier. The word is supposed to be something that does not have anything to do with anything, like *kumquat* or *funicular* or *Gerald Ford*. You say *Gerald Ford* and right there everybody knows you mean business. But this only works if you agree beforehand. Things start to get out of hand and he says *Gerald Ford*, and for all they know this means he wants them to play tug-of-war with his testicles. He is screaming *Gerald Ford, Gerald Ford* while the women twist them as if pulling figs from a tree.

The key is to come up with a word that, even though they haven't agreed upon it, they will immediately recognize means in a seriously nonsubmissive way, I need for you to stop. Though what such a word would be he has no idea. He once read that among non-English speakers *cellar door* is regarded hands down as the most beautiful term in the whole lexicon. It doesn't sound like it at first because you just think of the scarred and battered portal at the back of the house. But say *cellar door* twenty times in a row and it sheds the semantic for the purely phonemic. You start to hear the song in the sounds.

But whether he says *bookcase* or *avocado* or *light bulb* or *Russia* or *shampoo* or *cellar door*, these will just be words to the women, mere noises. Of course when you think about it, all of language is just noises, random sounds—*oohs* and *phttts* and *baas* and *clonks*—that really mean nothing in themselves, but put them together just right and they mean everything. He marvels now at how anybody ever understands anything. Maybe we really don't. Maybe we run around making noises that we think are profound or heartfelt or deeply revelatory, but to everybody else it just sounds like *cheepie cheepie cheepie*. He wonders if he has possibly hit upon a deep but rarely acknowledged aspect of language, rarely acknowledged because if it came to circulate widely, it might well spell the ruination of humankind.

The blackness from behind his blindfold now feels total. He, too, had been afraid of the dark as a boy, though he would never for a moment admit it. Between the ages of two and eight—he was ten, though his memory has long since occulted this fact—pitch-darkness frightened him. It did not frighten him in the way that it frightens other children. He was not afraid of the creatures that might emerge out of the darkness to grab one of his legs or wrench his head from his torso or scratch off his face. He was not afraid of what the darkness hid. He was most fearful of the possibility that the darkness hid nothing at all, of the emptiness that stretched endlessly, of the void that lay in wait.

Martin tugs once more at the ties around his wrists and ankles. Once more, he is impressed; a swabbie could not have done better. He thinks at any second now the women will surely return. The thought again makes his heart gallop. Yet if we leave off all the metaphysical gadzookery, what really concerns him is not that he will be in some way harmed or humiliated, but that in the process of being harmed or humiliated he may say or do something that will make his pleasure in such harm or humiliation manifest. He worries there may be truths about him he does not want the women to discover. Even worse: There may be truths about him he does not want to discover.

One autumn early in their relationship, he and his wife flew to the West Coast for the wedding of a classmate of hers from college. He and Lily were still relative strangers; every day he learned something new about her. On this trip he learned she always sat on the aisle because she was certain that should the plane crash, the window seat would turn into a flaming death trap; she refused the serving of mussels during the in-flight meal because a sous-chef friend of hers had told her they often sit in the refrigerator at the back of the kitchen for days on end, stewing in their own urine. She was not about to lunch on bivalve pee. When they arrived, Martin discovered her former classmate was marrying an heir to a California almond fortune. This was his first inkling she came from a class pitched far, far, far above his own. The rehearsal dinner featured toasts over flaming glasses of amaretto liqueur, the cake icing was marzipan, and at the reception they ate wild trout almondine. After the ceremony he and Lily decided to drive up the coast and find a seaside inn in which to stay, but just south of Eureka they encountered a forest fire gone out of control. Hastily erected traffic signs diverted them east. They joined a flagging line of cars, refugees fleeing the flames. The skies were ribboned with bands of maroon and cinnabar, apocalyptic hues. They ended up spending the night in a campground affiliated with a casino on tribal lands, the only vacancy they could find, sleeping in a nylon tepee equipped with Wi-Fi and three premium cable channels. In the morning they took a walk through the village and came upon a Quonset hut with a shingle outside that promised your fortune for five dollars. Lily insisted they go in. The seer was an old crone in a bathrobe and a swami hat. They sat in lawn chairs at a card table while she read Lily's palm. She said Lily's life would be hard but Lily would be harder, and happiness is a state of amnesia, and honey always tastes better to the bear than it does to the bee. The woman made several more gnomic pronouncements and then it was Martin's turn. But when she looked at Martin's hand, her features darkened. She eyeballed him intently for several seconds, slid a pad of paper and a pencil toward him, and said, List your three greatest fears and I will circle your most heartfelt desire.

By this point the women have been gone for what seems a truly long time, though he understands more than most just how unreliable such subjective determinations can be. Kant showed time does not exist out there in the world but is instead one of the ways we have of organizing experience. It seems the most real and obvious and ubiquitous and undeniable thing of all, when it is simply one of the cubbyholes in the hutch of our thinking. Still, Martin is certain they have been gone an unreasonably long time. This makes him irritated at Lily. She has promised to love and cherish him. Lying here cinched to the bed, he feels far from cherished. He tugs again at his ties, though they prove more secure than ever. It comes to him that somebody else in the same situation, one made of softer stuff, might soon start to thrash and scream. He right away wishes he had not had such a thought, because it makes him want to thrash and scream. His panic rushes up all at once. He jerks at the ties and twists back and forth as a fateful dread breaks over him. He is suddenly on the brink of going so out of control he will no longer be Martin, but instead the animal beast that resides within, unknown and unannounced and unrecognizable until now. He feels a yell launching from the pit of his stomach and powering its way up his gullet to hammer at the roof of his mouth, prying his jaws apart to spring itself on the world, but at the very instant his ability to contain the yell is at its end, the door to the room opens. It does not just open but flies open, followed by footsteps approaching with disconcerting speed. Here the blindfold is torn from his face to reveal Lily looming over him. When she says, It's your mother, he thinks for a second that his wife is playing some weird game, full of Oedipal sickness.

But she gestures with the phone in her hand and says it again. She says, It's your mother.

Lily says, Martin, I am so, so sorry.

CHAPTER TWENTY-SEVEN

A S ONE OF HIS SISTERS EXPLAINS LATER, his mother had run to the store to pick up a roasting hen for Sunday supper. It was a dish his father had always liked. When she got home, the house was quiet and she assumed her husband was upstairs taking a nap. When the meal was ready, she climbed the steps to tell him to come down and discovered he was not in the bedroom. She searched all over the house for him, calling his name, but still he did not show. She went out into the yard. She looked in the garage and beneath the hedge. Maybe he had fallen. She went next door and asked the Murchinsons if they had seen him and then she went across the street to ask the Wilheits. Nobody had a clue. It started to get dark. She called Martin's eldest sister, who called his other sisters. They all arrived with their husbands and children to gather outside the Fowler homestead. The entire clan—minus Martin, of course—scoured the neighborhood until almost midnight. His mother wanted to call the police, but Martin's youngest sister said, They won't do anything until the missing person has been gone for at least twenty-four hours. Martin's mother said, I'm calling them anyway. It turned out that, as the desk sergeant explained, this was one of those untruths you see passed along in police procedurals on TV. He said, Maybe it is how they do it in

South Bend or Terre Haute or any of your bigger cities, but that is not how we do it here. Here at the Nice Police Department if somebody is missing we get on it lickety-split. Two squad cars drove around the rest of the night and all the next day until the following evening late, when Martin's mother happened to open the door beneath the stairwell in order to look through the boxes of old tax documents and records they stored there. She had just about decided that maybe her husband of fifty years had an entirely other secret family, as you sometimes hear about, and had gone to be with them in Utah or wherever men keep second families, and if so she might discover documentary evidence in the form of secret love letters or canceled checks or dusty deeds. She had never been of a suspicious turn of mind. This quest, however cynical or punitive it may first appear, was in truth an expression of the deepest love. She loved him to such an extent that she would rather learn he had betrayed her in the most undignified and appalling of ways than discover that some harm had come to him. Yet this was when she found him sitting stiffly in the dark. The coroner had to work to pry the nickel from the corpse's hand.

Sartre says you don't become a man until your father passes. Martin flies home first thing the following morning, feeling more like a six-year-old than a man. Twice during the flight, he has to get up and go down the aisle and lock himself in the toilet so he can blubber away. He tells himself he can best help his mother by displaying a sober and thoughtful presence to act as a counterweight to what he is certain will be her own overwrought and weepy response. He wants to cry all his tears out now so he won't have any left for later. He arrives to shocking greenery and high humidity. Summer comes early to Indiana. The dogwood blossoms have long been out. His sisters are all at the house. His mother has taken to bed. Yet with his first glimpse of her, his features collapse and his anguish is loud and unstaunchable. It's as if all his crying on the plane was merely a rehearsal for this moment. His mother, on the other hand, propped up on pillows in her bedroom, presents an eerily placid demeanor. With her husband gone she no longer recognizes her life. She no longer recognizes herself. She rises only for the funeral. Martin has been asked to say a few words and has been awake much of the previous evening preparing them, but when the time comes, he manages to utter a small homily that sounds in the light of morning so hackneyed and threadbare that he feels as if he has poisoned the social memory of his father forever. Back at the house, platters of sandwich meat appear, complemented by small cubes of American cheese, each run through with an individual toothpick, along with bowls of jarred olives and gherkins. The mourners stay on for what to Martin feels like an unconscionably long time. Immediately after the wake, his mother returns to bed. He sits with his sisters in the living room, where they insist on discussing the patriarch's will. While the man has left most of what little there is—the house, a modest insurance policy, the tow truck—to his wife, there are also small bequests for each of the children.

Do we have to talk about this now? Martin asks. He has a blinding headache. He is weary from lack of sleep.

Not all of us live in a New York high-rise, the middle sister says.

That night, lying in his old bedroom amid the souvenirs of his youth—the plastic models with the decals of a Japanese Zero and a British Spitfire suspended by fishing line, still contesting the Battle of Guadalcanal in the air over his bed; his abandoned ant farm sitting in the window, the arid tunnels empty save for a single thoracic casing; his collection of *Sports Illustrated* annual swimsuit editions (1991–1997, including his personal favorite, the improbably bosomed redhead of 1995) secreted in the box beneath his bed; the pennant heralding the fighting barn owls of Indiana A&M and the college motto (*Esse quam videri*: To be, rather than to seem) in the school colors of butterscotch and bone—Martin finds himself so exhausted that the full reality of what has happened has yet to sink in. He is in the middle of one of life's most transformative experiences, an experience to which he would like to devote the whole of his attention, but he finds his energies sapped by minutiae. He thinks not about his father but broods instead on the cheap and bitter and almost undrinkable coffee his mother stocks, or on the fact that his rental car shimmies wildly whenever he goes over thirty miles per hour, or on the way his hay fever caught fire due to the Indiana tree pollen.

The day after the funeral, he wakes in his childhood bed

to a downpour outside the window. He takes his mother a mug of tea and urges her to get up and move about, but she refuses to climb out from under the covers. She refuses to speak at all. His sisters have asked that he stay on for at least another day or so out of respect, and he has agreed. He has agreed if only because he remains on standby at Indianapolis International. But he quickly realizes that he has miscalculated gravely. His siblings have returned to their lives with all due speed, as having him here excuses them from seeing to his mother themselves. He has little idea of what to do. The fact that he gets back to Indiana no more than a few days every year or two has made his mother, her needs and wishes, alien to him. He understands that in his sisters' eyes, his long absences leave them with a huge number of emotional chits they now aim to redeem. He peeks in on his mother twice more that morning, but she lies in bed motionless and refuses to answer him. Throughout the day, people arrive to drop off an assortment of covered dishes and plastic tubs of prepared food, but when he reheats a tuna casserole for his mother's dinner she won't eat, turning her face stonily away. Just as he has started to wonder whether she will remain forever mute, he wakes in the middle of the night to hear her talking through the walls. Her voice is matter-of-fact. Though he cannot make out the words, he lies there for some time listening to her go on in a conversational lilt, a one-sided dialogue interspersed with long stretches of silence. When he finally goes down the hall to investigate, he discovers her sitting up in bed, addressing the bench beneath the bay window.

She stops when she sees him and says, Your father and I were just talking about you.

Mom—

We don't think you should go to New York. Your father and I think you should stay behind and finish your dissertation, no matter how long it takes.

She says, There is no reason you should give up your dreams.

Martin stares at his mother. Despite her gentle nature, she has always been a thoughtful woman with a keen moral sense, though duly skeptical of all manner of spiritual hokum, from talk of horoscopes and personal auras to appeals for dubious health fads. Coconut oil is not a cure-all. The daughter of a union organizer in the steel mills of Gary, Indiana, she met Martin's father while she was attending the university in Bloomington. She had driven south to research a paper on nineteenth-century utopian communities. There had been one such settlement not far from Nice. It was now a dilapidated ghost town, but in its heyday some 2,200 freethinkers had lived there. They rejected private property and were wary of printed money. They espoused polyamory and vegetarianism. While wandering the grounds she came upon his father, who was just emerging from the woodlands. He had been hunting pheasant and quail. He had already bagged three. Taking note of his shotgun and filled with Laputan sentiments, she lectured him on the outrageously lax gun-control measures then—and still—typified by Indiana state law. The Fowler line has, for the most part, been populated by diminutive women prone to agree. He had never before been so harangued by a female, especially one of such

Rubenesque proportions. He was smitten. He was smitten in an almost biblical sense. He felt he had been clubbed over the head. He asked her out. She said, Give up hunting and I will, never once imagining he really might. But he laid his shotgun down and never picked it up again. She dropped out of school six months later to marry him.

But Mother, Martin reminds her now, as gently as he can, Dad's gone.

To his surprise, she laughs. She laughs and says, Of course he is. But when I talk to him and remember him he's still here, in a way. He talks back to me—I hear him talk back to me—and so he is still here.

When he looks unconvinced, she says, But I thought you knew: That's all we are in the end. That's all anybody is. A voice in the head, the memory of a glance.

You make us sound like spooks, he tells her.

Your father will always be more real to me than Tina Wilheit down the way or Brother Probus at the church or the president of the United States. He is more real to me than this moment here and now. Don't you see?

She looks at him steadily, the ruffles of her nightgown scattered all about her. She looks at him until he forces himself to look away.

Tell me how I can help, Mom. Tell me what I can do.

She shakes her head. There is nothing anyone can do.

He returns to bed but is unable to sleep. Her mother's words keep coursing through his head. He does not know whether to be depressed or strangely cheered by the notion that we may be little more than characters in a story, mere figments, a memory—the refrain in someone else's song. He rises at dawn, more exhausted than ever. The day unfolds much as the previous one. His mother again refuses to eat. That afternoon, he attempts to sort through his father's finances. In recent years the old man's penmanship disintegrated into a loose approximation of ancient Babylonian stylus writing, and so Martin makes little headway. For dinner, he takes his mother a ham sandwich on a tray and some apple juice, but when she sees him she sits up and says, I would like chicken. He says, You would? I think someone brought some chicken sal— She says, I want the barbecued chicken from the All You Can Eat Bar-B-Que Grill & Takeout with the signature Habancro Hades sauce out on Indiana State Road One sixty-eight, along with a can of malt liquor. He is not put off by her request, but happy that she has at last responded. She has never surrendered to melancholy, and with these words she is reasserting some of her old appetite for life, if only to demand fowl over pig. It gives him, if nothing else, a concrete course of action.

Mindful of his rental car's unreliability, Martin takes his father's tow truck and heads into town. He stops at the package store for a six-pack of malt liquor and then makes for the All You Can Eat Bar-B-Que Grill & Takeout. The parking lot is packed, and once inside, Martin attaches himself to the end of a long line. He waits some thirty minutes, but when he finally reaches the front he learns that the take-out window is on the other side of the dining room. He waits for another quarter of an hour in this second line. As it winds around the outer perimeter of the dining area, he lets his gaze range among those seated at the tables. He finds his eyes lingering unbidden on a booth in the corner, until he suddenly realizes he is staring—has been staring for some seconds—at the unmistakable countenance of Wendy Chalmers. She has put on a bit of weight but haven't we all. And instead of memory's mass of wavy brown curls falling halfway down her back, her hair is now platinum blond and just grazes her collar. Still, there is the identical profile and the pensive quality to her features he remembers from long ago. She is sitting next to a large man in a billed cap and bushy sideburns. On the other side of the booth sit three children, two boys and a girl, all of whom mercifully take after their mother. Martin regards the quintet for some moments until the next thing he knows—it happens that quickly, as if he has been forcibly drummed into service by his own future—he is marching up to Wendy Chalmers's table, where he stops and says hello.

The man with her looks up first, followed by the kids, their small faces lifting, and only then does Wendy turn toward him. Her recognition seems to come from far, far away and is a long time in arriving, as if all recollection of him has been interred at a place in the most remote mine shaft of her brain, buried there decades ago by a consciousness bent on self-preservation, and so now must be painstakingly dredged back up into the light of day, past the sediments of lived experience carefully layered over the wound, upending the accumulation of years, rewriting each memory so as to deliver her here, to this moment; though he also senses there is a piece of her, some small but stubborn element, that is intent on entombing once more all remembrance of him.

Her face is the site of a pitched battle, forces of light and darkness warring in her eyes.

And then Wendy Chalmers is whispering, Holy shit, and just as quickly putting her hand over her mouth, as if she might stuff the oath back inside.

She introduces Martin to her husband and the children. Martin shakes the man's hand. Martin asks how she is and Wendy says she's fine, and he says he is fine, too. He realizes only now that he has been looking forward to this very meeting for the past seventeen years, though in his mind it was to be much different. He cannot pinpoint a single instant in all this time when he thought to himself, One day I will talk to Wendy Chalmers again—his pessimism always ruled when it came to her—but he understands that he has at some level been readying himself for this encounter all the same. It was to be the two of them alone and unrushed and quiet. Here the noise of the restaurant forces them to shout. He is convinced that if he could just get Wendy Chalmers off by herself to talk for ten minutes, he would reach a new understanding about his life that he has never come close to before. He suddenly has so much to say and there is so much he wants to know, but standing here amid the roar of the diners and the fussing of the children as they squirm in the booth and in the crosshairs of her husband's stone-cold stare, he feels the chance fatally slipping away. And then the husband is saying, It was nice meeting you, but we should be going, and he and the children stand. They stand in the booth and then Wendy Chalmers stands. They can't get out because Martin continues to block the way, and when he realizes it he murmurs, Sorry, and starts to move, but right here he notices a small smear of the signature Habanero Hades barbecue sauce on Wendy's left sleeve. She is wearing a light blue sweatshirt that says SAVE THE PLANET 2015 on the front, as if the decisive opportunity has long since elapsed. Something about the noise in the restaurant and the banality of the message and the rust color of the sauce on her sleeve, the blood hue, and the unnatural platinum tint to her hair, makes Martin incapable of getting out of the way. He does this instead: He drops to his knees before the table and looks up at Wendy Chalmers. This creates considerable consternation among Wendy's family, as well as among the diners seated at adjacent booths. Wendy looks down at him, her features softening in spite of herself. Martin experiences a jarring sensation deep inside, a great unsettling, and then he lays his cheek flat against the cool table and kneels there in front of Wendy Chalmers, continuing to gaze up at her. He has no idea what he is doing or what he will do next. He has absolutely no idea where any of this is going. But he kneels there, feeling the coolness of the laminate on his face, and peers up at his past. In that moment the intervening years seem to collapse like one of those dynamited buildings you see in aerial videos, the upper floors crashing through to the foundation, and all of a sudden it's as if it was never there. These years are as good as never having been. History is not the record of what once happened; history is what we don't know has happened. It seems now as though he has really spent the last decades in this exact position, absolutely still, kneeling before Wendy Chalmers. His mind goes to the photon, that most princely of all particles, the very stuff of light. From its point of view, the entire universe is frozen in place. Time stops. Time never got started. It is no longer a thing bought and sold, divided and subdivided again, an element of exchange in the great circle of commerce, a simulacrum of movement, but exists only in the dead silence that comes with his ear pressed to the table. He wants to stay just like this, forever and ever. He wants to say, Nobody move.

But then the youngest of Wendy Chalmers's children begins to cry. The grown man on the floor has frightened the boy. The sound of the tyke's bawling sets the world back into action once more. Wendy whispers to Martin, Get up, please, while her husband reaches for the crying child and mutters, Christ, Wen, do something, and then here comes the manager, a small man in a string tie, who asks if there is a problem. Wendy says, No, no problem, and she looks at her husband, who agrees there's no problem. Martin, lying with his face against the table, opens his eyes, and, seeing the manager, he stands and says, No problem, sorry.

Martin follows Wendy Chalmers and her family to the parking lot, where they flee in a battered white van—DEGRAFF'S WASTE HAULAGE on the side—before the crazy man can pull something new. He returns inside and waits in the correct line for another forty minutes to order barbecued chicken. Bag in hand he walks back out to his father's tow truck, only to find that he left the high beams on and now the battery is dead. Martin opens the hood of the truck, but this marks the frontier of his automotive know-how. He phones his roadside assistance service and gets a call center on the other side of the world, where a man speaking in heavily inflected English asks to be called Chip. Martin explains that he needs a jump. Chip promises to call back in ten minutes. Martin drinks one of the warming malt liquors and eats a drumstick. Exactly eight minutes and twenty-two seconds later, his phone rings and Chip gives him a local number. Martin dials and hears his father's voice on the answering machine, his father saying leave me your name and your number and your location.

Martin's father says, I'll be right there with a tow before you can say boo.

CHAPTER TWENTY-EIGHT

J UNE, THIS MONTH OF WEDDINGS. The Fowlers go to three separate ceremonies. The days are unseasonably warm. Despite the roar of the air conditioning, they sit sweating through the vows. At one reception the tiers of the wedding cake list dangerously; the rolled fondant roses have bled into the white frosting. Martin and Lily arrive home to discover Maeve and the boys sunning on the rooftop. The light is blinding off the windows of the adjacent buildings. The twins run barefoot in their cutoffs, the hot tar scalding their soles. The nanny wears a modest one-piece she ordered online, the cut high along the neck and low at the thighs.

Lily reaches for the sunblock. Come here. You're about to roast.

She daubs the lotion along the lengths of her sons' arms, up and down their legs. White war paint beneath their eyes. You, too, Lily says, and Martin watches his wife rub the white cream into the girl's shoulders, at her nape. Maeve closes her eyes and leans forward. Three tiny rolls of flesh form beneath her suit at the waist, each no thicker than a number 2 pencil. There is a bug bite on her thigh.

Standing at the railing, Arnold looks back. Can you jump? he asks. His face has filled out. He has the fabled Van

Slyke cleft in his chin. In another ten years, he'll display the
bruised good looks of the prodigal.

You could, Martin says, but you wouldn't want to.

You'll die, Gavin says.

You'll die, Arnold says.

Quiet, you two, Lily says. Or I'll throw you both off.

Their days slow. The minutes falter in the heat. Life feels like
less of a race. They go to see a performance of Shakespeare in
the Park; they attend a weekend concert on the Great Lawn.
Manhattan sunsets, a vast blaze in the wide, wide sky.

The newspapers that summer are full of talk of the eclipse.
Martin draws the boys a diagram to illustrate the disposition
of celestial bodies. His sons couldn't care less, of course; they
are asleep anyway long before the drama begins. Maeve, on
the other hand, is intrigued by the sketch. She takes it with
her when she and the Fowlers climb the north fire escape at
three in the morning to watch. While waiting he points out
various features on the lunar surface: the Sea of Serenity and
the Sea of Tranquillity, the Tycho Crater, the Montes Archi-
medes, a mountain range. He mentions the Mare Desiderii,
the Sea of Lost Dreams, which the Russians thought they
had discovered on the far side of the moon, though it turned
out it was no sea at all, but only an illusion of shadow and
light. Maeve listens with keen interest. Despite the late hour,
she is visibly excited by the drama. Ancient peoples regarded
eclipses, planetary transits, and comets as dire augurs. Perhaps some racial imperative still flows in her blood. He, too,

grows intent when the earth's shadow begins to overtake the moon. But as the key minute of totality approaches, he looks over and sees the two women sitting side by side on the fire escape, their heads lifted in what appears to him to be a kind of adoration. And it is from over their shoulders that he watches the moon darken, the color deepening until it hangs like an immense copper coin suspended in the sky.

The following Saturday he happens upon Maeve in the study. I was just going to check the markets, he says, but I can—

No, it's all right.

She stands before the cage, three fingers of her right hand through the bars. Aristotle, the African gray, preens and bobs, running its head against her thumb.

Birdie, she murmurs.

Martin sits at the desktop and checks the yen, the euro, the British pound. He checks the Norwegian krone. It continues to ride the roller coaster of world oil. Twice in the last week he has received blunt memos from Pierce at work, demanding to know what is going on—as if Martin mans the roller coaster, as if it is Martin at the helm.

Little Ari, she says. The creature presses against her hand, its eye closing and then opening, quivering with happiness at her touch.

He watches her before saying, It's never going to talk, is it?

Maeve regards Martin for an instant and then bends to open the cage door. When she slips her hand inside, Martin experiences a curious fear for the girl. It's just a bird, and yet the act appears to involve liberties he would not take himself. But the parrot allows itself to be gathered in her palm. She gingerly draws the bird out into the room and places it on the table next to the giant globe. She closes the door to the cage. Martin peers at the bird. He has only ever seen it through the bars.

The parrot looks at the globe. It looks out the window. It looks at Martin.

A full minute passes, and Martin is on the point of going back to his work, when the bird begins to strut, its head darting and stabbing. It travels back and forth along the table for some seconds more, and then with a sudden spread of its wings—its span is surprising and alive in the room; it makes Martin start—the parrot leaps back to the cage. It clings to the bars of the door with its claws. It extends it wings again, slowly this time, and with a thin rustling sound gathers its feathers once more closely around it. The bird adjusts its grip and says, Put me back.

The voice is small and childlike, not at all the squawk of pirate epics, but disconcertingly human.

Martin stands there, surprised, and looks at the girl. She returns his gaze, her eyes direct and unflinching.

The bird again says, Put me back.

What else can it do? Martin asks, his tone framed with wonder.

Isn't that enough? she says.

⮾

The week before the Fourth of July holiday, Schlüsser-Bonhoeffer settles. It is a stunning, an unexpected victory. After so many years and so much work, it does not seem real. The announcement is made at a firm meeting that afternoon. All eyes focus on Lily. As the lead attorney, the success is hers—just as the failure would have been hers. Her career would not have been over, but she would have been consigned to an office two stories down, the number of cases coming her way diminishing with the passage of years. Now, however, the *Journal* devotes six column inches to the story. All afternoon long, staff members and junior counsel stop to congratulate her. At the end of the day, the managing partner appears at the door of her office. Lily sits behind a huge bouquet, individual blooms nested in a bedding of snapdragons, ferns, and dusty millers.

Who died? Alan Sawyer asks.

She laughs. They are from her client. He stops to count the roses.

One for each million, he says.

She arches an eyebrow. Something like that.

Have a drink with me in celebration, Alan Sawyer says.

She gestures toward the papers on her desk. I wanted to finish before—

One drink. Humor an old man.

You're not that old, Alan, she says.

But he is. He turned seventy the previous month. He began with the firm almost five decades ago, fresh out of Yale Law, following a stint in Vietnam. He didn't have to go.

He had his student deferment. But he joined the marines. He hoped to see the elephant, he explains whenever anyone asks. He came back with a Navy Cross, two Purple Hearts, and a steel bar in his femur. After a mere twelve years of practice as an attorney, it was his name that topped the firm's stationery. Law and war—it's really all the same in the end, he will tell you.

Lily follows him back to his office. It is much larger than hers, a suite, really. The main room shows the skyline from floor to ceiling on two sides. He takes a pair of drinking glasses out of a drawer and pours three fingers of a single malt into each.

I'd offer you ice, but with a scotch this good you would disappoint me gravely if you said yes.

This is fine, she says.

They sit across from each other and sip their drinks in silence. The light outside the windows is quickly fading. The wall behind his desk is filled with photographs: Sawyer shaking hands with the ambassador to the Court of St. James's, Sawyer receiving an honorary degree from Cornell, Sawyer's wife sitting in the garden with Hayek, their blue Persian, asleep in her lap.

How is Catherine?

He shrugs. Some days are better than others. One doctor says maybe a year. Another says three. He swirls his drink in the glass and then drains half of it. They don't know a goddamned thing.

I'm so sorry, Alan.

He refills her glass. She tries to wave him off but he ignores her.

I want you on Universal Paper.

If it's okay with Daniel, she tells him.

I want you to replace Daniel.

Alan, I can't do that.

Daniel is her friend. They started together straight out of school, years ago.

Sure you can, he says. We'll keep him on as second, but I want you to lead on the case. If you want something done right— he begins. And suddenly his hand is on her knee.

She peers down at it for a long moment, refusing at first to understand. His wristwatch is large, the hands spears of gold light striking at the heart of a dark dial, stripped of numbers. He doesn't need numbers. His mind keeps time all on its own. She gently lifts his fingers from her leg, as if they were talons, and returns them to his lap. She sets her drink down and stands, smoothing her skirt.

Lily— he begins.

She shakes her head no. Only she is allowed to speak. Daniel will do fine, she says.

Hours later, Lily is still talking about it. I didn't know whether to put my hands around his neck or laugh, she says.

She and Martin are sitting on the sofa, drinking glasses of iced gin. Martin offered to take her to dinner, but Lily did not want to go out. She did not want to sit among other tables, surrounded by strangers. Instead, they ordered in, though she hardly ate.

Okay, she says: I wanted to put my hands around his neck. This was supposed to be my day.

What happened next?

What could he do? He was suddenly scared, I could tell. Understand: He survived jungle firefights, monsoons, murderous Vietcong. But he was terrified.

She shakes her head before going on. I don't know how men live with themselves.

He says, We find women like you who put up with us.

Maeve joins them, settling in the upholstered chair, holding a large, beaded glass of her own. She has put the children to bed. It is warm outside. The girl has opened several windows. The breeze moves through the room. It carries the faint odor of bilge, fungal and vaguely carnal, from the South Street Seaport.

It reminds me of home, Maeve says.

Martin looks at the girl for a moment before saying, Do you know, it'll be a year next week that you came here.

The girl inclines her head. It doesn't seem like a whole year, she admits. But then at other times it does. A year and more. Like I've lived here always.

A lot has happened, Martin says.

We should celebrate, Lily says.

He swirls the ice in his glass and says, We are. Remember?

CHAPTER TWENTY-NINE

L ATER, IN THE BEDROOM, Lily is unable to finish. While
Martin works doggedly, after twenty minutes she is
no closer. It galls her to think, not for the first time, that
her happiness so depends upon others. The skylight overhead, suffused with rain clouds, mirrors her mood. Frus-
trated, she finally climbs from bed and steps toward Maeve.
The older woman takes the au pair's arm to draw her up
out of the chair. Yet when she gathers the fabric of the girl's
nightgown in her hands to lift the hem, Maeve says, But
Ms. Fowler—

Call me Lily. Now reach for the skies.

The girl pauses before slowly—finally—raising her
arms over her head.

She is long-waisted, with slender shoulders. Her hip bones
flare sharply. Yet from behind she has the faintly muscled
back of a farm boy. Her breasts veer away from each other as
if annoyed by your staring. Between them lies the tattoo of
a Celtic Trinity knot some three inches across. Its presence
is shocking, an unexpected primitivism that seems in an
instant to recast entirely their view of the girl. The points

of the triquetra are limned in forest green. It stands out against her alabaster skin like a mark of ritual scarification.

Martin, quick to understand, dutifully retreats to the opposite side of the room. A piece of him longs to join in, but the situation inspires a Hoosier courtliness. Ladies first. He feels excited but also a little intimidated. If in these past months he and Lily have tentatively ventured a toe across the marital frontier, this is something new, a reconnaissance deep into the libidinal unknown, where there is no going back. This is Hudson embarking on the fatal traverse of his bay. This is Cortés landing on the beach at Veracruz, burning his boats. This is cannibalism in the sexual sierras. He has thought a number of times about what it would be like to have Maeve join them, though now that the moment has arrived, he feels woefully ill-equipped for whatever is to come next. Seeing Lily with the girl, he had expected to experience a tinge of jealousy but is surprised to find it is not like that. Instead, he has to keep reminding himself that this is indeed his wife. This is her nose and that is her hair and these are her legs, but when she caresses the nanny's flank or kisses her neck, it is like watching two strangers. He feels more puzzled than proprietary.

What strikes him above all is just how unhurried the women are. Their arms and legs undulate as if they are underwater. He understands for the first time how his own amatory routine is marked by a hapless velocity. This must be common among men. Get in there and do your business before she experiences a change of heart and kicks you out of bed. Watching the scene unfold before him, he realizes that, left to themselves, women have all the time in the world. The two seem in thrall to a present neither is anxious to leave. He soon suspects they have forgotten all about him. He might as well be in the living room, reading a book.

Lily wishes he were in the living room, reading a book. She would like to be with the au pair out from under the male gaze. The girl's clavicle is linear and finely edged, like a castle fortification seen across a plain. The silken handful of hair below looks shockingly dark and lush at the fork of her pale thighs. Her underarms give off the heady scent of wild chives. Lily darts here and there over the young woman's body, like a hummingbird unable to choose among the profusion of blossoms.

Despite such ministrations, however, Maeve's responses are muted. Lily suspects Martin's presence as he stands in the corner and gawks above a preposterous erection likely does not help. Perhaps the girl fears her performance might disappoint him, or that his regard for her will be diminished. What if after watching her cavort over the bed, he decides she is unsuitable to tend his sons? Say he decides she is a degenerate. Maybe she worries she is in fact a degenerate. You cannot emerge from a small isle overrun for a millennium by retrograde Catholic norms, a land that came late to divorce, a woman's right to vote, and abortion—the flames of Gehenna must scorch your dreams—without suffering a profound degree of moral fallout.

Or she may be concerned that Martin will feel threatened in watching another frolic with his wife, and conclude Lily likes making love to her more than making love to him. Say he fears the two might abscond together, heading out into the patriarchal wilds to sow gender mayhem, a Bonnie and Clyde to upend social convention, except this time it will be a Bonnie and Bonnie.

Though possibly, it occurs to Lily, this gets it backward. What if the girl is conflicted not because she worries Martin might think she wants to run off with his wife? What if she is conflicted because she wants to run off with his wife? Perhaps she has been smitten with Lily all along, and so burdened with both a crushing guilt and a spiraling desire. The more Lily considers the possibility, the more plausible it appears. She imagines the two of them running away to Los Angeles or Paris or a hut on the beach or a cabin in the great north woods. She imagines them awakening to the smell of wood smoke in a yurt in Outer Mongolia.

Meanwhile, Martin continues to stand in the corner, eyes big. If only he would leave and go off to the kitchen to make himself a sandwich or head down to the study to check the markets online. He is always checking the markets right when you need him, when you want to talk to him or would like some company or two minutes before you both are slated to be somewhere, but he never checks the markets when you want him to be checking the markets. Lily is positive that were he to get up suddenly and go down to look at the latest quotes on the Haitian gourde or the Kyrgyzstani som or the Malaysian ringgit, the girl could cast off her inhibitions, her affections free and unconstrained and quite unlike anything either has ever experienced before. Lily tries to signal with her eyes that he should vanish, but Martin is in no state to heed even the most obvious of hints. He is not a man with an erection; he is an erection with a man.

The more subdued Maeve's demeanor, the more exasperated Lily grows. The older woman is still nowhere near to finishing. Between her husband's sexual ineptitude and the girl's reticence, it is no wonder. You look forward to something and you look forward to it and then when it finally happens you think, What happened? Time to regroup. In the end she kisses Maeve lightly on the lips and turns to Martin, crooking her finger as if they are members of a tag team. Making his way back across the room, he can feel his heart racheting in his chest. By this point in the evening more storm clouds now choke the skylight above, giving the room the air of a grotto. But when he places a knee on the bed he hesitates, unsure of what to do next. His first inclination is to reach for his wife; otherwise, she might be hurt. Yet he does not want the girl to feel excluded. And if he offends the nanny his wife could—in the name of all women, everywhere—be offended in turn. The safe harbor of monogamy feels impossibly remote.

Lily decides the matter for him. She scoots down to the other end of the bed, leaving the two up at the headboard, and swivels around to watch.

If it was odd to see the two women together, it is odder still—it is bizarre—to have Lily look on while he and the au pair do what they do. If he has thought at times about what it would be like to be with the girl, or what it would be like to see his wife with the girl, he never really dwelled on what it would be like to be seen by his wife when he was with the girl. They say there are so many possible permutations in life that the mind must exercise a kind of triage, blocking out some so it can give full attention to the rest, no doubt guided by this or that evolutionary imperative. Apparently, evolution sees little percentage in the threesome; such close-quarter sexual competition likely leads to close-quarter hand-to-hand combat, and before you know it the whole species would be rendered extinct. Now, however, with Maeve in his arms, he becomes acutely aware of his wife's searching eyes ranging from behind. He takes special care not to look back at her—his wife, not the girl. He can look at the girl fine. He could look down on her all day. The line of her neck stretches long and lean. Her shoulders stand out small and naked and white. As he rocks above her, she lightly holds the back of each of his arms up near the shoulder, though he cannot tell if this is out of genuine affection or a simple need to check any rambunctious displays on his part. If asked he would say she gives off an aroma closer to dill, or possibly sorrel. Her carnal grip on him is disconcertingly snug; this no doubt all changes once several infants have tunneled through on their way out into the world.

Outside, the rain has begun. It taps against the skylight
like something wanting inside. Sprawled above the au pair,
Martin remains ever mindful of the power of Lily's gaze
as it continues to come at his back. He is determined not
to let it interfere with his enjoyment. This is the first and
for all he knows the very last time anything like this will
ever happen, and so he aims not to waste it. Unfortunately,
the girl is not so impervious. She appears to be straitjack-
eted by a thoroughgoing self-consciousness. No doubt the
prospect of romping with a man while his wife—mind, the
girl's employer—sits across the way must be fraught. Who
knows when Lily might turn outraged or accusatory or
mocking. You cannot live in the household for more than a
few days without having experienced the rising tide of his
wife's sarcasm. Or maybe Maeve is worried she may inadvertently say or do something that Lily will regard as an
affront, crossing some invisible line the girl did not even
know existed. Say Lily decides he and the girl are having
too good a time together, a better time than Martin has
with his own wife. Or she decides that deep down the girl
dreams of making off with her husband, of stealing him
right out from under her, of running away from the city
and over the hills to a pastoral setting far removed from
the urban hubbub and the crowds and the street ads and
the knifings. . . .

At this instant the girl sighs softly—it could register
impatience, or boredom, or even indigestion, though Martin interprets it as an obvious expression of pleasure. From

this he takes new inspiration. For all he knows, she really does want to run away with him. This sounds far-fetched on the face of it, but think about it. From above the girl, he thinks about it. He imagines the two of them sneaking out at three in the morning and climbing into Lily's car (his is newer, so he will leave his wife that; it is the least he can do) and launching on a cross-country spree where he will show her the real America, not the America of the strip malls and take-out burger huts, not the America of the office parks and auto dealerships, not the America of nail salons and mobile-phone shops and hotel chains, drinking glasses clothed in protective plastic wrap and reconstituted scrambled eggs at breakfast, but the America of the out-of-the-way B and B and the small country inn, with a four-poster bed and mismatched coffee mugs and an egg yolk staring back at you like the sun served on your plate—not the America of some halcyon past, because the past was never halcyon, including as it did human chattel, child labor, genocide, and theocratic fanaticism, but the America that was not and yet should have been—the America of fireflies, apple fritters, the ring of horseshoes, and the man who comes around knocking on your door every April offering to sharpen your knives, honing stone in hand; the America of canned gooseberry preserves in the root cellar, of homemade peach ice cream—the sound of the hand crank, grains of rock salt underfoot—on the porch, of a bowl of wild walnuts in the parlor next to the carved nutcracker face that uncannily resembles the mien of your uncle Fred; the America of a frosted stein of root beer so cold it hurts to hold in your hand; the America where nobody steals your morning newspaper, an America where there still are morning newspapers; an America where you adopt the ugliest hound in the pound because the look on its face is so wretched and defeated, you know no one else will. And then later, once they have seen enough of America, once she is sated with America, once she is fed up with America, she might invite him back to Ireland, where he will be welcomed by her family, who will take him in and seat him at a place of honor at the dinner table. They will teach him how to anchor fence posts and fix a tractor, while he will teach them about hedge funds and tax derivatives. Martin, the girl beneath him, pictures waking next to her every morning on mattress ticking stuffed with hay, to mists coming off the green fields through a cottage window, the slice of soda bread coarse.

She licks the glistening film of lemon marmalade from the blade of a knife.

Consider the scene in all its ramifications. Outside, the rain has stopped. While water continues to drip from the eaves, the room seems the site of a sudden calm. There is Martin braced above the au pair, her legs scissoring his middle; there is Lily behind, watching her husband as he falls into the divide between the girl's thighs again and again. And then there is Maeve, who in truth is not overly concerned with what the other woman thinks. Nor is she preoccupied with how Martin might judge her. The girl does not want to introduce him to her father or abscond with Lily to a yurt.

She is tired—too tired to touch on shadings of guilt and recrimination, the calculus of social opprobrium, or the ethics of the marriage vow. She rose at daybreak to feed the twins a breakfast of French toast sprinkled with powdered sugar, accompanied by the tuliped melon slices they like so much. Half an hour later, she made Martin's whole-wheat bagel with low-fat cream cheese and Lily's protein shake with a side of granola. She prepared them each (oat milk for her, half-and-half with three packs of artificial sweetener for him) a coffee to go. Later that morning she pressed Martin's shirts and mopped the kitchen floor. She fixed the twins a lunch of grilled cheese sandwiches with homemade applesauce. After eating they went for a walk in the park, where Arnold suddenly bolted out into the street and barely missed getting run over by a delivery van, and Gavin threw a tantrum because he could not catch a pigeon. On the way home she picked up three of Lily's suits at the dry cleaner's, as well as a whole ham and fresh fruit for dinner. While the boys napped, she scrubbed the toilet in the master bathroom and dusted in the living room and den. She changed a light bulb in the Fowlers' bedroom, the battery in one of the smoke alarms, and the water filter in the carafe in the refrigerator. She cleaned the inside of the microwave oven. When the boys woke, she served each a glass of milk and three cookies and parked them in front of the TV for their afternoon cartoons. She spent the next two hours readying the ham, scoring its flesh with a knife and applying an apricot glaze dotted with cloves. She mixed onion and stout to make a gravy and composed a salad of romaine and radicchio. For dessert she whipped up a pavlova with raspberries and passion fruit. Following dinner it took her an hour to clean the kitchen and then another hour after that to bathe the boys and put them to bed, because Gavin refused to go to sleep. She does not worry what Martin thinks about her body. She is too weary to wonder if Lily might be jealous. Her mind is on tomorrow. She ought to clean the refrigerator and wash the bed linens. She ought to dust the blinds and wipe down the ceiling fans. She needs to water the plants in the living room and change the parrot's bedding. She will prepare a dinner of either roast chicken or seared scallops with cremini mushrooms—she hasn't decided which. The drain in the kitchen is sluggish, she saw ants along the baseboard of the food cupboard, and she needs to buy more of the special spray Lily insists on using on the granite countertops.

Through the skylight, the clouds overhead have started to disperse, edging away from the moon. A ghostly luminosity washes over the bed. Martin, lingering above the girl, suddenly hears, Look at me, in a whispered, urgent voice. He peers down to find her gazing up at him intently, her normally blue eyes appearing in the weak light as dark opals, rich ebon pools that reflect his face back to him in surprising detail, his features looming nearer and then receding as he seesaws above her. Her breasts tremble with the movement, framing the tattoo of the triquetra, toward which his attention is ineluctably drawn:

Despite the near-pornographic setting, the specialist in him cannot help but detail an array of numerical relations: Each lens-shaped segment is formed through the intersection of two circles with the same radius, such that the center of each lies on the circumference of the other inscribed within a larger circle; the ratio of the width of each segment to half its height will always be √2, while that of the width to its full height is √3; the ratio of the diameter of the outer circle defined by the points of each segment to its widths is √5—irrational numbers all, running to eternity without the repetition of any set sequence. Spooky business, said to terrify the ancients. (If asked, Martin would be happy to relate the story of Hippasus, the Pythagorean disciple who first discovered irrational numbers while idling away long hours on a voyage home to Magna Graecia, at which point he was promptly thrown overboard and drowned.) It is as if nonsense has taken up lodging in the very heart of all meaning, the darkness of unreason inscribed at the core of light. Martin assumes the three points of the figure must approximate in some sense the Christian Trinity; it will be years before he learns they originally symbolized in Celtic mythology the stages of womanhood: maiden, mother, and crone.

Look at me, he hears again, as though the tattoo itself has spoken. He stares at it hard, but when he glances once more up to Maeve's face, he finds she has craned her neck to stare over his shoulder at Lily, sitting behind him—whose own focus, he can feel, still streams powerfully at his back, completing the circuit. In that instant, the triadic trope inked into the girl's flesh seems to have found its exact expression in their bedroom. And here, without any warning whatsoever, the very dilemma that has beleaguered him the whole of his adult life unexpectedly vaults into view: If everything must be seen before it can exist, who sees the Seer? Which means we need something else to observe God, and then something still further to observe this something else, and on and on and on, following the line of an infinite, inescapable regression—unless it is not a line at all but instead a growing encirclement, one in which each term on its own is always needed but never enough. We see God just as He sees us, and we both require something still further to confirm our seeing, this subsequent term—Plato speaks of the "third man" in his *Parmenides*—itself being seen in turn by the first two: an inaugural daisy chain from which flows the whole of existence. Never before has sex felt so much like syllogism. What is worship but the litany of prayers expanding outward, a mushrooming call-and-response beseeching the Other to recognize us, to redeem us, to save us in the end. The Big Bang as the first-ever game of peekaboo.

The realization rains through his brain like a shower of sparks, the triquetra looming up and falling back as he plunges into the girl again and again, his thinking having come completely uncoupled, and in the thin light the stark lines of the figure appear eerily primeval, as if it is indeed a message from the time before all time.

He finishes with a splash. The girl lies beneath him, unmoving save for the shudder that seizes her head, like a sheep with its throat cut.

Martin collapses at her side, his chest heaving. They are both shiny with sweat. He glances over and sees the girl's fine dark hair plastered to her brow.

This is when Lily again says, Look at me.

He and Maeve both incline their heads to peer down the length of their bodies to where his wife continues to sit cross-legged at the foot of the bed. For a long second, she remains shrouded in silhouette; the shadow of her profile is turned sideways, like a mare in a stall. And then the last of the clouds part overhead, and the moon comes completely unshuttered, pouring through the skylight to bathe her in a pearlescent sheen.

Come, the girl says.

She has raised herself to her elbows, and she speaks in a voice of uncommon tenderness: Come join us.

Only now does Martin recognize Lily's fingers moving at her center. His wife's expression is one of profound concentration, as if she were playing an ancient and venerated instrument requiring enormous skill and years of dedicated practice, an instrument reserved for only the most sacred of occasions. Are you looking? she whispers. Her entire body shakes; he can feel it through the mattress. She seems all alone and very far away, as if there were entire continents no love could ever traverse.

Do you see? she asks once more, though it comes out a choking cry. Her spine goes suddenly rigid, her head thrown back. Her face clenches like a fist.

CHAPTER THIRTY

IN THE MORNING THE MOOD is subdued. Lily leaves early for work. Martin pauses in the doorway to watch the au pair load the breakfast dishes into the washer. The boys sit at the kitchen table, drawing goatees and horns on world leaders in a weekly news magazine their father has yet to read.

Maeve—

It's all right, she says. She bends to slot another saucer into the wire rack.

For dinner the girl makes fried cabbage with bacon, a dish Lily likes. When Martin offers to open a second bottle of wine, both women say no. The following evening, the three of them try to teach the twins the alphabet song. Arnold makes it as far as *L*; Gavin, *F*. On Thursday, Lily schedules an appointment for the girl at her salon, and Maeve emerges with her hair cut close; it hugs her scalp like the pelt of an exotic animal. Saturday the Fowlers have the Davenport-Finkelmeyers to dinner. Little Tzipporah Davenport-Finkelmeyer eats with the twins on TV trays in front of the television, while the au pair serves the adults in the dining room. During a meal of poached fish, George Davenport mentions that the biggest salmon he ever caught—it was almost eighteen pounds; his eyes swell at the memory—was on the river Eriff, and when he learns Maeve has swum the river Eriff, he does not leave her side for the rest of the evening. At the door he says, If I were twenty years younger—

Hannah Finkelmeyer gives her husband an affectionate tug on the ear and says, She would be one.

Later that evening, Maeve and the Fowlers listen to music while playing a round of three-handed pinochle. The girl plays with verve, slapping each card down like a dare. She hates to lose. At the top of the hour during the news, Lily says, Martin, listen.

The full extent of the damage won't emerge until the next morning: a large spill off the Pacific, of the kind that blackens the coastline for hundreds of miles. The front page of the *Times* will display a pelican mired in dark crude. The price of a barrel begins its long climb.

I don't understand, Maeve says. She looks from one to the other. She holds her cards in both hands like a small fan.

The krone, Martin explains.

Thank God, Lily says. I thought we were going to have to hock the Waterford.

Martin shakes his head. You know, sometimes you can be such a—

Bitch, Lily says, finishing for him. She can still make him laugh.

It seems a corner has been turned. They discuss the future guardedly, glances hesitant, as if they were planning a heist. In the fall, the boys will be enrolling in kindergarten. Martin brings home brochures from Pace University, close enough to walk. He spreads them on the kitchen counter. She can take classes in the morning and be out in time to pick up the twins. They have programs in elementary education, in art, in history—whatever she wants. Lily speaks to an immigration attorney. Changing her visa shouldn't be that hard.

The girl wipes her cheek with the back of her hand.

Their lives slip into a series of rhythms: meals, jobs, the weather. A business publication interviews Lily about Schlüsser-Bonhoeffer for an in-depth feature. Maeve receives an email from Padraig. In the photo, a grinning young man holds a baby up for the camera. She squints beneath a mop of carrot orange hair. They've named the child Siobhán—meaning God is gracious. Martin has been contacted by another investment house. They want him to head up the currency desk. He will start out as a fully vested partner; he can expect double his current annual bonus—three times or more, in a good year.

These evenings of late summer, the quality of the light turns marine. The bushels in front of the greengrocer are tilted to display the apples, the eggplants. The slaps of chess clocks sound in the parks. From the wharf at Bayonne to the industrial canyons of the Bronx, the shadows flee the dying sun. There comes that singular moment, a lone instant, when all the obstacles melt away, when that final happiness, the end toward which the whole of existence aims, lies once and for all within reach.

This is the summer they all head east for vacation. They overnight in oceanfront cottages in Barnstable and Yarmouth, driving all the way out to Provincetown at the tip of the Cape, at the very edge of the country. Maeve and the boys stay in an adjoining room. Once the twins fall asleep, she and the Fowlers stroll the beach, pausing to search the sky for meteors. The surf tumbles up the shore. Ocean thermals lift Maeve's hair. She gathers whelk and cockle shells by starlight, carrying them in the folds of her skirt, her thighs standing out whitely against the sands made pewter in the darkness. Back in their room, she stores her finds in a large mason jar with a cork stopper. And later, the three of them standing naked in the mirror.

She tastes soft-shell crab for the first time, and lobster bisque. She goes back four times for servings of oysters on the half shell at an all-you-can-eat establishment in Truro. They return along the Cape road, stopping at historic Plymouth to see the rock, which disappoints her—her da used to move bigger ones with his draft horse—and then continue on to Boston, where they stay for three nights at an inn that served as an armory during the Revolutionary War. The girl visits Southie, the famed Irish ghetto, which has been gentrified beyond recognition. A fabled tavern still stands at its heart, where you can order nine kinds of stout, and they have a corned-beef brunch every Sunday, yet the barmaid is from Krishnapur and the cook speaks only Tagalog. They travel to Thoreau's pond, though the hut is long since gone, its pieces cannibalized in the late nineteenth century to repair a farmer's barn.

On their final Saturday they head out to the Public Garden. It is a warm day with a southerly wind. They ride one of the swan boats out into the middle of the lake, Arnold trailing his hand in the cool water, leaving a small wake all his own. Later they wander past the flower beds along the shore, and then to the stands of trees beyond, overflowing with horse chestnuts, dawn redwoods, and ginkgos, and then onto the Common itself. At the playground off the Frog Pond, the boys tear here and there, crawling through the tunnels and spinning on the roundabout. A vendor sells hot dogs from a cart next to the swings. Behind him, an older woman is picking up after a toy collie, and behind her a young couple—they can't be more than fifteen or sixteen, Lily thinks—neck ferociously along the bank.

Just before noon, Gavin falls from the upper stair leading to the top of the slide. Lily sees it all clearly. He goes to put his foot on the final step to hoist himself up for the long swoop down, but somehow he misses, his leg striking through dead air, and before she knows what is happening her son is twisting off the ladder and pitching backward toward the ground. He lands with a thump that sounds absurdly loud, and lies absolutely motionless. Lily experiences a great lifting sensation from deep inside, as if her internal organs have leaped up from their place in her body to drive her forward, to propel her out of her seat on the bench. She is not yet halfway across the playground, however, when the girl is already there. The au pair kneels at his side and gathers the boy up. He lies limp in her arms for a long and unendurable instant—during which Lily thinks to herself, He is dead; I am the mother of a dead child—and then his arms rise slowly, like one swimming to the surface, to come about Maeve's neck. His hands lock at her nape. He hugs her to him, his face pressed into her breasts. He hugs her with all his might, with a desperation that has nothing to do with the fall. He pulls back for a moment to stare at the girl, and from where she stands Lily can see the urgency with which the boy's eyes move over the Irish au pair's face, and then he hugs her once more. He hugs her as if he fears losing not just her but the world, and this is his last link to it, this is the only hope he has of not being lost forever.

Lily cannot remember the last time someone hugged her like that. She cannot remember when anyone has ever looked at her in quite that way.

And then the world is moving once more, Martin kneeling at the girl's side to take his son from her arms, Martin saying, It's okay, moving his hands over Gavin's small frame for a moment, checking for injury, for broken bones, but the boy is squirming to get loose. Arnold is already mounting the steps to the slide once more, oblivious of the drama, and Gavin does not want his brother to have all the fun.

Lily starts to call to the boys, to say, No more playing; we're done. Let's go back to the inn, where it's safe—but she knows this would be useless. Martin would turn to her with one of his looks, a look that says, Don't be that mother. Still, she is shaken. She makes her way over to the bench to sit once more. Martin has paused on the other side of the playground with his phone to his ear; she watches as he gestures to an invisible caller, intent on making this or that point. She tries to imagine he is not her husband but instead a complete stranger, and she wonders what she would think if she saw him there, what kind of man would she conclude he was, and whether she would find him handsome or interesting or worth knowing. The hair at his crown is starting to thin. His shoulders slump in a way she has not really noticed before.

Lily sits with her head back and her eyes shut. She feels one of her migraines coming on. She hears someone approach, and then the au pair's voice: They're probably hungry. Lily, her eyes still closed, says, Look in my purse and buy them a hot dog. She listens to the clasp of her pocketbook and the sound of Maeve calling to the boys. She hears the sound of their feet thumping against the playground surface as they rush over to the vendor. The brothers argue about what should go on their food. Arnold wants catsup. Gavin wants catsup and mustard. Arnold says in that case he wants catsup and mustard and relish. Gavin says in that case he wants relish and more relish. Arnold says. More relish is just relish, stupid. Gavin says, Don't call me stupid, stupid. Lily hears the nanny speaking to the vendor, and then a long silence, during which she imagines her sons looking on as he prepares the food, followed by the sound of money passing hands.

What do you say to the man? Maeve reminds the boys.

Tank you, Lily hears them both reply, and she opens her eyes.

❧

Two evenings after they return home, Martin happens upon his wife sitting on their bed. Her rosewood jewelry box lies open before her. She has taken all the pieces out—the diamond necklace, the ruby setting, the gilded choker—and spread them on the bedcover.

My earrings, she says. She blinks up at him. My sapphires.

They're probably in—

I've looked.

Did you look in the—

I've searched everywhere, Lily says.

Maybe we left them in the hotel.

I didn't take them with me.

Martin hesitates for a moment before saying, They'll turn up.

Lily shakes her head. They're gone.

They go through her other jewelry boxes, including the cedar heart on the bookshelf and the marble round in the living room. They search her bureau drawers and the cubbyholes of the secretary. They look in the tops of closets and rifle through the end tables. He crawls beneath the bed to hunt there.

They're gone, she says again.

They sit at the kitchen table. The buildings through the windows are like shafts hurled down from high above by angry gods.

Lily says, I think it's pretty obvious.

Is it? he asks. The color has left his face. Is it really?

What does she have? Lily asks. She has nothing. Next to nothing. She has only what we give her.

Martin goes to the sink to draw a glass of water. He drinks half of it and, with his back still to her, he says, Why?

My earrings—

Why, Lilith?

When she doesn't answer, he turns to face her. For just once I wish you could see yourself, he says, in a voice so quiet it seems to belong to different words altogether.

Her head snaps back as if she's been struck. Anger enters her features like a fever, and she says, I see myself. I see myself fine. It's you I can't stand to look at.

Martin spends the rest of the evening in the study. He sits at the computer and watches the numbers scroll the screen like electric currents shimmering down a spine. Later he hears the two women talking, their voices rising and rising through the walls. (Lily, don't do this. That's Ms. Fowler to you, and I'll do whatever I want.) He hears a door slam, and a second later footfalls approaching down the hall. Maeve enters without knocking. She hesitates when she sees him but then continues on to the cage. When she removes the shroud, Aristotle takes two steps sideways on the crossbar and yawns. She reaches to stroke the creature, and with a quick glance at Martin she says, Talk to her, please.

He cannot look back at her. He focuses on the keyboard instead. Things have gone on that Lily doesn't like, he finally says. I don't know that it's any more complicated than that.

Or maybe she likes them too much, the au pair says.

She lifts her gaze from the bird to peer at Martin. Her eyes seize him straight on, as even as the horizon.

We'll give you a good recommendation, he tells her.

She continues to pet the parrot, and speaking softly, so softly that Martin realizes he is holding his breath to hear, she says, My mother died slowly over months and months. She could not bathe herself and then she could not feed herself and the day came when she couldn't use the toilet. Toward the end she lay in bed moaning. At the very end her moans turned into screams. Me da sat at the table in the kitchen with his head in his hands and listened to her screaming, knowing there was not enough morphine in the world for the kind of pain she felt. But when she finally went, it was not a relief as everyone always says. It was bloody horrible. It was inconceivable. It was inconceivable in the same way that a round square or a four-sided triangle is inconceivable. I could not make sense of it. It was not just that my mother had passed but that something had gone terribly wrong with the world, and my father and I were the only ones able to see just how wrong everything had gone while everyone else remained ignorant. I was sure at the time I would never recover. I could not stand to be in the same house my mother had lived in and walk the same paths and hear the people she'd heard. I could not stand to breathe the same air she'd breathed. When the opportunity to move here arrived, I jumped at it.

Martin says, I'll write the recommendation myself.

Here her brogue thickens still further, the vowels growing hard and bald, and the girl says, You hear all your life about America, though that is just talk and pictures. But when you arrive, the landscape and the people and the sounds in the streets and the lights in the sky are nothing like you expected. When you and Ms. Fowler hired me, I was terrified. I worried I would never fit in. It was almost more than I could bear. That first week I must have come back to my room a dozen times to cry. I was desperate to go home. I could have phoned me da and said, I don't want to stay, and somehow he would have gotten together the money for the plane fare.

Martin says, Better yet, you write the recommendation. Write whatever you want, and I'll sign it.

The bird continues to preen beneath her touch. But Maeve is not finished. She says, The only thing that kept me from going was the twins. Her voice turns husky with sudden emotion. Martin has to strain to understand as she says, They remind me of my brothers. Gavin is just like Paddy was at that age. If I go away now, they will think that I don't care and never cared. Think about that.

Think about your boys, she says.

When Martin doesn't answer, she shakes her head. He senses a rising anger he has never felt from her before, a fury he would never have guessed she might be capable of. She says, You and your wife spend all day, every day, moving big words and long numbers around as if they are the most real things in the world. They are not real. But because you don't understand this—because you believe in them—you are hardly real yourselves. You can't cook and you don't clean and you are clueless when it comes to raising your sons.

I think we may even have some friends who are looking for a nanny.

You can't even fuck on your own, she adds. And she replaces the shroud over the cage as if to save even the bird from having to look at him.

It will be almost two years before Martin comes upon the earrings. He discovers the felt-lined case at the bottom of the bedroom closet, in a box along with some old bank statements, an expired passport, a pair of boarding passes for a flight to Paris, and a copy of his tax return from a decade ago. He knows what it is the instant he sees it. The hinge opens with a rasp. The light reaches into the very heart of the blue stones, flinging the color back into his face.

By this time, Lily will have transferred to her firm's West Coast affiliate. She and the boys move to a three-bedroom bungalow with a fountain and an abandoned bocce court on the grounds. From the road the terra-cotta tiles look like rose petals on the roof. They send Martin digital photos each month, and he phones at least once a week, often more, though his sons' lives are busy; they don't always have time to talk. Arnold is on a Pee Wee baseball team; Gavin attends an alternative school in Mission Viejo. Lily wants to send him to a residential program upstate in the fall that specializes in spectrum disorders. When the boys do get on the phone, they tell Martin about the beaches and the taco truck in the park, the gulls circling overhead, and their trip to Catalina where they came upon a snake hidden in the dunes.

For a while, they talk about an uncle Phillip, and later an uncle Jake. He wears a ponytail, Arnold tells him, but he's not a girl.

Martin had offered to move himself. She and the boys could stay on at Maiden Lane. She could have Maiden Lane. But I need a change, Lily told him. She was tired of the apartment. She was tired of New York.

She was tired of Martin.

In retrospect he wishes he had insisted. Memories haunt these rooms. He hears the clang of crockery in the kitchen, the tap of footsteps down the hall. If he listens closely, he can hear the sounds they made in the bedroom. Their noises seem to spring from the very walls. It has been months since he last wound the grandfather clock. The hands stand frozen, as though they are pointing in a direction he will never go. He roams about like a pensioner, the slanting sun as it comes through the tall windows seizing the motes in the air, as if life itself were disintegrating at the molecular level.

He has taken to sleeping in the study. The ghosts are fewer there. He makes himself a bed on the small sofa. He lies in the darkness. The bars of the cage glint dully with the ambient light of the city. Aristotle rustles every so often. Otherwise, the parrot sleeps with its head tucked beneath a wing.

Martin's dreams have grown fitful. He dreams the boys are involved in traffic pileups, they drown at sea, seismic tremors bring buildings down upon their heads, wildfires overtake the bungalow. California dangers.

Several months back he met someone himself. Her name was June. She was the hostess at a little grill just off Wall Street where he went for dinner. She noticed the man sitting alone in the booth in the corner who always ordered the meat loaf. He told her one evening he hadn't eaten meat loaf in twenty-five years. It reminded him of his mother's. He was from the Midwest; she could not remember where.

On the job she wore a short skirt and a sequined blouse. Her thighs were plump beneath the skirt. When she slipped it off, she kicked it as if making an extra point. Hers was a smoker's laugh. He pretended to believe her when she told him her age. She had a son in the navy, a daughter who worked as a police officer in a small hamlet upstate, and a late husband she hoped was at this very moment burning in hell.

Martin never took her back to the rooms on Maiden Lane. They went to a hotel instead. The front desk staff glanced at one another knowingly, trying not to smile. He liked to stand in the corner and watch her from across the room.

I can do this on my own, she said when she ended it.

I don't need you.

His insomnia turns chronic. Most mornings Martin is up early, already at his desktop in the study by two, maybe three o'clock. It's just as well; the world markets have been open for hours. As head of the currency desk at his new firm, his responsibilities have ballooned. He charts the paths of the rand, the rupee, the South Korean won. On the screen their trajectories rise and fall like waves. The krone holds steady, the great black wealth still pumping up out of the earth. Sometimes he checks his wife's social network pages, and sometimes he goes to travel sites. He thinks about taking a trip: the Seychelles, the Great Wall, Mayan ruins—anywhere that might cause him to look back and tell himself a different story about his life.

And sometimes he sits at the keyboard and watches a woman squirming atop a man. He watches two women together. The joy they take in each other is, he thinks, as simple and pure as a stream. He watches a woman with two men. One man is heavy; the other is heavier. The woman has a bit of a belly herself and a hard, hard face.

He comes to Day for Knight. Day reclines as she always does on the bed, in her wig and sunglasses. Also a string of pearls hanging from her neck, an added touch. Knight, meanwhile, lies next to her, massive purple plume growing from the helmet. The camera looks at them from on high, mounted three-quarters of the way up the wall.

On this morning, however, there is a difference. Martin cannot put his finger on it at first. He sees as always the harsh definition of Knight's body, the bulging plates of muscle, heavy shadows among the biceps and pectorals, the sheer mountain faces and cliffs of his physique. Only then does Martin notice. Usually as rigid as steel piping, on this morning it curls uselessly on the man's thigh.

Day, in her wig and sunglasses, does what she can. But after some minutes it continues to string limply from Knight's middle, like tack hanging from the peg on a stable

wall. Martin's sympathies go out. For the first time, he wonders about Knight the man, what it is Knight does, if Knight
has a family. If Knight is a good and dutiful son himself, if
he is a Catholic or a Presbyterian. He wonders if Day is a
Quaker or a Jew, a Democrat or a Republican, or a socialist,
or a member of the underground animal liberation front.
For all he knows, she could be a stripper or a housewife
or a school-crossing guard. She could be second flautist in
the Pittsburgh Symphony. He does not know if Knight is a
bouncer or a construction worker, a computer programmer
or a professor of theology or stay-at-home dad.

Here is what he does know. He knows that at the very
instant of pleasure, Knight likes to bite her shoulder, and
that Day likes it, too. He knows that when Knight finishes, a
slight tremor seizes the man's left foot. He knows Day's habit
of holding Knight between the thumb and three fingers of
her left hand, her pinkie aloft, as if he were a small pitcher
from which she could pour. He knows, in other words, what
you would never know if you met them in the street, or
worked with them, or went to church with them, or served
them coffee in a diner, or taught their children geography.

Watching now, Martin is moved to consider what anxiet-
ies from the world of light penetrate here, what terrors or dis-
appointments have crossed over to sap Knight of his sexual
vigor. What effect will the memory now being forged have
on Knight's waking hours, what trouble may it bring tomorrow. Though it comes to Martin that maybe noon needs
midnight. As if these evenings make possible the office-
going you, the child-rearing you, the steak-eating you, the
whole SUV-driving TV-watching shoe-tying bed-making

online-shopping egg-cracking nap-taking coffee-drinking pencil-sharpening check-cashing you. The dark side of the moon could be dark for a reason.

⬿⬿

Here, unfortunately, Knight's helplessness causes Day to giggle. She is not malicious but tired. Tired of Knight with his unending demands. Yet Martin wishes she hadn't. He can tell even if she can't: You do not laugh at Knight. There is no audio, but the grin stands out broadly on her face. While Knight, looming under his helmet, looks as imperturbable as ever, Martin sees the cords in the man's neck stiffen.

But he is unprepared for what comes next. When Knight shoves Day Martin stands, knocking his chair over. Martin is afraid. He is afraid for the woman. Day is not. She shoves back, causing Knight to grab the pearls at her neck in anger. But instead of choking her, the string breaks. Day, watching the rain of gems, hoots in the man's face. Knight pushes her again, and this time she goes crashing off the bed and onto the floor. She is wearing an absurd pair of stilettos, six, seven inches, and she goes down hard. Her legs splay wide, the furrow between narrow but dark and rich, glistening, in contrast to the white-blond hairs of the wig on her head. Her piercings below leap with light.

Day, from the floor, remembers the camera. Martin watches as she points to it and laughs once more. He wants to warn her not to.

If Knight was angry before, his rage now turns incandescent. He kneels on the bed and lunges for the video mount, both arms shooting out. From this side of the screen, his hands swell so dramatically and without warning the sight makes Martin step back. Day, still on the floor, will not stop laughing. When Knight rips the camera from the wall the world tilts suddenly, the angle dipping and ranging, as though he has grabbed hold of Martin's head.

The room careens—edge of bed, wall, ceiling—and then reverses, the universe somersaulting. The camera rises and falls, and then rises again. We see Day, her arms flailing. A small inkblot of blood appears in the lower left quadrant of the lens. Martin, standing, shouts, Stop, but of course Knight does not hear. There is no one left to hear. Day writhes, twisting. Martin would feel sexual if he didn't feel so horrible. Her body on the floor seems to jump on its own. The camera rises and falls, and it rises again, the world windmilling, as he beats her to death with your face.

Acknowledgments

WITH DEEPEST APPRECIATION to Tim Keppel and J. Jordan Phelps for their detailed comments and criticisms; to Molly Friedrich and Hannah Brattesani of the Friedrich Agency for their unflagging encouragement and support; and to Erika Goldman, publisher and editorial director of Bellevue Literary Press, for taking a chance when others refused to.

BELLEVUE LITERARY PRESS is devoted to publishing
literary fiction and nonfiction at the intersection of
the arts and sciences because we believe that science and the
humanities are natural companions for understanding the
human experience. We feature exceptional literature that
explores the nature of perception and the underpinnings of the
social contract. With each book we publish, our goal is to foster
a rich, interdisciplinary dialogue that will forge new tools for
thinking and engaging with the world.

To support our press and its mission,
and for our full catalogue of published titles,
please visit us at blpress.org.

BELLEVUE LITERARY PRESS
New York